On t

Huey Cobra gunships were up and circling the launch site. The sign above the road at the base camp entrance was swinging from the takeoff blast.

It read:

WELCOME TO 5TH SPECIAL FORCES GROUP
(AIRBORNE) RECON
COMMAND AND CONTROL NORTH—
REPUBLIC OF VIETNAM
''WE KILL FOR PEACE''

Dangling below the sign were seven enemy skulls.

COMMAND AND CONTROL

Command and Control really existed, with an annual casualty rate near 200 percent. Author James D. Mitchell is a retired U.S. Army Green Beret sergeant who lost an eye running recons with C and C. Like his hero, he is a tough guy and an incurable romantic.

COMMAND AND CONTROL

by

JAMES D. MITCHELL

BERKLEY BOOKS, NEW YORK

COMMAND AND CONTROL

A Berkley Book / published by arrangement with
the author

PRINTING HISTORY
Berkley edition / December 1989

ISBN: 0-425-11777-4

DEDICATION
This book is dedicated to those britches-ripped, hollow-eyed, smelly grunts who gave their lives to defend freedom in Southeast Asia—American mettle of the highest caliber.

ACKNOWLEDGMENTS
Grateful acknowledgment and thanks to my wife, Amelia, the members of the Trinity Arts Writers Association, and my editor, Jim Morris, without whose collective support, encouragement, and critique this story would not have been possible.

Preface

Prior to 1966, the primary mission of Special Forces in Southeast Asia was counterinsurgency operations within South Vietnam. In mid-September 1966, that mission was expanded with the creation of a separate top secret entity called Command and Control.

Command and Control was tasked to conduct covert combat operations and reconnaissance into denied areas.

Command and Control North was the staging base created for the planning and support of operations into Laos and North Vietnam. C and C North was positioned on the coast just south of Da Nang.

There were two other Command and Control projects: C and C South and C and C Central. Central, located in Kontum, targeted Cambodia. C and C South, based outside Ban Me Thuot, worked both sides of the fence—Laos and northern Cambodia.

Every Special Forces soldier involved with the C and C projects was a volunteer. Not that all Special Forces personnel in 'Nam weren't volunteers—they were. However, duty with C and C was a step beyond that, and generally viewed as patriotic masochism.

Command and control teams were small—six personnel. Two Americans, designated One-Zero and One-One, comprised the leadership element. Four indigenous personnel, usually Montagnards—Yards—made up the firepower augmentation for the team.

The seven primary missions of C and C teams were: area reconnaissance, bomb damage assessments, enemy prisoner snatches, friendly POW recoveries, body recoveries, wire taps, and assassinations.

Each C and C volunteer, on accepting the assignment, was required to sign a statement that essentially acknowledged: ". . . if in the conduct of covert combat operations into denied areas, you are killed or captured, the United States will disavow any knowledge of you."

Chapter 1

Hot downdrafts and near choking exhaust fumes swirled through the open troop cabin as we sat huddled inside our chopper waiting for our dual Cobra gunship escort to launch. Once the Cobras were airborne, our slick would launch and follow them to the target area.

I glanced over the team. Recon Team Texas, two Americans and four skinny Yards, were no strangers to Laotian real estate. During the past eleven months I'd run every type of mission C and C handled, except one.

This was my team's first body-recovery mission, a downed and burned chopper located sixty klicks northwest of the tri-border junction in Laos—target designator, Hotel-5.

The crew of three had bought it while trying to exfiltrate RT Kansas four days before.

Kansas had managed to fight their way off the landing zone and escape. They were successfully extracted from their alternate exfil point the next day. The chopper had not been so fortunate.

The One-Zero of Kansas told me the slick took heavy automatic weapons fire on approach and blew and burned when a chi-com B-40 rocket ripped into its tail section. Kansas, low on ammo and with one wounded, barely had time to drop their rucksacks, and run. The One-Zero also told me he'd seen a bald NVA for the first time ever, and it was the bald bastard who fired the rocket into the chopper.

Aerial photos of the crash site showed both pilots badly charred and still strapped in their seats. The third member of the crew, the door gunner, couldn't be seen in the photos. It was my guess he was still in the troop cabin or had been captured by Chuck, the NVA.

I met with four other team leaders the day I was assigned the body-recovery mission and picked their brains for anything I could use during mission planning. All four had conducted prior body recoveries. About the only thing they agreed on was that each situation was unique, but none was a cakewalk, not that any of our missions were. On an assassination, wiretap, or enemy-prisoner snatch, we could go in with some semblance of stealth, either by parachute, strings—ropes suspended from a helicopter—or even walk in.

On body recoveries, we had to go in to Chuck's turf like a goddamn brass band. Since he knew we'd be coming to try to recover our dead, you could bet your hottest love letter he'd be waiting.

After the other team leaders left the meeting, I sat alone with Sergeant Swede Jensen. Jensen was a seasoned One-Zero, hardened by twenty-six back-to-back months in 'Nam. He was a tall lean man with a proud but not arrogant style, and hair as blond as his first name. He had been in Chuck's backyard so many times that he knew most of them by their first names. I didn't know Jensen well, but his reputation almost qualified him for sainthood, provided you overlooked his mouth.

He usually referred to the VC and the NVA as, "Those fucking scum-sucking pigs."

I began our conversation with, "Congratulations on your Silver Star, Swede. That's number two, isn't it?"

He leaned back in his chair, crossed one leg over the other, and said, "Yeah, wonderful isn't it? I figure if I take both of them, sit 'em on a bar somewhere back in the world, along with a dollar or two, I might just be able to buy a draft beer. That is, of course, providing the bartender isn't some antiwar puke."

I didn't share Jensen's feelings about the antiwar types back home. I figured protesting was their privilege and this war was my privilege. Even though I was in Vietnam defending their continued right to disagree with me. Nonetheless, I gave a token smile at Jensen's comment.

After a short silence he looked at the floor, then directly back into my eyes. His voice was serious this time. "Look, Yancy, if you're taking heavy fire out there and your shit starts getting flaky, you can skip the bodies, but at least get their heads. Hell, most of what you try and pull outa that cockpit is gonna come apart in your hands anyhow. It's a shit-stench mess! Anyhow, take a machete and some empty sand bags to put the heads in, just in case."

I felt a hard frown knot my face. A heat seemed to sweep through my blood on hearing words I didn't want to believe, words that seemed sick, spoken by a legend whom I damn near worshipped.

The thought of brutally hacking off the heads of three comrades, three American patriots, infuriated and sickened me. My jaw tightened and my eyes narrowed involuntarily.

I stared directly into his eyes and said, "What makes

you think for a goddamn minute that I'd even consider a demented thing like that? You're sick, Jensen!''

I stood and backed away from the table with my fists clenched at my side.

Jensen remained seated and slowly looked up. He spoke with a calm voice. "Look, Sarge, you handle it your own fuckin' way, it's your show. But if you don't bring back some positive means of body identification, then those guys are going to be listed MIA, not KIA, until long after this war is over. You and I know they're cold and dead, but that's not good enough.

"This isn't World War Two, where you just wade into a field of corpses and yank their dog tags off. The medical bureaucracy here isn't going to buy it until they have indisputable proof of death. Taking a hand won't do it. It's got to be the body or at least the heads.

"Think of their families." His voice had graduated to a growl, while his eyes stayed fixed on mine. "Those bodies are so burned and charred now that they can't have an open coffin funeral anyhow. They won't know if it's a head or a goddamn dog in that coffin. But at least they will be confirmed dead, and at least their families will have something to cry over. Then they can collect the insurance and get on with their lives and not be praying and clinging to an empty hope.

"If you don't think you can handle the mission, mister, then pass it to me or someone else."

He paused for a moment, then lowered his voice. "You think about it Mister One-Zero, because a lot of people are getting ready to risk their lives to get those bodies back. If you start hesitating, there's going to be another stack of corpses for another team to go out on the same weak fuckin' limb for.''

Jensen stood, tilted his head downward as though in silent prayer, and finished calmly. ''I don't know if it helps any, but Headquarters endorses the decapitation if you have to do it. It won't be the first time it's had to be done.'' He walked to the door, stopped for a moment, and as though talking to the door, said, ''By the way, Chuck may have the whole area rigged with booby traps, including the bodies, so be alert.''

A moment later, I moved to close the door. Dazed, I slumped into a chair. It seemed to take an eternity before it all sank in and I admitted to the reality. Jensen had given me some straight-from-the-shoulders, non-sugar-coated advice, and he was right.

But why was I so devastated? In the past eleven months I had learned to kill, kick ass, and not worry about the size or sex of the enemy in my sights. Why, all of a sudden, was I having trouble living with another brutality, particularly when that brutality was in the best interest of a fallen comrade?

''Comrades. One night you were drinking in the club with them. The next day you were lifting their bullet-riddled bodies off a chopper, laying them in the hot sun, gently rolling them into a plastic body bag, and trying not to cry while doing it.

Comrade. That word had grown more sacred to me than words like *home, family, love,* and *freedom.* Perhaps those words were sacred, too, but they were distant. *Comrade* was here and now, and the thought of having to mutilate their charred remains twisted into my soul. I didn't even know these particular guys, but they had died in the flaming cesspool; and they were sacred to me. I stared at the wall and wept for a moment.

Later that night, I sharpened my machete, wrapped three empty sandbags around it, and strapped it to the side of my rucksack.

Chapter 2

Our gunships, two Huey Cobras loaded for bear, were up and circling the launch site. I felt the upward surge as our slick lifted off. I peered back through the swirling sand at our base camp. We hovered a few seconds, then moved up and westward. The sign above the road at the camp entrance was twisting and swinging from the takeoff blast.

It read:

WELCOME TO 5TH SPECIAL FORCES GROUP
(AIRBORNE) RECON
COMMAND AND CONTROL NORTH—
REPUBLIC OF VIETNAM
"WE KILL FOR PEACE"

Dangling in the wind below the sign were seven enemy skulls. It had been eleven months and fourteen missions since I first read those words, "We Kill For Peace." Killing for peace is about as insane as raping for virginity, I thought to myself.

We clattered through clear skies at ninety knots and three thousand feet. Our ETA on target was 0830 hours,

roughly one hour and fifteen minutes of flight time—
Good Lord willin'—and a 37-mm antiaircraft round
don't rise.

I leaned forward to shout into the door gunner's ear,
so he could hear above the incessant *whop-whop*. ''Tell
the pilot if we can he needs to bring us in from a westward approach! The sun will make it a little tougher
for Chuck to get a rocket on us!''

The door gunner, a short Hispanic with a mustache
that looked like a well-used Brillo pad, smiled back and
gave me a thumbs-up response. He pressed the button
on his headset and relayed my message to the pilot. A
moment later, a gray-gloved hand twisted back out of
the cockpit, thumb up.

The gunner leaned away from his M-60 and toward
me. He shouted, ''This one's gonna be hot, ain't it?''

I yelled back, ''Roger that, amigo. Gunfight at the
Not-so-OK Corral!''

His mustache immediately drew back, revealing a
wide ivory smile. Patting his M-60 affectionately, he
shouted, ''That's all right, amigo!''

I liked his spirit. His faded flight suit told me he was
no beginner at this business. His confidence spread to
my entire team, watching our muffled conversation.

He then yelled with a friendly smile, ''How come
you recon dudes don't wear mustaches, man?''

I yelled back, ''My girlfriend kept complaining about
runs in her panty hose!''

He laughed. ''Now I know why you gringos call them
womb brooms.''

Tuong, our tail gunner, barely sixteen, was the most
curious of my cowboys. He'd been watching, trying to
decipher our chatter. No matter when, if he heard or
saw something he didn't understand, you could bet there

would be a question about it. He strained to lean over two other team members seated on the floor between him and me. "Sar Brett, what funny?"

I smiled back, opened my mouth wide, darted my tongue in and out of my mouth, then finished the charade with a wink.

It was important never to ignore the little people. They relied on us. They trusted us, loved us, and even died for us. No matter how trivial the question or the need might seem, it warranted genuine attention and a response.

He'd heard it before. He smiled and nodded his head. His curiosity satisfied, he settled back to his position and leaned his head against Rham's shoulder.

Although the little people didn't fully understand some of our Yankee ways, they still enjoyed laughing about them.

If there was one merit to this war, it was that it elevated a man's appreciation for two things: a good home-cooked meal and some long-lasting round-eyed loving. The home-cooked meal was in a distant second place.

It had been two months since my R and R to Sydney. The feeling of a round-eyed woman wrapping her gripping thighs around my body was still a vivid memory.

I reached into my pocket and pulled out a photograph wrapped in plastic. It was Vonnie holding a stuffed koala bear I had won for her at a circus shooting booth in Sydney. She was my link with love since my fiancée had "Dear Johnned" me. Her letter had knocked me to my knees for a while. But sometime later I reasoned if she couldn't handle my being off on an exotic working vacation there probably hadn't been much staying power to her love in the first place.

I did see her side of it. Without much notice, her

"handsome and windblown lover" quit in his senior year at the University of Texas and joined the Army, volunteered for parachute training and Special Forces, and, if that wasn't enough, did everything but buck the line to get to Vietnam. She had good cause to question my sanity, not to mention feeling like she'd been instantly relegated to fourth place in my life—all at a time when a lot of people were having trouble seeing any merits in this war in the first place.

For a while, I tried to explain my feelings in late-night letters. I told her it boiled down to a simple and indisputable truth. There is a savage Communist effort here being leveled against a people who should have the privilege of freedom and the right to evolve into a democratic government, or any other government they choose. They deserved that free choice and were fighting for it.

"If I chose to ignore these people and let them fall to the Communist bastards without a fight, it will forever eliminate the pride I feel when I hear our national anthem play, or see our country's flag dancing proudly in the wind." I went on to explain I had a free choice of will, bought and paid for by patriots. Win or lose, I was where I wanted to be: on the field; in the combat arena for freedom.

After weeks of writing unanswered letters, it became apparent I was directing my urine into high-velocity breezes. In CCN we'd been using those euphemistic phrases like *urine into high-velocity breezes* since our commander, Colonel Ivan Kahn, had gotten his nipple in a roller with some uninhibited commentary during the inspection of a particularly obnoxious senator. We had a whole roster of them: pendulating Richard; defecation in the cooling apparatus; *cabeza de Ricardo*.

I closed my final letter to her, quoting not John Wayne, but Casanova: "Ours were happy moments which time can never erase and which death alone will make me forget."

I looked over my shoulder to check the team. They were all asleep. My eyes shifted back to the photograph in my hand, back to more recent and more pleasant memories of Australia and Vonnie. She had a smile on her face like the sparkle of a diamond kissed by a sun ray.

We had met in a nightclub my first night in Sydney. I was mesmerized from the first moment I saw her. Tall and slender she was, with long, silky blond hair that moved with a happy rhythm when she danced. Her shapely buttocks were supported by athletic muscular legs. Under a silver satin mini the fabric had teased her braless nipples into two alluring points. It was lust at first sight.

After a dance, much to the irritation of several other admirers, I bought us a beer. Standing at the crowded bar, I looked her directly in the eyes with my best smile and said, "I must warn you, I am highly trained and skilled in subversive activity. My plan is to get you drunk and take advantage of your luscious body. You may have difficulty ever settling for hamburger again."

I realized it was possible I'd overdone it, which is my habit sometimes when the spirits are flowing. Luckily, I was wrong. She laughed, sympathetic and enchanting.

"Yank, that sounds like a challenge to me. You may not know it yet, but we Australians rarely avoid a sporting challenge." The contest was sealed with a kiss.

As the evening continued, I learned the hard way about Australians and their stout beer. I was knee-walking drunk by midnight, but Vonnie was so sober she could probably have performed a trapeze act for Barnum and Bailey. The last thing I remembered was trying to sing "Ballad of the Green Berets" while climbing the stairs to her flat. Fortunately for me she not only had a sense of humor but a tenderness for drunk gladiators.

Vonnie accepted me immediately. She loved me without inhibitions, and filled my six days of R and R with tenderness, laughter, and caring. I was elated, stunned, that one woman could give so much to a stranger. During the six days we shared, she never resisted my needs, questioned or complained.

One afternoon we lay recovering, pleasantly exhausted, in the tangled sheets of her bed, she massaging my back. "Everything about you pleases me, Yank, your muscularity, your wit, and your China-blue eyes," she said.

About the time I was starting to feel the need for a larger hat size, she leapt up from the bed, slapped my buttocks, and said, "But your ass is so big!"

I rolled over, still feeling the sting from her love tap, and smiled into her laughing eyes. I spread my legs and said, "You're probably right about that, darlin' . . . but a man can't drive a railroad spike with a tack hammer, now can he?"

She tilted her head and raised her eyebrows. "You have a point there, Yank, and I have to admit you drive very well. Besides, I was just kidding. Your butt's perfect."

She knelt beside the bed, gently kissed me on the forehead, and spoke with misty eyes. "I'm going to miss you, love."

I pulled her naked beauty across my body and cradled her head against my chest. Stroking her soft hair, I listened to her whispered sniffing until she drifted into a restful, childlike sleep.

When I awoke there was a note on the nightstand saying she had gone to pick up some groceries. Below the note was a poem:

If I'm asleep when you want me, wake me.
If I don't seem to want you, make me.
For this blissful moment, you are my chosen man,
So take me.

Love, Vonnie

The morning prior to my departure, Vonnie took my beret and carefully hand-sewed a pair of her black silk lace panties into the lining. Finished, she inspected her work, then came over to the couch and sat beside me. She handed me the beret with palms up, much as though it were a ceremonial presentation.

She spoke softly, with a slight downward tilt of her head, perhaps indicating doubts about my approval. "This is a little keepsake for you, something to help you keep me on your mind. If you know what I mean?"

My smile brought her head up. I briefly examined her gift, carefully positioned the beret on my head, and said, "Thank you, honey. But just for the record, my heart won't need reminders. It would take a three-dog-night in the outback to make me even begin to forget you."

I lay back on the couch and pulled her tall body on top of mine. Smiling, I said, "You know, maybe I should sew a pair of camouflage underwear inside your umbrella. Might be quite a conversation piece at the bus stop on rainy days."

She looked into my eyes and said, "Don't you dare," then leaned to kiss me.

Our kiss became passionate. We slowly removed our clothes. I watched her eyes close while she drew the soft edge of her lower lip between her teeth.

"Oh, Brett . . ." she whispered. "I love it."

Glistening beads of sweat rolled across the naked sway of her breasts and into her cleavage. Her hands gripped into my side, her mouth sucked in full labored breaths.

As her thighs tightened around my hips, she whispered in an almost inaudible climaxing breath, "Brett, oh, Brett . . ."

Her words faded and her soft eyes opened slowly. I drew her body down onto my lips and tasted the salt-laced moisture of her kiss. It would be a democratic day in the Kremlin before I ever forgot that moment.

My thoughts returned to reality when my One-One, Sergeant William Washington, nudged my leg and pointed toward the valley below. He handed me his binoculars. "Feel like venison for supper, boss?"

I took the field glasses and scanned the terrain below. After a moment, I looked back at Will. "I don't see a thing, partner."

Will shifted his position to lean nearer the open troop door. While pointing his finger down, he shouted, "There in that draw. A big buck, man."

I quickly pulled the binoculars back to my eyes, looked toward the draw, and saw what looked like a ten-point buck disappearing into the trees. I smiled and shouted back to Will, "Damn, partner, that makes my mouth water, and I was just getting used to rice and fish heads."

Will laughed as I handed him his binoculars. He took one last look at the deer fading from sight beneath the jungle canopy and said, "You know, man, this is really a beautiful country. Be a great place for a vacation if they'd just stop trying to kill us tourists."

We both grinned.

Washington was the best One-One a team leader could ask for. He was short, black, and almost as skinny as one of the yards, but he could hump a sixty-pound ruck up a mountainside like Jim Brown charging through a line. Will claimed he was hung like a stud field mouse, couldn't sing, dance, or play basketball, so he joined the army and set his sights on being a Green Beret.

Whether or not any of it was true didn't amount to a hill of beans to me. Will was a friend and a damn good soldier. He could make the right decision when needed and would follow an order impeccably and without hesitation. I counted on Will, sometimes beyond the normal boundaries of my leadership position. Frequently the CO asked him to take his own team. He would have been a good One-Zero, but he always declined, saying he preferred to stay with RT Texas. We had been through a lot together. It only took one trip into Chuck's country to discover Will had balls of brass.

He was a family man, from Memphis, Tennessee. He missed his family. But you had to know Will for a while before you could see fully the love and allegiance he held for them.

To many single guys, like me, the war was the focal point of our lives. We automatically planned to extend when our tour was up, and stay with it.

But Will never deviated from his loyalty to his family. Whenever anyone asked if he was going to extend, he laughed and answered, "Man, are you crazy? My wife's done wore out three sets of knee pads praying for me while I'm here. I ain't staying in this fuckin' war a minute longer than I have to. I got chitlins, chilluns, and Chunky waiting for me back in the world, and they're counting the days till I get home, just like I am."

Chunky was his nickname for his wife. "Best cook in the world, next to my mama."

Regular as clockwork, Chunky sent him a candy-and-cookies care package every week from home. Will always shared it with the team. If anybody wanted an argument about Chunky being "the best cook in the world," they'd never get it from a member of RT Texas.

While most of the other team members had pictures of *Playboy* centerfolds hanging by their bunks, the wall by Will's bunk was solely dedicated to pictures of Mom and Dad, Chunky, and his two daughters. It was a regular family gallery around his bunk. Given the chance, he would tell you about them all, at length.

There was something else impressive about Will—his sense of humor under stress. Two months before, we had run an Ashau Valley target. The mission was supposed to be an ambush and enemy POW snatch. But it went bad when we made unexpected heavy contact and almost got our asses shot off. We were running hard from them and getting short on daylight. Will was on the radio every step of the way as we ran, tripped, and stumbled through the bush. He was trying to get some simpleton base-radio operator to understand our "right-fuckin'-now" need for some air support.

The base-radio operator came back asking, "Just how close is the enemy in pursuit?"

Will, pissed off to the maximum, shouted into the

handset, "Hang on a second, asshole, and I'll let you talk to one of them!"

The base response came back immediately. "Roger, Texas, understand. We'll have two F-4s on target in fifteen minutes. Come up on the guard freq when you get a visual on them."

It was that kind of under-the-gun response to high-pressure situations that made me feel proud to be out here on freedom's anvil. Working with guys like Will Washington made all the fear, anguish, and sweat worth it. It didn't matter to me how big, small, or nonexistent a man's stack of medals were. Every one of those hollow-eyed, smelly, britches-ripped grunts was a hero.

A sudden blast of warm air hit my face; we were descending and must be nearing the target.

I checked my watch: 0822 hours. In the distance I saw our gunships dropping altitude. At the same time, the door gunner turned, gave me a stern look, and held up one hand with five fingers spread wide. We were five minutes off-target. I reached into my shirt, pulled out my one and only thirty-round magazine and held it above my head, signaling the team to lock and load their weapons. Thirty-round magazines were as rare in 'Nam as virgins on Tudo Street, but I had managed to scrounge one for each team member to use on infil.

I thrust the magazine firmly into the magazine well, hit my bolt release, and flipped the selector to full auto. The team followed suit, each being careful to keep his finger clear of the trigger.

My muscles tensed and my adrenaline started to pump as I leaned to check the team and give them a last-minute dose of confidence. It was my habit each time right before infil to look each one of them directly in his eyes, give him a rigid thumbs-up, and wink.

There were times when empty-gut nausea may have diluted my inspiring performance, but I figured it was just stage fright, something we glamorous actors had to learn to live with. But, then, in itself, that ever-prevailing will to survive had a way of keeping a man's wits alert. It was like being charged by a violent two-thousand-pound water buffalo; you really didn't need words and winks to encourage you to get your shit together.

Our ship dropped to eight hundred feet and slowed to fifty knots to allow our Cobras to get more lead. They needed about a minute's distance on us to make their ordnance run on the LZ. As planned, one Cobra would skirt the LZ with high-explosive rockets and the other would roll in behind with white phosphorus. I had asked for WP in preference to napalm. I knew the Willie Pete would cause some small fires. But if I'd specified napalm, it would turn the place into an inferno. Once the Cobras had completed their LZ prep, they would still have a fifty percent ordnance reserve in case our proverbial stool really got runny.

The LZ had a radius of seventy-five-meters, barren of trees but covered thickly with five-foot elephant grass. I counted on the grass to give us some concealment from direct fire even though half of it had been burned away by the fire from the downed chopper.

The burned slick was centered on the LZ like a macabre toy in a seemingly abandoned, overgrown child's sandbox.

Will leaned out the chopper door and held on to the door gunner's leg with one hand while scanning our forward approach with his binoculars in the other. Wind velocity from the rotor down draft flapped his shirt collar violently about his neck, his cravat dancing wildly like some faded battle streamer.

I hadn't told the Cowboys—Yards—about possibly having to decapitate the bodies, but I did tell Will. It would be he and I making the actual recovery on the bodies while the Cowboys provided a four-corner perimeter around the chopper.

In a private moment before launch, I told Will once we made a quick check of the bodies, I would decide whether to recover them intact. I told him they would be badly decomposed, that most of what we tried to pull out of the cockpit was going to come apart in our hands, and that the stench would be sickening. I had hesitated to tell him the details, but I didn't want him hit with any surprises. I told him to wear his cravat tightly drawn around his face just below eye level to help filter out some of the stench and swarming flies.

Will took it all in stride. He handled it a whole lot easier than I had when Swede Jensen hit me with it. I also told Will that if we were under fire, we wouldn't have much choice about bits and pieces.

Will pulled in from outside the chopper door. "Looks clear and dry, boss. Maybe we can skip the mud bath this time."

I hoped that would be the case, but you could never be sure how dry an LZ was going to be until your feet hit the ground.

I leaned toward him and pointed over my shoulder, indicating for him to turn my radio on. He switched the PRC-25 to the on position, checked the whip-antenna base for tightness, and gave me a thumbs-up.

Pulling the handset to my ear, I made a commo check with the pilot. "Raven leader, this is Texas. How copy? Over."

The pilot responded, "Roger, Texas, this is Raven leader. I gotcha loud and clear. Let's hope it's this good when we get some distance between us. We're about two minutes out. You ready to rock and roll back there? Over."

It was a relief to hear his calm, joking voice. "Roger, Raven, ready for showtime. Just keep the meter running, buddy. This is Texas, out."

Our plan was fairly simple. After the Cobras made their ordnance prep, our slick would drop in quick, hover at four feet, just long enough for us to clear the ship, then take off. Our slick and the Cobras would stay on-station until I popped purple smoke for abort or yellow smoke for exfil.

The pilot had asked during our mission briefback why I wasn't using conventional red smoke to signal abort and green for exfil. My rationale was that Chuck knew how we operated. Since Chuck also had smoke, all he had to do was set up an ambush, hurl a green smoke grenade, and, presto, in would come another candidate for crispy critters. By using an abstract combination of yellow and purple, Chuck wouldn't know what to throw. If the pilot saw any color but yellow on the LZ, he would know it was time to beat feet and leave us to our alternate escape-and-evasion plan.

The bad news was, they only had about twenty minutes' station time before their fuel gauge started pointing toward home. Although I figured we only needed fifteen minutes on-site, I couldn't be sure about it.

Chapter 3

Our lead Cobra made its ordnance run, diving at full speed. Its front Gatling gun began a blazing growl. Red tracer rounds streaked through the sky. A hundred meters out, the Cobra leveled off and sent two high-explosive rockets ripping into the northern edge of the LZ. The pilot quickly triggered two more in rapid trail. All four rockets impacted with thunderous explosions, gray clouds of smoke billowing up through the jungle canopy.

We were still a mile off-target when the trail Cobra dived sharply and hurled four white phosphorus rockets in rapid succession into the southern side of the LZ. The explosions spewed white-hot flakes out through the trees and into the LZ. As he strained to pull out of his run, I got on the radio to the lead Cobra: "Hatchet Leader, this is Texas. Over."

"Go ahead, Texas, Hatchet Leader. Over."

"Roger, Hatchet. You boys do know how to start a show. Were you taking any fire on your run? Over."

"Roger, copy, Texas. Negative on ground fire. Them cats know better than to throw a rock at a beehive. If he's in there, he's wishing he had asbestos drawers. Over.''

I laughed. ''I copy, Hatchet Leader. Thanks for the fireworks show. You guys keep the lipstick off your dipstick. We may need an encore in a few minutes. It's show time. Texas out.''

Wind drift swirled the awesome smell of freshly exploded sulfur through our cabin, bringing with it an ominous scent of impending combat. That all-too-familiar smell had been a fragrant friend at times, an emissary of death at others. Right now it was a friend moving through the jungle ahead of us. In the next moment, it could turn and become a deadly adversary.

We were on final approach. I positioned my cravat over my face and tightened it. We scrambled to our door positions . . . three at the right door, three at the left door. Our legs dangled in the air, just above the chopper struts. My eyes watered from the wind blast. I squinted to peer through the rising smoke. The ground started coming up fast. I quickly scanned the target, searching for any wire or cord that might reveal a booby trap. None.

I caught a peripheral glimpse of movement in the line of trees. A B-40 pointed right at us. I yelled to the door gunner, who was half stooping over his M-60, his finger fixed on the trigger, ''Two-man rocket team. Three o'clock!''

''Roger! Got 'em, amigo.'' Without hesitation, he pivoted the M-60 and swung the muzzle forward and down toward the enemy. The weapon hammered ripping well-aimed lead along the base of the line of trees. His strong body jerked in violent harmony with the machine gun's vicious rhythm.

Rham, my M-79 Cowboy, brought his grenade launcher up and triggered a round into the same spot.

Will and I opened up in unison with the door gunner pouring full automatic bursts into the enemy.

Our rounds hit target. The NVA holding the rocket lunged upward, then backward, as our barrage of lead ripped into his khaki-clad torso. The B-40 dropped to the ground.

I shouted to Will, "Good shooting, Quickdraw!"

Keeping his eyes focused on the fallen NVA, he shouted back, "Not good enough! One of the bastards got away!"

The door gunner continued riveting five- and six-round bursts along the trees.

I felt the upward heave of the chopper come to hover. The rotor blast whipped ripples through the elephant grass, laying it down as though clearing the way for our descent. I gripped my CAR-15 against my chest.

Rising forward, I thrust my free arm outward and yelled, "Let's go!"

En masse, we plunged into the tall grass.

The chopper accelerated quickly and rose forward through the looming smoke. In a moment it was gone, and silence descended.

The team hastily gathered near me. Will lay on his side, a painful, strained appearance on his black, sweaty face. I crawled to his side and spoke, trying to whisper, "Are you hit, buddy?"

Will grimaced while loosening the laces on his left boot. "No, man, I just took a hard lick on my ankle. I'm okay, but I'll sit out the next fast dance if you don't mind."

While my head moved cautiously from side to side,

I peered through the grass and responded, "That's okay, buddy, you can't dance anyhow. Let's move out."

A gentle morning breeze drifted the smoke, foglike, across the LZ.

Half crouching, I led out slowly through the tall grass toward the chopper. The team followed in line at five-meter intervals.

When we reached the burned-out edge of the grass, I halted the team, knelt, and gazed toward the blackened, lifeless chopper thirty meters to our left front.

A small grass fire near the chopper scattered patches of smoke across the clearing in front of us. The smoke drifted over the chopper as though it were a helpless ghost ship floating in a calm sea.

My ears strained to hear something, anything, in that strange silence. The only sound was the distant fading crackle of burning grass.

Will crawled quietly to my side and whispered, "What do you think, boss?"

"I think it's too damn quiet. I don't hear a bird or even a fuck-you lizard."

Turning to the rear, I signaled for Tuong to come up. His sense of hearing was as fine as a wine connoisseur's sense of taste. He'd been raised in the jungle. Tuong knew the sounds that belonged there, and the ones that didn't.

Tuong crept slowly through the grass and came to my side. I turned to him, cupped a hand to my ear, and pointed forward.

Intently, he looked out into the LZ. He listened. A moment later, he whispered, "Too quiet. I think Chuck here."

I turned to Will and motioned for him to give me the binoculars. I carefully studied the chopper. The gruesome profiles of the charred pilots were visible in the cockpit. Next, I searched the troop cabin for the door gunner. Empty. I checked the surrounding ground for his body. Nothing.

Handing the field glasses to Will, I said, "Looks like a two-out-of-three day, partner. I can't find the door gunner anywhere."

Will repeated the search and retorted, "Shit, where can he be?"

Easing a few short feet back into the grass, I pulled the radio handset to my ear and whispered, "Hatchet Leader, this is Texas. Over."

"Go ahead, Texas. This is Hatchet."

"We're in a four-o'clock position thirty meters off the target. No casualties. Site recon shows both pilots right where they're supposed to be, but no door gunner in sight. We're ready to move on target. Can ya'll roll in and spray our flanks before we move? Over."

"Roger, Texas, where do you want it?"

"Both sides of the trees. North and south. Be gentle, partner. I'd like to stay a virgin on friendly fire. Out."

I checked my watch: 0836. We were already five minutes into a twenty-minute game. The first quarter was over.

I felt the hot Asian sun beginning to bake into my neck. I reached over my shoulder to wipe the sweat and reposition my rifle-carrying strap under my collar. The muffled thunder of our Huey Cobras drew nearer.

Suddenly Will, who'd been scanning the area with the binoculars, began rising slowly out of the grass, his mouth gaping. His glasses stayed fixed forward toward the nose of the charred slick. "Shit! Those bastards . . . shit! I don't fuckin' believe . . ." His voice faded as he handed me the field glasses and slowly knelt in the grass. "There, twelve o'clock off the slick. Back in the trees. It's him."

I took the glasses, rose, and peered beyond the blackened chopper into the trees. There I saw it. The hideous, stretched profile of the door gunner hanging inverted from a tree. His olive-drab flight suit was unburned. He had evidently been thrown free of the chopper when the rocket exploded into it. I hoped to God he was dead before they got to him, but the fact that his hands were tied behind him told me it wasn't likely.

He was strung up by his feet. His arms were dangling outward from his back in a bent, grotesque arch, his hands still bound. A gray, blood-soaked burlap sack was strapped over his head.

I'd heard the demonic bastards did this, but now, the jerking movement within the sack confirmed it. The Communist butchers had tied a sack of live rats around his head while he was still alive.

His final moments must have been filled with panicked, helpless agony. Why hadn't the deviant bastards just shot him? Why this?

A gripping chill swept through me, blurring the vision of my shocked eyes. My knees weakened, and nausea twisted my gut. I sank back into the grass and stared pathetically at the ground, feeling broken . . . stunned . . . senseless.

I felt a violent squeezing urge to hurl my rifle into God's face, to rip off every stinking stitch of combat garments covering my body and run.

In those brief seconds of insanity, it was only my comrade's words that saved me. Not God, not discipline, but comradeship.

Will gripped my shoulder hard and shook me. He

spoke with a determined whisper. ''We'll get the bastards who did this, man. They're waiting out there.''

His words jerked me back to consciousness and the mission. I knew we couldn't get sidetracked on a vendetta no matter how justifiable. Our job here and now was to recover those bodies.

Chuck was counting on us to react to the horror. He knew it would hit us hard. He was counting on it to effect our timing, our thinking, and our performance. We couldn't let him dupe us into rage, or shock us into cringing.

It was time to let him see American mettle.

I turned face-to-face with Will. One of us had to get the door gunner's body. Time was not on our side. I would have to split the team, and it should be me on the pilot recovery. If the heads had to be taken, I couldn't give that job to anyone else. I asked Will, ''Partner, how's your ankle?''

''It's okay, boss. I'm ready for Friday night.''

''We gotta move fast. I'm sending Rham and Tuong with you to recover the door gunner. When the Cobras pull out of the run, we'll move in. I'll handle the pilots. You get to that tree as fast as you can, cut him down, and drag him back to the north edge of the grass line. Wait for us there.''

''Roger, Brett, we got it handled.''

''And, Will, don't take the sack off his head. If you can, cut one end open and turn those fuckin' rats loose. But leave the sack on. If the shit hits the fan, break contact, and try to link up with us. If you can't, then move out to the alternate exfil point.''

Will nodded. I handed the binocs to him. He tucked them down into his half-open shirt.

Turning to the Cowboys, I pointed to Tuong and

Rham, then at Will. They understood they were to follow him. I then pointed to Lok and Phan, indicating
they were to stay with me. I didn't like splitting the
team, but it was my only choice. I remembered what
Swede Jensen had told me a few days ago: "If you start
hesitating in the middle of this hot fiasco, then there's
going to be another stack of corpses out there for some
other team to go out on the same fuckin' weak limb
for."

This was no time for hesitation.

The trees suddenly erupted with earsplitting cannon
fire from the Cobras. The rapid synchronized scream
of their lead venom ripped through the jungle canopy
in thunderous symphony with the rotors. The strike was
perfect. They rose proudly into the sky at the end of
their run, scattering the lofted smoke in their path.

Up and forward we lunged, sprinting through the heat
and smoke toward the target. As we cleared the protective cloak of the tall grass and came into the open, my
nostrils filled with the smell of burning grass and
scorched earth.

My ruck bounced hard against my sweat-soaked
back. We ran full-stride toward the dark chopper.
Within seconds, we reached it.

I kneeled at the lower edge of the open cockpit door.
Phan and Lok hurriedly crawled underneath the slick's
black belly. They lay prone. The muzzles of their weapons rested in vigil on the rounded struts. Will, Tuong,
and Rham rushed on by us, headed for the gruesome,
inverted body of the door gunner.

Will struggled and limped with his injured ankle. A
cloud of burned ground dust filtered into the air as he
hopped and dragged his foot along the parched earth.
He, with his damn pride, had lied to me about his ankle

being okay. He knew full well if he hadn't lied about it, I would have made him stay back in the protective grass.

I broke the silence and shouted, "Damn it, Will, hold up! Let Tuong get him!"

He ignored my plea and limped onward into the grass, never looking back.

Then it hit me—the awful smell of stale, burned flesh. It slammed into my senses the instant I gazed up into the open cockpit at the charred pilots. The hot morning sun streamed through the clogging mass of swarming flies and mosquitoes. The filthy sight and fetid smell of lumped flesh on their encrusted, rotting remains churned a choking nausea up from my stomach.

My hand involuntarily jerked to my mouth, cupping over my wet cravat. I tried to swallow as the foul vapor of the nightmare flooded over me.

My eyes narrowed. I was dazed by the ghastly, dark creatures above me. The cloud of flies and mosquitoes droned their frenzied, rapacious chant over the corpses.

The fire-ravaged face of the right-seat pilot was arched upward toward the ceiling of the aircraft. His jaw was open wide, as though straining to emit an agonized, silent scream. His last futile cry must have echoed through the roaring flames and into the surrounding jungle during those final burning moments. A mesmerizing flash engulfed me. I wondered if in his dying seconds he had smelled the terrifying odor of his own flesh melting away.

As a field soldier, I'd pictured my death coming in a barrage of enemy lead tearing into my chest with only a quick second of suffering. As pilots, these men had lived with the knowledge that fire would likely be their final reaper.

Death. I remembered part of a conversation with Will about death. We had been sitting on the floor of our team hooch, sharing a bottle of Mateus.

Will leaned back against his footlocker, looked up at his gallery of family pictures, and said, "We don't likely have no real choices about how we die. If we're lucky, we may just have a little choice about the cause we die for. If the cause is noble, and your life is right with God, then he's got a slot waitin' for you in his army."

I stood, positioned my rifle muzzle down, and leaned forward to check the pilot's seat harness. The nylon straps had been completely melted. My hands reached in to grip the pilot's blackened, shriveled arm. I tried to pull him down and out of the seat. As I gripped tighter into the charred, encrusted flesh, it oozed a dark, thick sap through my fingers.

The rigid corpse seemed fused in place. I gripped and pulled harder. I began to feel the burned, moist inner flesh come apart in my hands and slide off the bone as if it were a greased shaft. A mad furor of flies and mosquitoes pierced and bit into my neck. I struggled in vain to pull him out. My soaked face scarf molded into my mouth as I gasped for air through the stench.

Finally, after what seemed like an eternity of futile effort, I dropped to my knees exhausted. The salty sting of sweat poured into my blurred eyes.

I reached blindly over my shoulder and fumbled to find the protruding handle of my machete. My foul wet fingers trembled as they wrapped around it and drew it slowly out of the sheath.

I rose, stood facing the gruesome carnage, and whispered through my wet cravat, "Brother, please forgive me."

With all my strength, I swung the sharp steel blade powerfully up. It bit savagely into his neck. The skull fell slowly over the blade and dropped into his cradling lap.

I yanked the blade loose from the seat back and reached alongside my ruck to pull the sandbags free. After stuffing two of them into my side pants pocket, I took the third and worked it carefully down over the black skull. Pressing both hands against the sides of the sandbag, I lifted it and quickly turned the sack upright. The head dropped to the bottom. I fastened the end with cord, leaving a small loop for a handhold.

I drew the sleeve of my shirt across my sweat-dripping brow. Without looking up, I retrieved the head-laden sandbag, grabbed my machete, and moved quickly around the nose of the chopper to the other door.

Phan and Lok were directly beneath the chopper. I knelt, handed the sandbag to Lok, and whispered, "You keep. Don't lose."

"Okay, boss." He took the bag, inserted his small hand through the loop, then positioned it with him behind the strut.

I stood and looked toward the tree where the door gunner was hanging. He was gone. The thick grass obscured my vision, but I made out the vague figures of Rham and Tuong moving half humped and slowly toward me. Each grasped one of the door gunner's legs. They were straining to pull his corpse feet first through the brush.

Will limped slowly behind the struggling procession, his dark face silhouetted against the dull green grass.

They were nearing the burned-out edge of the grass. In another moment they would be in position.

I turned and faced the decaying pilot hunched before me. He was bent forward, as though he had fought to free himself and been paralyzed into position by the torrid flames.

I brought my blade up, then swiftly down through the mass of flies. It cracked hard into the back of his neck. His head fell with a soft thud onto the cockpit floor. The cavernous hollow eyes of the head peered up into mine. I hurried to stretch the opening of the sand-bag over the skull, closed and tied it.

Suddenly, the silence was shattered by the stuttering blast of full-automatic weapon fire.

I had heard that ominous slow cycling rate of fire before, spewing its potent 7.62 lead at me. It was AK-47 fire, and it was right on us.

I dropped the sandbag to the ground and jerked the muzzle of my weapon toward the fierce enemy fire. During the movement, I saw Will take a hit in his back.

He arched backward, still standing, as though an ax had been driven into his lower spine. His mouth gaped. He screamed to Rham and Tuong, *"Didi mau!"*

They instantly dropped their burden and sprinted toward the chopper.

Will pivoted to face the savage attack. His CAR-15 erupted as three khaki-clad figures raced on-line toward him. The spewing lead from Will's oscillating weapon bit directly into them. The impacting lead twisted and jerked their bodies, then sent them surging backward and lifeless into the tangled grass. Still firing, he turned. His rounds ripped into a crouched rocket launcher near the tree line.

The NVA slumped face forward over the rocket tube.

A dark red circle soaked the back of Will's shirt. As Rham and Tuong slid beneath the chopper's belly, I yanked my cravat from my face and yelled, "Cover me!" and rushed toward Will.

The Cowboys opened fire, paralleling my movement. Their tracer rounds streaked by me like burning red stars cutting through the elephant grass.

Will turned and began to hobble toward me. His arm trembled as he reached out to me.

Without warning, a hammering burst of AK-47 fire came from a tree behind him. The enemy lead tore into Will's back, slamming him face down into the matted grass. The steady, cracking bark from the sniper's weapon continued.

I screamed, "Stay down, Will! I got him!"

I tilted the barrel of my rifle up toward the tree-shrouded figure and triggered a burst of fire directly at him.

The sniper's body crashed straight down through the foliage and came to sprawl in a forked lower limb of the tree. He rolled quickly over a limb, and hung there a second at arm's length, then dropped to the ground.

There was no time to pursue the bastard. The last thing I saw was his skinny frame and clean-shaven head disappearing, limping into the foliage.

Frantically, I dived forward to Will's side and knelt to gently roll his blood-soaked body over onto his back. The assassin's rounds had penetrated through him and ripped a blood-squirting, fist-sized hole in his chest.

Will's dark eyes began to open. He squinted at me with silent bloodshot agony. I supported his head with one hand and strained to smile into his eyes while madly jerking a first-aid packet from my web gear.

"Damn, partner, you've been a regular one-man

show over here," I said, forcing a calm tone. "I hope you don't mind me butting in on you."

A weak half smile came across his face. Red drool filtered through his teeth as he spoke softly. "Naw, man . . . I was needing to reload anyhow."

I ripped his blood-wet shirt open and slammed the bandage over the red flow. Trying to stop the blood gushing from his chest with the small gauze pad was as useless as a postage stamp on a cracked dam.

I laid his head carefully back into the red, matted grass, then furiously yanked the cravat from my neck. I hurriedly folded the cloth into a square and placed it over the red, oozing hole. I felt the wet, sucking wound grasp the textured cloth as I applied a firm pressure with my hands.

The covering fire from the team ceased. I swung my head back toward the slick while keeping both hands pressing down on the wound.

I shouted, "Rham! Tuong! *La dai!*"

My glance went back to Will's head and saw his eyes beginning to close. "Will, don't go to sleep, damn it. You know about shock! Don't go to sleep . . . and don't fuckin' die!"

Abruptly, his hand reached up and gripped my arm. His head tilted forward. He tugged weakly to draw me near his face. I reached to cradle his head in my hand and leaned to hear his slow words.

He coughed. A thick dark syrup rolled through his lips. "Tell Chunky . . . I'm goin' 'cross the river, man. I'll see her and the kids . . . over there. Might even see you there, boss."

His eyes began to roll slowly back into his half-closed lids. As his body shivered, I bent, whispering into his ear, "I love you, Will. I'll give your message to Chunky, don't you worry, partner."

The moment eclipsed. His eyes froze as though peering into another world, and his strong neck went limp in my trembling hands.

My teeth clenched hard to halt the swelling tears. I pulled his blood-drenched body up into my embrace and kissed his wet, spongy hair. His warm blood soaked into my chest and the sweet odor of his sweat filled my nostrils.

I shouted up into God's face, "Goddamn you and this sick fucking war!"

Chapter 4

A faint cracking noise came over the radio handset. "Texas, this is Raven. Over." I ignored the voice. It blurted again, louder: "Texas, this is Raven. Over."

I laid Will gently back on the grass, drew in a deep, heavy breath, and pulled the handset to my ear. "This is Texas. Over."

"This is Raven. We're running short on time, Texas. Y'all about to wind things up down there? Over."

The urgency in his voice drew my attention to my watch: 0851 hours. We were in overtime. I answered, "Roger, Raven. Fuckin' mission accomplished. I got one dead, no wounded. Lima zulu clear. I'm going to need you to sit down so we can get the bodies loaded. Over."

"Roger, Texas, understand. We're comin' in. Do we need a Cobra prep on the lima zulu? Over."

"Negative, Raven. I say again, lima zulu clear. We wasted a squad-size NVA element. If there's more of the bastards out there, I don't think they want any more. Over."

"Roger, copy, Texas. Whip some smoke on us. Raven out."

I yanked a yellow smoke grenade from my shoulder strap. Looking around, I saw Rham and Tuong kneeling over the door gunner's body, gazing silently at Will. Tuong's lip was quivering as if he wanted to cry, but wouldn't.

Tuong had been closer to Will than the other team members. He had given Will his first Buddha, actually a matched set.

That hot afternoon, Will and I had sat on the steps of the team hooch to clean our rifles. Tuong marched proudly up to us and held out two small Buddhas carved in stone. Each dangled from a thin gold chain.

Will looked up at him, smiled, and said, "What you got there, Babysan?"

Tuong, swelling with pride, said, "For you, Papasan."

Will reached out and gathered both Buddhas into his hand. "Wow, you must think I'm in for a heapa trouble, giving me two Buddhas."

Through a playful smile Tuong replied, "No *dinky-dow*, one for you and one for Mamasan Chunky. You send one Mamasan, she be okay then. You no have to worry for her."

Will's eyes gleamed down at the Buddhas resting in his hand. "Okay, Babysan, *merci beaucoup*. How 'bout you givin' me a picture of you. I'll send it with Buddha to Mamasan Chunky, okay?"

Delighted with the opportunity to send his picture to Chunky, Tuong quickly yanked a canvas wallet from his hip pocket. He carefully studied each picture as he sorted through them. Finally, he selected one and handed it to Will.

Will took the photo and placed it and the Buddhas into his shirt pocket. Glancing back at Tuong with a polite but puzzled look, he asked, "How 'bout Brett? Don't he get one?"

Tuong laughed. "No, him already have *beaucoup*. Him need *beaucoup*. You, one!"

I smiled at Will and explained. "Partner, that's a compliment to you, just needing one. The little people think I need more protection than you do, me being a terminal sinner and all. If I wore all the Buddhas they've given me in the past eight months, I'd need a damn back brace."

The moment ended with Tuong, Will, and me all laughing. Then, true to form, and although he had been part of it, Tuong asked, "Sar Brett, what funny?"

I jerked the pin and threw the smoke grenade toward the center of the LZ. Hissing yellow smoke bellowed from the canister engulfing the area in its rising jaundiced cloud. I quickly reloaded my weapon and motioned for Rham and Tuong to retrieve the door gunner's body. "You carry. Follow me."

I turned, picked up Will's rifle, and slipped the carrying strap over my neck beside mine. I grasped Will's arm and bent to pull his limp body up and over my shoulder. Draped over my back, his chest rested on the radio pack. I gripped his legs tightly against my stomach and trudged into the pale yellow fog. Rham and Tuong tugged the rigid corpse along the ground behind me.

As we approached the blackened chopper, Lok and Phan scurried from their positions beneath its belly. Lok had already picked up the other sandbag I had dropped. He stood holding both of them at his side.

The acrid mist from the grenade smoke stung my nostrils and watered my eyes. My labored breathing drew in more of the foul sulfur vapor. Vomit surged into my mouth. I bent to spit out the bitter liquid while continuing to plod forward.

Our slick was on final approach. The slow whopping thunder drew nearer. Its drab shadow began descending into the haze. When the claws of the struts reached for the ground, the rotor's hot draft scattered the smoke and sent a wave of charred ground dust gusting into my face. I squinted while moving ahead. After a brief hover, the chopper sat down.

The Hispanic door gunner leapt out and ran toward me. His eyes narrowed as he came closer and saw it was Will I was carrying. "Oh, man!" The gunner groaned loudly. "I didn't know it was your partner that got hit. Is he—"

I shouted, "He's dead, damn it. Help the Cowboys with that body."

His eyes turned to see Lok run by us and toward the chopper. The head-laden sandbags gripped in his hands were bouncing and swinging.

"Wh-where are the other bodies, man?" the gunner said, stuttering. "I—I only see that one." He pointed to Rham and Tuong tugging the corpse past him.

I yelled, "This is it, man! Now, give 'em a hand damn it! Let's get the fuck out of here."

He stared fearfully down at the bloody sack covering the stiff corpse's head. A shocked look came over his face. Stunned, he stepped back. His dark eyes teared. Recovering from his shock, he quickly lunged forward, grabbed the shoulders, and began moving ahead with Rham and Tuong. When they arrived at the door of the chopper, they swung the body up into the cabin, as though it were a sack of potatoes being thrown into a truck. We had body bags on board but there was no time for formalities.

I was the last one to the chopper. I bent forward at the edge of the door and gently tilted Will's body from my shoulder and onto the floor.

Tuong shuffled over the door gunner's body between us, then carefully pulled Will toward the center. He laid Will's head on his lap. Tears streamed down Tuong's face as he stared at the small bloodstained Buddha hanging from Will's neck.

I jumped into the crowded troop cabin, hurriedly scanned the team, and checked to make sure Lok still had both sandbags. All present. I thrust my arm forward and shouted, "All clear!"

I quickly turned and sat facing outward. My legs hung over the door edge as the chopper's turbine revved. I watched the smoky terrain fall away and studied the stage and the scene that marked the final moments of Sergeant William Washington.

Before these moments, I could have perhaps walked away from this fuckin' war and felt I had done my share. But now I felt a stronger sense of commitment, not just blind loyalty to a cause. My stronger commitment was a firm promise to Will. A promise to return and to kill the bald bastard who'd taken his life. And a promise to keep Texas, the team Will had been such a proud part of, pressing on with the same spirit and performance that he had helped to mold and maintain.

As we rose higher over the trees, our Cobras swooped in from the surrounding canopy and sped into their lead position. Although I hadn't noticed it during exfil, they had evidently stayed on-station at low altitude. They had deliberately exposed themselves as easy targets for ground fire, so they could aid us faster if the shit hit the fan during those final moments before lift-off. They knew their close presence would make Chuck think twice.

All of our air assets had performed outstandingly. It would be my privilege to write it up and recommend them for appropriate decorations. But right now there was something else that needed to be written. I turned, motioned for the door gunner to switch off my radio, then reached into my pocket and pulled out a small green notebook and a pen. I leaned back against the gray quilted pad covering the interior wall of the troop cabin and began to write:

On August 28, Recon Team Texas, operating in conduct of a body-recovery mission at target designator Hotel-5, engaged hostile elements of the North Vietnamese Army in a heavy exchange of combat fire. As team leader of RT Texas, I submit the following account of events as authentic documentation of what occurred during that action. This account is submitted as valid basis for recommendation of award for one team member who distinguished himself far beyond the requirements of duty.

At approximately 0828 hours, RT Texas infiltrated the target via air assets provided by 1st Air Cavalry, Da Nang AFB. Enemy contact was made during infiltration. Upon assessment of the situation, it became necessary to split the team in order to perform the recovery. I assigned Sergeant William Washington the task of leading an element to recover a door gunner's body, which was hanging from a tree approximately forty meters from the downed helicopter. It warrants mention that Sergeant Washington had sustained an ankle injury

during infiltration, but did not reveal the seriousness of the injury so as not to impede the mission.

In pain, Sergeant Washington led his element
into the area and retrieved the body. During his
return to our location, at the center of the LZ,
Sergeant Washington sustained an enemy gunshot
wound in his back. He then, without regard for his
personal safety, directed his personnel to return to
the main element. Sergeant Washington then
turned and provided covering fire to protect their
withdrawal. I observed Sergeant Washington kill
at least three of the enemy at close proximity to
his position as they attacked him. He then turned
and killed an NVA B-40 rocket-launcher operator.
After the hostile exchange, Sergeant Washington,
wounded and with an impaired ankle, tried to return to our position. During that time, Sergeant
Washington was hit with heavy sniper fire and fell
to the ground. I returned fire. Sergeant Washington died in my arms a few moments later.

To say Sergeant Washington's uncommon display of valor and unselfish dedication to duty were
"in keeping with the highest traditions of the military service" is not true. Sergeant Washington
exceeded those standards.

It is formally requested that Sergeant Washington be recommended for our country's highest
award, the Medal of Honor.

Details of the aforementioned engagement will
be available in my after-action report, to be submitted upon return to base.

Respectfully submitted,
SSG Brett A. Yancy
Team leader RT Texas, CCN

I pulled a piece of fire-retardant canvas from my pocket, wrapped it carefully around the small notebook, then pushed it under my belt and down into my crotch. I reasoned if we took a hit somewhere between here and base and went down, at least part of Will's story might still have a chance to be told.

I pondered the words I'd just written. It seemed wrong that the final valiant moments of a good man could be boiled down to a few paragraphs. So much more of Will's story needed to be told. My hand reached to touch my friend. My fingers gripped the damp matted tangles of his dark hair.

I whispered, "Someday, partner, I'll tell your story. I fuckin' promise."

My eyes turned slowly to the Hispanic door gunner seated beside me. He seemed mesmerized as he gazed at the jungle some three thousand feet below us. I remembered the laughter we'd shared on the way to the target, and his moment of fear when he first witnessed the carnage on the LZ. Now, a sadness showed in his eyes, and I sensed what was troubling him. I nudged his leg.

He jerked from his trance and blinked, as if I had shocked him.

I moved closer to him, extended him my right hand, and strengthened my voice to a tone of anticipation. "Amigo, it seems like I ought to know your name by now. Mine's Yancy. Brett Yancy."

He raised his right hand from the machine gun and moved it slowly into my grip, saying, "I'm Hector. Hector Gomez, El Paso, Texas."

His eyes avoided mine. He seemed reluctant to talk.

I planned my words to try to take some of the edge

off his somber mood. "Man, that almost makes us cousins or something. I'm from Texas too. Mineral Wells." I glanced back with a grin. "What I want to tell you is, y'all did a great job for us today. Tops."

With a meek smile, he looked into my eyes and gave all the credit to someone else. "Thanks, man, but it's these pilots who do it. They're great."

For a moment, Hector avoided my eyes. Then he looked back at me and said, "Look, man, I feel a little uncool with that shake scene I dropped on you back there at the target. I'm real sorry. It was—"

I interrupted him. "Hector, you don't have to apologize. Believe me, you handled it better than I did when I first saw it. Shit, I came un-fuckin'-glued!"

I was starting to sound like Swede Jensen.

I looked back at Hector and changed the subject. "By the way, you handled that M-60 like you grew up with it."

A spark of enthusiasm lit up his face. His voice raised above the steady, soft roar of the chopper. "Thanks. My dad was a range instructor at Fort Bliss. I could field-strip an M-60 before I learned how to heat the springs on my dad's '60 Chevy."

Puzzled, I responded, "Excuse me for asking a dumb question, but what the hell are you talking about? Heating springs?"

He gleamed with an amused grin. "You Anglo dudes aren't into low-riders. Well"—he moved his open hand up and down as if it were an important part of the story—"the best way to turn a gringo-mobile into a low-rider is to take a torch and heat the springs. You just lay underneath it, move the torch back and forth along the spring, and in a few minutes, presto, it starts to drop right down. The scientific explanation is that it takes the temper out of the metal and causes it to lose its strength. But you have to be careful when you do the rear springs.''

''Why's that? Seems like it would be easier to do the rear springs.''

''Well, you got the gas tank back there, see, and with that torch it has a way of igniting the fumes. My buddy, Raymond, found out about that the hard way one afternoon. He was doing his rear springs and should have put a wet blanket around the gas tank to keep the sparks away from the gas, but he didn't. Man, when that thing exploded, it blew him and his mustache clear across the fuckin' garage!''

''Did it kill him?''

''No, just burned him a little.'' He paused before continuing with a reminiscent grin across his face. ''But he never did find his mustache!''

Will and I had shared off-the-wall conversations about a lot of things. For the moment it was like being with him. It was good to see Hector shake off his depression. The conversation had helped take my mind off things for a while.

Smiling, I asked, ''Well, how did your dad like his Chevy when you got through with it?''

His head shake was as though my question sparked an amused but somehow painful memory. ''Man, he didn't like it one damn bit. He wore my ass out and told me I wasn't going to drive his car again until I replaced the springs. You know how much four new springs for a '60 Chevy cost? One hundred and eighty-five dollars, that's how much. It took me working most of the summer to pay for those springs. I never cared much for low-riders after that.''

I shared his grin. ''My dad laid the law down to me

a couple of times too. So what are you doing in the army? Get drafted, or just follow in your dad's footsteps?''

"No, man, I joined the army. Not for this fuckin' war, or to be like my dad. My dad is tops, and the army was a good life for us. But all I want out of this is a piece of that GI Bill and a chance to go to college when I get out. Nobody in our family ever went to college. My dad told me, and I can believe it, 'an education is the only thing in this life somebody can't take away from you.' ''

A gleam of pride shone in his eyes when he spoke of his dad. "What kind of degree you shooting for?''

He smiled and looked out into the clear sky. "Man, I know it sounds funny, but I want a B.S. in crop and soil science. I feel like I've picked enough fruit in my lifetime to fill up the Orange Bowl. I'd like to learn about the scientific end of it and maybe grow my own someday. I guess it's in my blood.''

I began to feel tired. "Hector, good luck. I think you'll do fine.''

I checked my watch: 0910. We still had about an hour to base. I looked around to check the team. They were all asleep. I noticed that Phan's CAR-15 was still on automatic. Stretching to reach over the bodies, I flipped his selector switch to safety.

I glanced back at Hector and said, "I'm going to nod out. If we take a thirty-seven hit, don't wake me up. I'd just as soon die asleep.''

He smiled back. "We're outa thirty-seven range. That's why we're at three grand. But, if anything does happen, I'll just say a quick Hail Mary over you.''

I winked back. "If you say Hail Maries over me,

don't say 'em too loud. You might just get us struck by lightning!''

He grinned, then looked intently into my eyes. "Look, man, I just want to say I'm real sorry about your partner. He seemed like a good dude. Man, I know it's tough on you losin' him that way."

His sincerity struck a lonely note in me. I avoided his eyes and replied, as though talking to the wind, "He was fuckin' great! He made this team. You know, the colonel wanted Will to form and train his own team, but he loved RT Texas, wouldn't leave. He'll always be with us. Every time we kick ass or have to run, he'll be with us every step of the fuckin' way."

I gave a quick glance to Hector Gomez, then leaned back near Will and slept.

Chapter 5

I awoke with Hector shaking me. "Yancy, we're about ten minutes out."

I leaned forward and smelled the familiar stink of Da Nang rising to greet us. Our common flight path back from Laos crossed directly over Da Nang. From there it was ten klicks southeast to our coastal base camp.

Da Nang's stench had a lot to do with its harbor. It was contaminated with everything from sewage and garbage to blood and bodies. Every year, the monsoons caused the city to flood, giving it a knee-deep bath in sewer residue. After centuries of an annual bath in sewage Da Nang smelled like well-seasoned shit.

When Bob Hope performed in Da Nang, he stepped off the plane that hot morning and was immediately hit with the odor. He asked, "What on earth is that smell?"

A sergeant, standing with the greeting party, answered, "Bob, that's shit."

Bob replied, "My God, what do they do to it?"

I turned toward Tuong. He was asleep and still cradling Will's head in his lap. I gently placed my hand over Tuong's mouth and nudged him. When his sleepy childlike eyes began to open, I signaled for him to wake the team.

Tuong turned to the man nearest him and placed his hand over the man's mouth, then tapped him. After waking, each team member performed the same steps to wake the man adjacent to him. I watched. They did it the way Will had taught them. I suppose it really didn't matter how someone was awakened up here in a chopper, but it did matter in the bush, and I wanted good habits maintained whenever possible, especially noise discipline.

Noise discipline was an important part of any covert operation. But, on Chuck's turf, it was critical. Since it was not unusual for Chuck to probe for our position at night, the slightest noise could suddenly become fatal. If a man was awakened abruptly, he might make a sound, and that would be all Chuck needed to lock in on us. Our team SOP, standard operating procedure, now required that a man be awakened in such a way as to prevent inadvertent noise.

The new technique had been invented by Sergeant William Washington.

Will had told me his idea on the same evening we returned from a mission—Will's first with Texas. It was a five-day wiretap and sensor plant on an NVA battalion located near Saravan, Laos. Our RON, short for "rest overnight," position had been so close to the battalion headquarters that if a man sneezed during the night, one of the enemy guards might have said, *"Gesundheit!"*

That evening, after filing our after-action Report, Will and I sat in the camp honky-tonk drinking well-deserved beers and enjoying the air-conditioning. Something was bothering Will. About halfway through the second beer, he leaned forward, placed both elbows on the table, and spoke with his slow Southern drawl. "Boss, what would you say if I told you that our RON procedure during that wiretap mission scared the hell out of me?"

I leaned back in my chair and thought about it. Will was the type of man who never complained, even when there was plenty to gripe about. Instead, he would see a problem, think about it for a while, then offer a solution. If his recommendation wasn't accepted, he would press on, live with it, and never bitch about the consequences.

Will leaned on the table, smiling as though he'd said his piece and was prepared to negotiate.

Looking into his shining dark eyes, I said, "Partner, I'd say you're not a man who's easily scared. So, maybe we need to fine-tune the SOP a little. But our RON SOP has always worked in the past."

Will caught my defensive tone, grinned, and responded with a slight sideward tilt of his head. "Brett, that last sentence sounds like something the captain of the *Titanic* might have said to his first mate about their iceberg procedure."

I laughed, tapped my beer can against his, and raised it in a toast. "Roger, buddy, you're right. What do you have in mind?"

Listening, it became immediately obvious to me that Will had given a great deal of thought to this procedure. He didn't hesitate or linger on his words as he outlined his idea. "It's pretty darn natural for a man to be just a little jumpy when he's done slipped up to sleep on the enemy's back porch like we did these last four nights. Once during the night, when I woke up Rham, he made a noise like he'd just been stung by a bee or something. Man, it scared the hell outa me! I thought sure Chuck had heard him. Anyhow, I got to thinking, and here's what I come up with. I call it Safe Sleep SOP.''

I listened intently and tried not to gape at the simple genius of it.

Will's idea was to have the team sleep in a wagon-wheel formation with our heads forming a kind of hub near the center. He recommended each man be required to maintain a one-hour, sitting-up vigil while the others slept. At the end of his watch, he would lean over to the next man, place his hand over his mouth to restrain any noise he might make, then nudge him. The watch duty would be passed around the circle at one-hour intervals to allow each man five hours of rest, providing Chuck didn't interrupt our beauty sleep.

If we were probed during the night, the man on guard would start the silent chainlike action to wake the team. I would then make the decision to move out or hold our position. The concept was a big improvement over our old haphazard, sleep-anywhere, wake-any-way method.

After Will completed detailing his concept, I sat up straight in my chair, narrowed my eyes in admiration, and said, ''Partner, I think it's great. In fact, I'd stand up and applaud, but I don't want your head to get too big for your beret. If I schedule some team training time for tomorrow morning, can you lead us through it?''

''Roger, boss, you got it,'' he said, smiling.

''Now, how about another beer?''

Will declined a third beer, saying he needed to get

back to the hooch and write Chunky and the kids a letter.

The next morning we all assembled on the shady side of the team hooch and Will showed us how he wanted it done. As he taught the class, I could see the Cowboys weren't really interested in the new method, and blamed myself for the poor response from them. It was always tough to get the little people to accept change. I felt like I had probably jumped too soon on this one. We had all just returned from a five-day mission and the Cowboys probably would have preferred being downtown in Da Nang getting laid, instead of learning a new way to wake someone up. In fact, that same preference was drifting through my mind at the time.

Nonetheless, Will gave a good class. At the conclusion of it, the team rehearsed the method with everyone in the wagon-wheel position. The performance from the little people was poor.

After the class, I complimented Will on his instruction.

He shook his head and replied, "Thanks, boss, but I guess the old saying is true."

"What's that, buddy?"

Will smiled back, looking up at me. "You can lead a horse to water, but you can't make him drink. So, I have an idea that just might start these little horses to sippin'."

Will didn't bother to explain what he meant, and I didn't question him about it. Just before daybreak the next morning, he made his point.

At dawn, Will awoke and moved silently through the hooch, waking each of us with his hand-over-the-mouth method. Upon awakening, he signaled for each person to sit up, maintain silence, and observe. While all of us watched him through the dim morning light, he crept to Phan's bunk. Phan was still fast asleep. Will deliberately avoided using his new method and nudged Phan abruptly. Phan jumped almost straight up in bed and shouted, ''Puck you!''

There was an instant chorus of sidesplitting laughter. The dazed and bewildered look on Phan's face was one I wished I had caught on film.

After the laughter died down, Will turned to the team, his point well illustrated, and said, ''You see, Chuck going to fuck you, if you no use my way.''

Not surprisingly, Phan became the most ardent practitioner of the new waking method and was forever after nicknamed Puck-you Phan.

Will's sleep formation and waking technique became well known around camp and was quickly adopted by all teams as SOP.

Our chopper dropped altitude as we neared base camp. Command and Control North was wall-to-wall sand. Except for the cement bunkers, the barracks, and the guard towers the SeaBees had built, the entire base was ankle-deep sand.

It was an uncommonly large camp, about two hundred meters wide and twice that distance in length. Although Special Forces ran the camp, we comprised only twenty-five percent of the total camp strength. The other seventy-five percent were Legs—nonjump-qualified soldiers—who were assigned here to perform noncombatant jobs. They handled the mess hall, motor pool, and the communications facility. Vietnamese soldiers functioned as guards.

In addition, there was a camp barber, a laundry, and house girls who cleaned the hooches. Most of the indigenous workers went back to Da Nang every day at 1700 hours.

The camp was bounded on the west by a marsh, on the north by a petroleum dump, and on the east by the South China Sea.

One hundred meters off the southern side of our perimeter stood Marble Mountain. It was a geographical freak of sorts, rocky crust dotted with scrub brush. The mountain spanned some one thousand meters in length, and protruded over two hundred feet out of what was otherwise a flat coastal landscape.

The mountain, as wide as it was high, housed a maze of caverns and tunnels that the local Buddhist monks used for religious retreats, and the VC used as hideouts. Although we maintained a continuous control outpost on the summit, Chuck occasionally lobbed a mortar round into our camp from the mouth of one of the many caves.

While we couldn't prove it, we believed the Buddhist monks played a Jekyll and Hyde role; robed monks by day and black-clad VC by night. We killed six of them back in April during a sapper attack, enemy suicide squads. They had slipped through our wire with satchel charges. Before it was over, they had cost us eight American lives and seventeen "indige" lives, plus a supply building.

Even after our heavy losses the Vietnamese government still wouldn't evict the monks. It seemed the monks were their religious reps, and nobody wanted to take the responsibility for pissing off God. So the monks stayed, and we endured.

But after the April sapper attack, our hindsight sharpened. We added three more double-high rolls of concertina wire around the entire camp and a ten-meter mine field between the outer and inner wire zones.

It was a damn shame we had to lose twenty-five men before somebody woke up to the need to beef up our defenses. It was kind of like a city back home that allowed children to be killed at an intersection before they saw the need for a fucking traffic light.

Chapter 6

As the Huey lowered us into a swirling cloud of sand, I saw Colonel Kahn standing at the edge of the chopper pad. Holding his beret in his hand, he squinted up at our chopper.

Dignitaries and death were the only events that brought a crowd to the chopper pad at CCN. Death was more often the occasion. About a dozen men, Americans and indige, were gathered to greet us and help unload. That was the way Colonel Kahn wanted it. He seldom had to issue an order to gather the needed personnel. Each man took it upon himself to lend a hand. Rarely did anyone have to tell another what needed to be done. We had all done it many times before.

The final jolt of our chopper jarred my spirit when the struts came to rest abruptly on the cement surface of the landing pad. The shrill whine of the turbine began to fade. A curtain of dirt and sand rolled away with a final dying breath out over the camp. We were home.

Colonel Kahn hurried ahead of the others and was the first one to the chopper. I stood by the troop door as he approached. The squinched skin of seasoned frown marks gathered in hard vertical lines between his eyebrows when he peered into the cabin and saw Will's body lying on the floor. The blue glint of his grim eyes turned to look into mine. It was the first moment since I had begun to live with Will's death that I'd truly felt another person's sorrow touch mine.

Tuong gently rolled Will's body over into my arms and the colonel's. I avoided the eyes of my comrades as we carried Will slowly across the landing pad and laid him on the warm sand. I felt Colonel Kahn's hand grip my shoulder as I knelt at Will's side. Each word he spoke rang into my senses like the tolling of a bell.

"Brett, it's the hardest lick a man can take . . . losing a partner like Washington. I've known that loss. It lives with a man forever. Keep his spirit alive inside you and press on, the way he would expect you to."

I reached and yanked the dark, bloodstained Buddha from Will's neck. For a moment, I pondered the irony of the smiling stone figure in my hand. It represented truth, honor, fidelity, and purity. Well, so did Will.

Will had lived, laughed, loved, fought, sweated, and died with honor. William Washington was real, and I was bitter and resentful of anything that cloaked itself in divinity. The truly divine lay lifeless beside me. I wanted to stuff the bogus stone god down the dying throat of the bastard who took Will's life.

The spirit of revenge overtook me. I remembered the shiny head of the sniper I had watched limp into the woods. I'd never seen an NVA with a clean-shaven head. I even knew the bastard's address. Before long, one way or another, I'd be calling at that address— target designator Hotel-5.

I stood and dropped the Buddha into my pocket, then reached into my pants and pulled out the notebook in which I had written my recommendation for Will's award. I tore out the pages and handed them to Colonel Kahn.

"This is important, sir. I'd appreciate it if you could give this your personal attention." My voice quivered. "It's the final chapter in a good man's life."

Two men approached with a plastic body bag. The colonel wiped the corner of his eye and cleared his voice. "Roger, Brett, understand. Look . . . we'll finish up here. Why don't you and your team get some rest?"

I removed my ruck, sat it on the ground, and walked away without looking back. I couldn't stand to see Will stuffed into a wrinkled plastic bag.

Tuong, Rham, Phan, Lok, and I walked slowly toward the ocean and onto the glistening sand of the beach. I sat down, surrounded by the silent Montagnards, and gazed out toward the horizon. Sparkles of sunlight danced across the shimmering water. It was a scene Will and I had often shared.

I lowered my head onto my arms and wept.

Chapter 7

A short time later the team assembled in the hooch for our usual postmission weapons cleaning. Afterward, I inspected each weapon then released the Cowboys for a three-day pass. I knew it would be at least a week, very likely longer, before we drew another mission.

Late in the afternoon, I met with Colonel Kahn and several staff officers in the command bunker to submit my after-action report. After reading the report they didn't question my decision to take the heads.

While there I queried Colonel Kahn regarding my Medal of Honor recommendation for Will. He assured me it had his complete approval, and he would submit it to higher headquarters along with his endorsement the following day.

After the meeting, I stayed in the small room and wrote four separate letters of commendation for the pilots who supported us during the mission. I also wrote a recommendation for awarding the Bronze Star to Hector Gomez. He had earned it. I hoped the bureaucracy didn't downgrade my recommendation to a hearty handshake and a smile. It wouldn't be the first time, if they did.

It was dusk when I exited the bunker and stepped into a light misty rain. Trudging through moist sand toward my hooch, I smelled the odor of burned rice. I peered toward two indiges squatting under a lookout tower cooking their evening meal before mounting the tower for night guard duty.

Their chattering always seemed happier when they were hunkered by a fire, stirring a steaming pot of rice. Warm vapor from the cooking pot rose lazily into the evening air as I walked by them. They didn't look up at me. The glow from the small fire flickered orange light across their faces. It was as though nothing else in the world mattered to them except that damn rice.

The muffled beat of jukebox music rose as I approached the camp honky-tonk. I started to pass by, but if I wanted a cold Coke to mix with the Jim Beam in my hooch, this was the only place to get it. When I walked into the club, everything fell quiet except the rasping beat of the jukebox. Feeling conspicuous, I walked over to the bar. I stood next to a massive man I didn't recognize. He leaned against the bar, staring down at an empty shot glass.

"*Lai day*, Fousi," I said curtly.

The pretty Vietnamese girl behind the bar scurried to me. Her grief-stricken face told me the whole camp knew about Will.

"*Hai* Coke!" My voice was tired and cold.

That wasn't fair, not to Fousi. She had been like a little sister to Will and me. Her parents had been killed by the Communists several years before. She had given me a Buddha. A special Buddha—the one that belonged to her father. Will and I taught her English, and she had tutored us in Vietnamese. Orphaned at the age of thirteen, Fousi had inherited the responsibility of supporting two younger sisters and her grandmother. She had had to grow up fast. It would have been easier and a lot more lucrative for her to become a prostitute—but she hadn't. There was a silent strength about Fousi. Will and I both had grown to love her. She was special, and she didn't deserve any crap from me.

She gingerly sat two cans of Coke on the bar and tried to smile. But a tear betrayed her. I wanted to reach out and wipe the tear from her face. But I couldn't. She tilted her head and hastily wiped the tears from her face.

A voice spoke beside me. I turned my head left and saw the drawn face of Swede Jensen.

"Real sorry to hear about Washington, Brett." He was too. It showed in his eyes.

As I started to speak, the large humped figure on my right side interrupted me. He blurted, "Yeah, I was sorry to hear about the nigger too."

A rage exploded inside me. My right arm coiled and drove a fist back and up into his ugly face. My blow lifted his slouched torso to full height, towering above me. A stupefied glare appeared briefly on his bloody face. My left smashed his mouth. He stumbled blindly backward, crashing into tables. I lunged forward. Jensen darted in front of me.

"Yancy! Don't kill the puke! He's out for the count."

I froze and stared at the unconscious, blood-spattered figure on the floor. A shiver of exhilaration swept through me. Breathing heavily, I turned and picked up the cans on the bar.

Glancing at Jensen, I said, "When he wakes up, tell him pain builds character, and he's in for more if I ever hear that word from him again."

Jensen laughed. "Roger that."

I walked through the crowd into the rain. By the time I reached my hooch the rain was heavy. Entering the large one-room hut, I pulled off my hat and flipped the light switch on. A gust from the monsoon swung the small bulb dangling from the ceiling, casting swinging shadows across the emptiness. Hard rain pelted against the tin roof. The room had never seemed so lonely.

In the center of the room was a big makeshift picnic table Will and I had built. The long benches seated three on each side. The table was our gathering place for chess games, letter writing, weapons cleaning, and drinking. Along the left and right side of the room there were six evenly spaced bunks.

I walked by the row of beds to the corner of the room unofficially designated as the team bar. A small diagonal piece of plywood nailed onto two short wooden braces.

Above the bar hung a large poster, a cartoon picture of a soldier charging up a hill through a barrage of enemy fire while returning fire with an M-60 machine gun. At the bottom it read: NEXT VACATION WHY NOT CONSIDER VISITING SCENIC VIETNAM? A full quart of Jim Beam sat on the shelf below it.

I blew the loose sand out of a cup and poured a fifty-fifty mixture of Beam and Coke into it. Lifting the cup, the aroma brought back a caravan of memories. Good memories. Memories of women, friends, and happier times. For a moment, my mind lingered with those memories.

I stepped across the room and pulled a pocket-size book from the shelf above my bunk, then sat at the large picnic table. It was the *The Prophet*, Will's second bible. He'd given me a copy for my birthday. He said it was the type of book that should be received

from a friend, not purchased out of curiosity. I opened
it to the inside flap and read the words he had written
into it.

> To Brett Yancy, July 9, 1969
> "Your friend is your needs answered . . . and
> when you part from him you grieve not, for that
> which you love most in him may be clearer in his
> absence, as the mountain to the climber is clearer
> from the plain."
>
>   Happy Birthday, Will W.

I sat alone at the big table, reading through Gibran,
sipping my drink. There was a hard knock on the door,
and then, swept in by the windy night, the lanky dripping figure of Swede Jensen lumbered into the room.
He slammed the door behind him, removed his soaked
bush hat, and slapped it hard against his leg.

Pulling a can of Coke from the side pocket on his
fatigue pants, he said, "Thought I might de-virginize
this Coke with some Jim Beam."

I closed the book and swirled down the remainder of
my drink. "Sure, come on in, Swede. Step over to the
Hobo-Hilton bar and I'll blend us up a couple."

As we walked toward the bar, Jensen lit a cigarette.
"Man, you fucked that boy up over at the club. Broke
his damn jaw."

I mixed two stout drinks and handed one to him.

Jensen continued while we walked back to the table.
"The man's name is Johnson. He's just a stay-behind
Leg. Works up in the teletype room at the headshed.
They had to haul him to the hospital in Da Nang. The

son of a bitch will probably apply for the Purple Heart while he's there . . . if and when he finally wakes up.''

I didn't comment on Jensen's after-action report. We sat at the table across from each other. ''There's probably some sand in your drink, Swede. That proverbial defecation's everywhere.''

Jensen smiled and raised his glass high above him. ''Here's to proverbial defecation, and here's to Colonel Kahn, and here's to Sergeant Will Washington.''

We brought our cups together, drew them back, and took a good drink. Jensen grimaced, then smiled. ''You're right, Yancy, damn sand's everywhere around this fuckin' place. Yesterday one of the house girls whipped some fuckin' on me, and it seemed like I felt sand in her.''

I laughed.

He looked up solemnly. ''Yancy, what I started to say before the shit . . . I mean, proverbial defecation, hit the cooling apparatus over there a while ago was—''

I broke in. ''No need for words, Swede. I understand. Thanks.''

''Did you get the bastard that killed Washington?''

The jabbing memory of the bald, khaki-clad sniper limping into the jungle burned again in my mind. For a moment it smoldered inside me. I stared into my drink. ''No, I didn't. But I will. I won't leave this fucking war until it's done.''

His eyes hardened with the look of a bull staring into a red cape, then he blinked several times and returned to the moment. ''I know what's gnawing inside you, Brett. I lost one of my Cowboys last month in that same area.

''Puan was his name, one of my best. He was on point when we fuckin' near walked into an ambush.

They hit him like a swarm of hornets. Nothin' I could do about it, didn't even get his body back.

"All we could do was run our asses off. But I still remember seeing lead rip through him, and the way his body twisted and jerked, and the fuckin' muzzle flashes! Shit, even after he was down and dead, one of the scumsuckin' pigs kept firing into him." Swede looked toward the ceiling and shouted, "Shit! You think I don't want some fuckin' payback on these heathen bastards too?"

A silent moment passed while he peered into his half-empty cup. Finally, he looked up at me and asked, "Did Washington have any family?"

I took a heavy breath, chased it with another drink, and answered, "Yeah. A wife and two little girls." I pointed to the pictures hanging neatly over Will's bunk. "Those are their pictures over there."

Jensen stood and walked over to look at the photos. A few seconds later, he turned, tilted up his drink, and slowly drank it down. He wiped his lips and walked back toward the table.

"Brett, I'd be proud if you'd appoint me your official contribution-fund manager for his family. I know most everybody in camp, or they know me. Don't get me wrong, I ain't promising no retirement fund, but his wife can probably use anything we can send her right now. It sometimes takes months before the Army pays up on death gratuity, and even when they do it's nothing to rave about."

I hesitated for a moment. Jensen's offer took me by twofold surprise. The sad part of it was, I hadn't even thought about a fund for Will's family. I knew if his Congressional Medal of Honor was approved it would mean one hundred dollars a month for Chunky. It would also open a lot of scholarship doors for his daughters someday. But what about right now? It was an enigma, the enigma of Swede Jensen. A rough-cut, hell-raising rogue, with more notches in his gun than a whole gang of outlaws, showing his inner core. It was a rare and unexpected moment for me.

I stood and extended my hand to his. "Swede, I'd be grateful for your effort. I know his wife and kids can use the money."

He accepted my handshake. "You don't have to be grateful for anything, Brett. It's the right thing to do. Give me a couple of days and I'll get it together. Shit, these guys around here ain't got no better place to put their money. And anybody who starts hesitating or getting skimpy about donating, I'll tell 'em flat out that they better dig deep 'cause I might just be collecting for them someday."

When I started to turn toward the bar, the door swung open and in strutted our squatty camp sergeant major, Rufus R. Twitty, radiant with obnoxiousness. Twitty's record with the Army was ninety-nine percent conventional administrative time. Somehow Special Forces got blessed with him in the twilight of his career. He was a sycophant's sycophant, with a flat nose to prove it, mounted on the front of a crew-cut head and directly beneath his gray beady eyes. When he got excited his voice sounded more like a loud squeal.

He squealed. "Yancy, what's this I fuckin' hear 'bout you playing barney-badass over at the club? Messin' up . . . shit, damn near killing one of my teletype operators. Listen, Slick, just 'cause you happen to be one of the dashing recon jocks 'round here don't make you imperious to the goddamn regs. Yancy, you're about to get your fuckin' ass court-martialed!"

Twitty probably meant *impervious*. He had a way of raping words. After another minute of verbal diarrhea, he looked up at me, then noticed Jensen standing there too. He didn't like Jensen's presence, but since Swede was a local deity, the sergeant major accepted it.

His high-pitched squeal lowered to a mumble. "Evenin', Swede."

"Rufus, just for the fuckin' record, your fuckin' teletype operator called Brett's partner a nigger. Brett proceeded to whip his ass. That's the long and short of it. Your boy Johnson just got a hard lesson in race relations, that's all."

Twitty placed his hands on his hips and drew in a deep breath, as if priming his bagpipes for another recital. "Well now, we all know there's Negroes, and then there's niggers, and just because some soldier gets his words confused don't justify damn near killing him about it. I'm probably as unbased as anyone but . . ."

My pulse jumped and my muscles tensed. I started walking toward him, shouting. "Twitty, get the fuck—"

Suddenly my vision caught the image of Colonel Kahn standing in the doorway. Jensen shouted, "A-ten-shun!"

We all snapped to. The colonel strode into the room. "At ease," he barked.

He'd evidently heard us. "Sergeant Major, what's going on here?" His voice was more demanding than inquiring.

Twitty began squealing again. "Sir, Sergeant Yancy here roughed up one of my teletype operators over at the club. Matter a fact, I had to put him in the hospital, and I—"

The colonel interrupted with a tone of sarcasm. "Sergeant Major Twitty, I don't expect you to fully understand this, not having the benefit of a combat background, but occasionally a combat soldier will react to situations in ways noncombat soldiers don't understand. It's called stress syndrome.

"I have some literature related to that area. It might behoove you to borrow it and update yourself on the subject since you are directly involved in the posttrauma effects of combat.

"Now, if you and Sergeant Jensen will excuse yourselves, I need to talk with Sergeant Yancy alone."

Jensen and Twitty turned and left.

After the door closed, Colonel Kahn removed his beret and poncho, and laid them across a footlocker. He stroked his fingers through his wet silver hair, saying, "I'm sure President Kennedy paid us the ultimate respect when he awarded the green beret to Special Forces, but I wish they'd made it a little more waterproof."

He motioned for us to sit at the table. Lighting a cigarette, he asked, "Brett, what happened over at the club?"

I told him, no excuses for my action. Afterward, I mentioned Twitty had threatened a court-martial.

"Don't worry about that," he said calmly. "It sounds to me like Johnson just learned a good lesson the hard way."

He snuffed his cigarette out, then turned his head toward the large Texas flag hanging at the end of the room. A draft rippled across the draped banner. "Are you from Texas?"

"Roger, sir, about six generations' worth."

"Well, that explains it. People from Texas are a little different. My wife's from a little town north of Waco called China Springs. Beautiful country out there, mesquite and cedar trees, rolling hills, grazing cattle, real tranquil. You ever hear of China Springs?''

"Yes, sir. My Dad's from Waco. We used to drive by China Springs on the way to visit relatives down there. It's one of those blink-and-you-miss-it towns."

He grinned. "Roger that." He pulled a pack of cigarettes from his shirt pocket. "Brett, I just received a directive from Fifth Group headquarters to send a team into the same target area you just came out of, Hotel-5. What they want is an NVA prisoner for interrogation."

My eyes narrowed when he mentioned Hotel-5. I also felt that sleeping sixth sense stir inside me. I wanted the mission so bad I could taste it, but I felt that Colonel Kahn was probably running a psychiatric pulse check on me to determine just how stable I was before he considered me for the mission. Could I handle it, or would I go psychotic out there and jeopardize the operation and my team?

Unspoken questions, but valid ones, in the mind of a commander about to make a decision on who to send in on a tough target, with an even tougher mission.

Chapter 8

Colonel Kahn pulled a small notebook from his pocket and began an entry. I sipped my drink and thought about the mission as he wrote.

Next to an assassination mission, a prisoner snatch was the most difficult assignment a team could draw. First, we had to go in and stalk an enemy known for tactical discipline on his terrain. Once we located an element, the preference being a small enemy patrol, we had to maneuver ahead of them, set up a hasty ambush, and kill all but one of the patrol when they were centered in our killing zone.

Stealth, knowledge of terrain, and timing were all critical to success. If we somehow got the ambush miracle accomplished without becoming the fuckees, we still had another hurdle. We had to escape and evade while dragging a defiant prisoner through miles of jungle to a predetermined exfil location.

I had conducted two prisoner snatch attempts—one successfully. I still don't know what the NVA military hierarchy brainwashed them into believing about us, but when they came face-to-face with the reality of being captured, they were scared shitless and would sooner die than submit.

I learned during the second mission that a good hit of morphine in the neck improved their manners considerably and still allowed them to walk, more like glide, through the jungle with us. Morphine turned a man into a starry-eyed kid on his first stroll through Disneyland.

But this time it didn't matter to me what mission or how difficult. It was a chance to get back into Hotel-5. A chance to get face-to-face with Baldy and personally extract the last breath of life from his gasping carcass.

I recalled a class on covert killing techniques I had attended at Fort Bragg. The instructor, a seasoned Special Forces master sergeant, said jokingly, "Given the choice, killing an enemy with a knife is the most personable way to convey to him your message of professional sincerity."

If I had any choice about it, I planned to be professionally sincere with Baldy.

Colonel Kahn completed his notebook entry, then described some of the reasoning behind the mission directive. "It seems the psy-ops boys down in Saigon are planning a big propaganda-leaflet drop along the eastern border of Laos sometime next month to encourage enemy surrender.

"But first, they want to get inside some NVA's head and analyze what his level of morale and motivation is. It's their way of determining if the leaflet strategy is geared in the right direction or needs some fine-tuning." He grinned. "It's our job to supply them with the warm body."

He continued while lighting a cigarette. "Personally, I'm not a big fan of psychological operations. I believe if you've got 'em by the balls, their hearts and minds will follow you."

I felt an urge to smile, but held it back. "Roger, sir, but I've heard of a couple of *chieu-hois*, surrenders, from leaflet drops, so maybe there's some merit in these psy-ops programs."

"Brett, your team has run a couple of snatches, and you're already familiar with that area of operation. How do you feel about going back in there on this one?"

It was like a prayer being answered before you even had a chance to say it. Trying not to sound ecstatic, I responded, "Roger, sir. RT Texas, or possibly Kansas, has the best knowledge of that AO right now."

I already knew Kansas was slotted for another mission and wasn't a contender for this one. "I'll need a One-One, or to borrow somebody from another team."

He frowned. "We're running too thin on personnel right now to break someone out of another team. But I do have a Spec-Four up in the admin office who's been bugging the sergeant major for months to get him on a recon team. His name is Binkowski. He's not Special Forces–qualified, but he is airborne. He's about all I can break loose right now. I will say this about him: If he turns out to be as good a field soldier as he has been a clerk typist, you won't have any problems."

My elation evaporated. I knew Binkowski. He handled most of the paperwork going in and out of camp: awards, promotions, R and R orders, and such. He was an eighty-word-a-minute whiz-kid typist, with a terminal lust to get his combat hymen broken. Worse, he was a Yankee, with a Boston accent that sounded like he'd just swallowed a mouthful of baked beans.

He did have a good military attitude and stayed in top physical condition. We had spotted for each other several times at the camp weight room. He had a flat-back bench press of 380 pounds, 40 pounds better than mine, and a squat of over 500 pounds. He looked like a Neanderthal man hunched over his typewriter.

Colonel Kahn was silent, awaiting my response. I knew the colonel wouldn't give me a dud. Binkowski might not be the first-round draft choice, but he was motivated. But courageous ambitions are sometimes second cousins to an impaired sense of reality.

I tried to sound positive. "He might work out fine, sir. I'll give him a try. A lot depends on how well he can work with the Cowboys. How much time do I have before we launch?

"I'm scheduling Texas for three days of isolation prep time beginning September eleventh. That's two weeks from tomorrow. Weather permitting, you'll launch on the fourteenth."

"So, if I start training him tomorrow, that'll give me two weeks with him before mission launch?"

"Not exactly. It'll be closer to ten days, Brett."

I was puzzled about the disappearance of several days. "Sir, I don't understand. I'll need to start with him first thing tomorrow while my little people are still on leave—"

He broke in. "That'll have to wait a few days. You're going to Bangkok tomorrow. I've got you scheduled on a Hercules out of Da Nang AFB at thirteen-hundred hours."

He leaned toward me. "You need a break, Yancy, and Bangkok is as good a place as any to get drunk, get laid, and get your mind rested. Don't worry about Binkowski. While you're gone, I'll have him study all of your after-action reports. That'll get him oriented on what to expect, mission-wise."

The colonel took a long draw on his cigarette. "This last mission put some deep cuts in you, Brett. It would have anybody. You need to get away and lick your wounds for a while, regroup. When you get back you can hit the track running. Who knows, after Binkowski reads through your AARs he may just decide stay-behind duty isn't so bad after all."

I was ambiguous about Binkowski. I knew him well enough to feel reasonably confident about his maturity. He had a kind of Yankee arrogance about him that made him want to excel.

I'd seen Binkowski's eyes fix into a trance doing bench presses. When he groaned and cleared the rack with 380 pounds looming above him, a powerful inner voltage seemed to radiate from him. He wasted no time or strength. He would swiftly lower the ominous steel down on his swollen chest, then, slowly, unrelentingly, drive it up to full arm's length above him. His physical strength was disciplined. If he could apply the same inner strength to combat, he would be damn good. But there was only one place to conduct the real test.

"Excuse my manners, sir. I didn't offer you a drink."

"Not tonight, thanks. I've still got to check the perimeter. We've had a rash of Vietnamese sleeping on guard lately. So, until we get it back to normal, I try to check them all twice a night.

"Last night I found one asleep in the southern guard tower. I didn't say a word to him. Just stood him up, put a grenade in each of his hands, then pulled both pins and climbed back down the tower. If he figured out a way to sleep with a live grenade in each hand he's got more balls than me."

I smiled and pictured the look that must have come across the guard's face, standing there with an M-26 fragmentation grenade in each hand. It must have turned him into a bug-eyed insomniac.

Colonel Kahn stood and shifted his poncho down over his stout frame, then positioned his damp beret onto his head.

As we walked to the door, he looked at me. "Brett, in spite of everything that happened out there today, I want you to know you did a damn good job. Don't get into some guilt trip and go blaming yourself for Sergeant Washington. It happens."

He opened the door, turned, and shook my hand as though he didn't expect a reply to his last words. "Have a good time in Bangkok. Try to get a room at the Siam Inter-Continental. It's where all the airline stewardesses stay on layovers. And believe me, they take layovers in a very literal sense. See you in a few days."

"Roger, sir. Good night . . . and sir, thank you."

He turned and stepped briskly into the dark cloak of rain. I watched him disappear into the blackness. A fresh clean scent filled my nostrils. A wet gust from the night blew over my face, as though trailing off the windblown cape of Caesar walking among his centurions.

For a moment, I thought about Colonel Kahn. I felt a deep sense of pride in being in his command. He was totally committed to our mission here and to the welfare of his troops. I'd seen him walk the perimeter many times, checking the guards and inspecting the mortar pits. I'd also seen him in the mess hall looking over the food before chow time. He believed in keen attention to every detail, but didn't overreact when someone made a mistake. If he saw a problem, he would let the person responsible know about it, and in the same breath provide his guidance to bring about a solution. It felt good to work for a boss like Ivan Kahn.

I closed the door and walked back toward my bunk while removing my shirt. I needed a shower, but right now I just didn't care. Taking off my shoulder holster, I felt the sting of an abrasion rubbed into my skin by the strap. I pulled the Beretta from the holster, checked to make sure it was still on safety, then laid it and the holster on the small table by my bed. The pistol had been a gift from my uncle. He'd given it to me when I was home on leave just prior to departure for 'Nam. His note on the inside of the box read: "Better to have it and not need it than need it and not have it. Uncle Steve."

So far I hadn't needed the pistol, but I carried it with me anytime I left camp. I also took his advice and kept a round chambered with the safety on. He'd said, "In the wrong situation, the time it takes to chamber a round can be too long."

I stripped off the remainder of my clothes, turned out the light, and lay naked on my bunk. I stared into the cool darkness and tried to let my mind go blank. My fingers moved across the dried, crusted blood tangled into the hair on my chest. Will's blood. My efforts to lose myself in thoughts of Vonnie, home, and Bangkok, all were clouded by sorrow. A silent rage, and plans for revenge, began to engulf me until finally I faded into the lonely shadow of a restless sleep.

As my eyes closed, I was vaguely aware I'd failed to lock the hooch door.

Chapter 9

"Yon-cee, Yon-cee. You wake please. Sar Yon-cee, you wake please."

A spark of panic stung my tired senses. My fingers quickly found the Beretta. In the same moment I reasoned that if the voice meant me harm, it wouldn't be calling my name. I loosened my grasp on the pistol, turned, and squinted into the darkness. The small curvaceous figure of a young girl stood beside my bunk. A dull tint of light outlined her long wet hair.

It was Fousi.

"Fousi, what are you doing—? Damn, I almost shot you! How did you get in? Never mind."

I rubbed my face and glanced at the luminous glow from my watch: 2145 hours. Evidently she had just gotten off work, ran through the stormy night, and came to me. She was soaked and shivering.

Her hands folded modestly in front of her while she gazed down into my eyes. The pleading look on her face matched a lonely note in her voice. "I no go Da Nang tonight. I wan stay wid you, Yon-cee. Okay?"

Love and admiration for Fousi welled in me. She had endured much: lost her parents to Communist butchers, accepted the burden of supporting the remaining children, suffered through poverty and put up with drunken GIs pawing her. But through it all, she never lost her capacity for caring. She had taken Will and me into her heart. Neither Will nor I had ever sought to trespass on Fousi's affection.

But now, she ached with another loss, the loss of Will. I wondered how much her battered young spirit could take before she retreated into bitterness and apathy.

I rose from my bed and hugged her quivering body. My hands stroked through wet tangles of soft hair as her tears broke. We embraced in the darkness, and as the rains poured from a troubled sky, we cried.

As our tears dried, passion grew. My head bent down to find her waiting mouth. My lips tasted the salt-laced tears as my hands roved over the smooth, damp silk of her dress, the contours of her body.

I drew her dress over her braless breasts, then carefully over her head. The white outline of her panties gripped her small waist and rounded hips. Her fine breasts blossomed full. She was beautiful.

Her soft eyes looked up, then frowned as her fingers reached to touch the abrasion left by my shoulder holster. Then her fingers moved to touch the blood-encrusted tangles of hair on my chest. She looked sadly into my eyes and whispered, "You lay, please, Yoncee. I wash you."

I lay on the bed as she removed two olive-drab towels from my wall locker. She wet one with the water from my canteen and silently washed Will's blood from my chest. Her relaxing hands moved gently over my body, dabbing, wiping, then drying each area.

Carefully, I guided her fragile, youthful beauty beneath me and heard her faint, labored whisper. "Yon-cee, I'm need you. I'm need love you, Yon-cee."

Somewhere, in those moments the wounds of our sorrows began to heal. And, somewhere in those moments my love and respect for Fousi overpowered selfish passion. I withdrew my climax.

I wasn't certain how or what disciplined me, but I was certain Fousi didn't need the burden of another child in her already heavily laden young life.

I wiped the remnants of tears from her eyes and cradled her head against my shoulder. As the night rains drummed against the tin roof, I pulled the cool nylon poncho liner over our warm bodies.

We nestled into a peaceful sleep.

Shortly after dawn the next morning, I borrowed the camp jeep to drive Fousi home. Although her grandmother lived with Fousi and helped care for her younger sisters, she needed to get home and make sure they were all right.

I draped my poncho over Fousi to protect her from the rain, then drove slowly out of camp. The night's heavy rains had flooded the narrow road. I could tell it was going to be a long ten miles to town. Fousi held my rifle across her lap as we plowed slowly through the watery, potholed road. The small windshield wiper slapped back and forth in the steady downpour.

Nine slow miles later we reached the steel-girder bridge spanning the southern end of Da Nang Harbor. The water level had risen several feet above the bridge roadway, blocking our path. I looked over at Fousi. Wind blew ebony strands of hair across her face. She looked at the flooded bridge ahead of us, then at me.

I asked, jokingly, "Can you swim?"

Her eyes first widened, then smiled after looking to

see if I was really serious. "Me no swim. Maybe need big helicopter."

"Well, Babysan, I don't have a helicopter right now. But we'll be okay. I'll just take it slow and easy."

The water was well over the road, but I felt we had enough clearance to make it across the two-hundred-meter length, providing the water didn't rise any more.

Fousi forced a reluctant smile as I eased the jeep onto the water-covered bridge. Her eyebrows raised with alertness. "Okay, Yon-cee, you take slow and easy, please."

I crept cautiously forward. The gusts of wind lapped small waves over the open edges of the floorboard. Six feet to either side of our path was a thin guardrail. It was the only thing between us and the drop-off. The jeep's engine purred through the waves. Fousi's face was tense. Her hands gripped the barrel of my rifle as though it were the safety bar on a roller coaster.

I said, joking, "Fousi, if you see any sharks, you shoot them. Okay?"

She jerked from her trance and quickly examined the gray waters dancing wildly around us. She gradually edged nearer to me while pointing the muzzle outward. "I'm think no shark want little snack like me. They maybe want *beaucoup*, like you."

A few minutes later we reached the end of the bridge and drove slowly up onto the paved high ground of the main road into Da Nang.

Fousi moved back to the center of her seat and announced, "You see, Yon-cee, slow and easy is good for us to cross bridge. Yes?"

I looked over at her and smiled. "You're right. Slow and easy. It's also good for loving. Yes?"

She tilted her head to one side with a soft smile, then

leaned and hugged my arm, damn near pulling me out of my seat.

As we turned onto the main street leading us into the inner city, the rains subsided to a gentle mist. The city's odor seemed to splatter beneath the wheels of the jeep, as if to tell me it disapproved of early-morning intrusion. Ancient ivy clawed the yellowing walls of stone-and-stucco huts. Emaciated limbs of old trees reached reluctantly toward cloudy skies, offering little cover to an old man limping along the road's edge.

I steered wide to avoid a large pool of water near him.

Ahead of us, a small motorbike strained to carry two armed Vietnamese soldiers. A gray fog of smoke trailed behind as they wove through the puddles and potholes of the narrow street.

Fousi recognized the familiar white stripes around their shiny black helmets before I did.

"Yon-cee, them Quan Canh," she warned. "You go slow!"

The QC were the Vietnamese equivalent of the Nazi SS. They strutted about arrogantly, decked out in smart military uniforms. They had the often-abused authority to kill on the spot anyone they suspected of antigovernment activity, no questions asked. They usually avoided confrontations with American, Korean, and Australian soldiers, but made no secret of their hatred for us. Recently, a QC had killed an American sailor when he'd caught him with his whore. His only punishment was a transfer to Nha Trang.

Fousi was right. The best thing to do was stay clear of them, if only for her sake—she had to live among the little bastards.

She motioned for me to turn right. I drove down the

muddy alley and stopped in front of a small shanty. Two little girls in tattered dresses squatted beside the shack, drawing figures in the moist dirt with sticks.

Seeing Fousi, their serious faces blossomed into smiles. They ran to greet her. Their smiles turned to bashful glances when they saw me. Before, I had only seen them in photos. The little girls were more beautiful than I had thought.

After fidgeting to free her arms from beneath the poncho, which swallowed her body, Fousi took each of them by the hand and led them toward me.

She introduced them in English. "This is Sar Yon-cee. I'm tell you about him before." She held up the hand of the smallest one first. "Yon-cee, this is Lon. She five year." Then Fousi raised a hand of the other. "And this is Ming. She soon be seven."

Their eyes looked up timidly. I knelt on one knee before them and spoke softly. "I'm very happy to meet you. Fousi tells me all about you."

They both cast an uncertain glance up at Fousi, as if wondering if her reports had been favorable.

I smiled. "She tells me you are both very good and very pretty, and now I know she is right."

Ming withdrew from her huddled position against Fousi. She gestured toward the figure they had drawn in the dirt, and spoke as if I'd been accepted as a new friend. "*Lai day*, Yon-cee."

There was the rough outline of a bird.

Ming bent down and brushed away some of the loose dirt. The image became clearer. It was a dove. She looked up at the sky and pointed to a break in the clouds. A streak of sunlight streamed through the opening.

Fousi explained as she stroked Ming's dark silky hair.

"Ming think dove bring peace and good things. She draw bird to bring happiness and take away bad." She paused to examine the clearing sky, smiled, and added, "Today maybe it work. You see, rain go away."

I reached down and took Ming up in my arms. Lon stood nearby, looking up at us. "Ming, did Lon help you draw picture?"

Lon remained silent, but smiled proudly.

Ming spoke, pointing to the oval around the bird. "Yes, Lon, she do here."

I bent down and gathered Lon into my other arm and lifted her up near Ming. "I'd say ya'll make a good team. Maybe someday, if I have trouble, you can draw a bird for me."

I turned to Fousi and couldn't help grinning. With the poncho draped over her, she looked like a walking tent with a smiling head peeking out the top. I twisted my arm under the weight of Lon to look at my watch. I needed to start back. It would be a slow drive and I still had packing to do.

Still holding Ming and Lon in my arms, I began walking toward the jeep. "I have to go now. Later today, I go to Bangkok. I've never been there before, but I'll bet they have coloring books and crayons over there somewhere. How 'bout if I bring some back for you?"

They smiled and nodded happily. I had already decided the best gift for Fousi would be a nice raincoat and an umbrella. My poncho didn't do a thing for her figure.

I sat the girls down, then helped Fousi out of the poncho.

As she started to hand it to me, I smiled and said, "Why don't you keep that poncho for now. It may rain again before I get back from Bangkok."

I winked, then walked around to the driver's side of the jeep. Fousi followed and stood at the door edge as I got in. "Where's your grandmother?" I queried.

"She go market. Be back soon." She glanced toward town, then reached into the jeep and took my hand between both of hers and smiled.

I wanted to kiss her, but Oriental custom frowned on public displays of affection. I whispered, "In my mind, I'm kissing you."

"Same in my mind for you," she whispered back.

Releasing her hand, I drove slowly away, returning a wave to Ming and Lon.

I looked back one last time at the huddled trio before turning onto the main street. I felt helplessness in the face of their poverty. They had never known anything but war. Even their parents hadn't seen or known too many years of peace.

One side of me felt good about being a part of the history that would eventually give freedom to the people of Vietnam. The other felt a nagging, growing anger. Why is this fucking war taking so long? Why is it dragging into its sixth year with no end in sight?

Chapter 10

I turned onto the main road leading back to the harbor bridge. The morning sun streamed through large breaks in the clouds, casting reflections on the pools of water gathered in the highway. I glanced into the rearview mirror, then took a closer look.

A QC jeep patrol was trailing me. They accelerated and followed, at a too-close-for-comfort distance. The little bastards had probably seen me with Fousi and decided to invoke a little police intimidation. I reached across the seat and pulled my rifle over my lap.

I glanced up into the rearview mirror again. They were laughing like a couple of thugs on a drunken joy-ride. I thought, How ironic. I'm being chased by two people I'm here to defend. They're driving a jeep, and carrying weapons given to them by my country.

I jammed the accelerator to the floor and felt the engine lunge. Fast approaching in the distance, I saw the gray steel of the bridge rising out of Da Nang Harbor. Coming toward me, I saw the dark canvas top of a huge truck chugging slowly through the high water. Within seconds the truck would block the entrance to the bridge.

I looked to my rear and smiled. The QC were right where I wanted them, right on my ass. Their forward view was smeared by the wet spray from my wheels, rising in a misty cloud behind me. It was impossible for them to see the approach ahead and the huge truck coming slowly out of the center of the bridge. I couldn't have asked for more perfect timing. Only a second from the truck, I hit my brakes and slipped into a skid off the road and into the soft mud of the shoulder. The pursuing jeep had no chance to stop. The QC driver only had a panicked second to decide if he wanted to impact head-on into the truck or steer haplessly into the flooded harbor.

Smart boys! They chose the water. Two long screams shrieked above the grind of the truck's engine as the little bastards hurled full-speed into the gray choppy waters. "Aeeeeeee!"

Within seconds their jeep disappeared beneath the waves while they babbled, bobbed, and splashed, trying to swim to shore.

The dented olive-drab truck chugged up the road and stopped near me. A gust of wind blew the acrid smell of burned diesel fuel across my face. The white block letters USMC appeared on the door beneath the massive arm of the stubble-faced driver. He leaned outward from the open cab window and spit a glob of tobacco juice into a puddle between his vehicle and mine.

The Marine looked down at me, smirking as he spoke. "It was nice of them little pricks not to smear theirself all over my front bumper." He looked back over his left shoulder and broke into a full grin while watching the two QC struggling to swim to shore, then added, "But I don't know how they're gonna explain losing a whole fuckin' jeep."

We both laughed. I replied, "Yeah. That's going to be a tough explanation all right. Looks like maybe their brakes failed."

The Marine spit again, then glanced at my beret. "You with that Special Forces recon outfit on the north side of the rock? The camp with all the skulls hanging from the sign?"

"Roger that."

"Our camp's just south of the rock, 3rd Amtrac Marines. Be advised, one of our patrols got ambushed last night. Hit hard, four killed. Just to let you know, if you're headin' that direction, Charlie is definitely in the fuckin' area."

I frowned. "Between the VC, the QC, and the NVA, they're fuckin' us coming and going!"

He grinned. "I know the feelin', buddy, but I'm gettin' short. Twenty days and a wake-up, then my mother's handsome son is headed home to Red River, New Mexico." He glanced at his watch. "Well, buddy, I gotta get on over to the air base. You gonna be able to get outa that mud by yourself?"

I bent and looked outside my jeep at the wheels. They were only about a foot deep in the muck. I yanked the shift lever into second gear to prevent the wheels from spinning, then accelerated and pulled easily back onto the paved road.

I looked up at him. "No problem. See ya 'round, and thanks again for the report on Charlie."

"Roger. Semper Fi. Don't let your meat loaf."

He revved the big diesel and pulled on by me. The exhaust stacks sent a thick cloud of black smoke swelling into the sky.

To my right front, I could see the two bedraggled QC trying to crawl up the slippery embankment at the water's edge. As I drove by them, I couldn't resist shouting, "Nice mornin' for a swim, boys!"

The one nearest the top of the embankment gave me a malicious glare, then, as he tried to flash me the finger, he lost his footing and began to slide helplessly backward, his arms waving wildly at his sides. The last thing he must have seen before hitting the water was my laughing face.

Chapter 11

Back at camp, I parked the jeep and walked inside to check my mail. The Vietnamese clerk handed me two letters, one from my mom and one from my brother.

As I left the mail room, Binkowski appeared from another room and strode, half hurrying, toward me. He was beaming. His voice rang out loud, almost melodiously. "Good mon'ing Sa'geant Yancy."

The Boston accent made the absence of any *R*s in his words sound like he suffered from terminal pneumonia. I stopped and turned toward him.

He shoved his open hand out to me and continued. "Colonel Kahn told me this morning I was going to be assigned as your new One-One."

I glared at Binkowski, deliberately ignoring his hand. His six-foot three-inch mesomorphic frame put him about two inches taller than me. His neatly pressed fatigues and spit-shined jungle boots contrasted sharply with my wet, wrinkled, and unshaven appearance. He smelled like a French whore with a pocketful of rose petals.

A hidden resentment stirred inside me when I thought of him replacing Will. I tried to subdue my prejudice.

I accepted his handshake. The texture of his palm was smooth.

I knew I should begin our association on an optimistic note, but Binkowski's attitude was more like a kid being accepted on the high-school football team rather than as a candidate for a Special Forces recon unit. I needed to get him down to a more serious and realistic level.

I looked into his still smiling eyes and spoke clearly, without expression. "Specialist Binkowski, I'm going to give you a straight-talk update right now. What has occurred is that you have been accepted on RT Texas on a trial basis for a period of training, to determine if you can hack it on a recon team. I've got ten days of prep time to get you ready for one tough mission. At the end of that training period, if I'm not satisfied with your performance, and confident of your ability, then I'm going to drop you and request a Special Forces qualified replacement.

"Laos is crawling with little khaki-clad bastards who want to kill me, and you too, if you achieve the dubious privilege of accompanying me there. I'm not about to risk my life, or jeopardize my team, any further than they already are in order to satisfy your thirst for adventure!"

His smile began to droop as I finished. "You need to understand straight out that you are not the new One-One on Texas. That is a position you'll have to earn! Now, does that lay it out clearly enough?"

Binkowski had involuntarily come to the position of attention. A lock of blond hair had fallen down over his eyes. He ignored it and snapped, "Yes, sir!"

I drew in a deep breath and expelled it before looking

back at him. "And don't call me 'sir,' damn it! I'm an NCO."

I became aware of my volume and lowered my voice back to normal. "Binkowski, you've been in another world working up here in this bureaucracy. I can understand that 'Yes, sir' has been part of your vocabulary here, but forget it with me. 'Roger' is a better word. It's more precise and easier to understand, particularly on a radio in the field. Try and get in the habit of using it."

I knew I was being abrasive with him, but he needed a mild shock to get him on the right frequency and keep his attention. Deep inside, I felt he had the right stuff to handle it, and along with that feeling there was a seed of admiration. He could have sat out his time in this war safely behind his typewriter. But something stirred a need in him for risk. I remembered Colonel Kahn saying that Binkowski was jump-qualified but not SF-qualified. I wondered what happened that had prevented him from getting into Special Forces. A man doesn't get through jump school wearing a size small jockstrap. He had the balls. Secretly I knew he was well aware of what he was getting into. In the days ahead, I needed to find out what lit his fuse, and, more importantly, what kind of explosive was on the other end of the fuse.

I wasn't about to say so, but I needed Binkowski. Without him in the One-One position, Colonel Kahn would have no choice but to scrub Texas from the snatch mission and insert another team. If that happened, it would kill any chance I had to get into Hotel-5 and find Baldy. Binkowski was a hinge on the trapdoor I planned to slam shut on Baldy's shiny skull.

For a moment, I relished my anticipation of the confrontation. I yearned to feel Baldy's frenzied struggle. I thirsted to see panicked horror in his eyes when my blade pierced his throat and dug the final terrified breath of life from his murderous soul.

I became aware of the time I'd allowed to pass in silence and looked back at Binkowski. A puzzled look, almost a frown, appeared on his face.

"Sergeant Yancy, are you all right?"

"Sure, I'm fine. What's your first name?"

"Arnold," he muttered. "But I prefer Ski," he added quickly.

I decided it was time to pick his spirits up off the floor and give him some pointers on recon at the same time. "Ski, call me Brett." I gestured for us to walk outside.

We stepped out of the small building into a crisp morning breeze and began walking to no particular destination. After several steps in silence, I said optimistically, "Ski, probably my biggest understatement of the day is that recon is going to be a new world for you. You have to learn fast, and you're going to have to trust my judgment most of the time.

"Trusting another man's judgment isn't always easy, particularly when your life is at stake during some of it. During your training—anytime, for that matter—remember this. The only stupid question is an unasked question. If you don't understand something, ask for clarification.

"One of my Cowboys, Tuong, is living proof of that. He'll ask a question anytime, anyplace. No team works well that doesn't have their signals straight."

Nearing a guard tower, Ski pulled a pack of cigarettes from his pocket and lit one, offering one to me in the process.

I responded critically, "No thanks. You know, I'm surprised you smoke, being a weight lifter."

"Yeah, I guess it is a little dumb, but being cramped up in that headshed all day behind a typewriter . . ." He tossed the cigarette away. "Well, it kinda breaks the monotony a little, you know."

His spirit had begun to drop again. Without looking at him, I retorted, "Ski, all the Yards on my team smoke. So it doesn't bother me. I'm not on any soapbox to get anybody to quit. But we have a rule on the team. When we go to the bush, leave your cigarettes in camp. Chuck can smell a gnat's fart a mile off; smoking is a dead giveaway.

"Also, I don't know what cologne that is you're wearing, but forget it when we go to the field. Same thing with boot polish. Throw it away. Anything that rattles or squeaks in your gear, either tape it down or oil it. Noises and smells, however slight, can get a team wasted in a heartbeat. I don't even like to take a shit out there."

We stopped and leaned against the sandbag wall at the base of a guard tower. A contemplative look came over Ski's face. I avoided interrupting his thoughts. I wanted to give everything I'd said time to sink in, and to see if he had any questions.

I studied the morning sky. A strong wind, blowing in off the sea, scattered clouds. Sunlight glistened off the tin roofs of the camp huts. I glanced westward toward Da Nang airfield. It looked like good weather for the flight to Thailand.

I looked at Ski. "By the way, you probably know I'm going to Bangkok in a few hours—"

He interrupted. "Yeah, I know. I typed your travel

orders this morning. Need to convert any money before you leave?''

"Roger. I'll come by the office before I take off. Thanks for reminding me. Listen, I put my Cowboys on leave. They'll be back in camp before I get back from Bangkok. Don't move your gear into the team hooch until I get back. They don't know about you yet, and I want to introduce you to them all in one gathering. You'll like the Yards. They're good soldiers. They'll do anything in the world for you if they like you.

"The Montagnards were the original people here, kinda like the American Indians back home. Just like the Indians, they got fucked over and pushed around until finally they withdrew to the central highlands. For my money, they're the best soldiers this country has. But understand this, they've been shit on so long by the Vietnamese that they don't have any allegiance to this war. Their faith is in us, as individuals, and we owe them our loyalty.''

I glanced at Ski, thinking he had a question, but he lit another cigarette instead. I continued, "While I'm gone, spend some time on the firing range. Don't worry about shoulder firing. Get used to firing from the hip, full-automatic, three- and four-round bursts. Practice from a prone position. Also, I want you to make a comprehensive map study of Hotel-5 while I'm gone. If I get zapped it'll be up to you to get the team outa there. So I want you to know that area inside out. Roger?''

"Yes . . . I mean, roger, Brett. Anything else?'' His voice rang with enthusiasm.

I sensed he'd absorbed enough for lesson one. I leaned away from the sandbag wall. "Negative, Ski. That should keep you busy for a while. By the way, rain or shine, we run every morning we're in camp. We make a three-mile run with gear and weapons. That's six trips around the inside of the perimeter. The sand makes it seem like twelve. But if Chuck gets on our asses out there like he's known to do, and we have to beat feet, it helps if we're the undisputed district track champs.''

Ski grinned halfheartedly, then looked around the camp as though making a silent assessment. A second later he tossed his cigarette away.

Suddenly, the unmistakable squeal of Sergeant Major Rufus Twitty shattered the morning breeze. He stood in the doorway of the admin shop looking at us. ''Binkowski, you planning on doing any work today? If so, get your ass back in here!''

I turned and looked directly at Twitty. He disappeared back into the small building. I glanced at Ski. The look on his face was like that of a teenager who had just been called by his mother.

Twitty was deliberately trying to embarrass him. ''I see Twitty's in his usual obnoxious mood this morning.''

Ski gave a dejected smile. ''Yeah, but you gotta give Twitty credit for consistency. He's an asshole all the time. There isn't any in-between.''

''Before I leave today, I'll ask Colonel Kahn to release you so you can get started on that map study and your range firing. It doesn't mean he's going to do it, but I'll ask him. Once you're assigned to recon, you won't see much of Twitty. His whip doesn't have much snap down there.''

Ski's spirits improved. ''That would be great, Brett, but I'm afraid it would take a miracle to get me out of there early. Twitty will be the main hurdle. He doesn't like you, and he's still got a case of the ass about your breaking Johnson's jaw. Says he'll be in the hospital for at least a week.''

''It would sure break my heart to piss Twitty off twice in twenty-four hours, but nobody ever told him being a stay-behind sergeant major was going to be easy.''

I looked toward my hooch. Beyond the gleam of the roof, the China Sea shimmered and rolled gentle breakers onto the beach. I thought about returning to the hooch and packing Will's belongings. I could put it off until I returned from Bangkok, but I felt it was important to get them to Chunky right away. At least then she would have something of his to cling to.

I turned toward Ski and offered my hand. ''I've got some things to do. I'll be by the admin shop before I leave, to talk with Colonel Kahn about getting you released.''

''Brett, I'm looking forward to working for you,'' he said sincerely. He gave me a firm handshake.

''You're not going to be working *for* me, Ski, you're going to be working *with* me. Me and four Montagnards. It's a team.''

Walking away, I looked back over my shoulder to see Ski, at an angle, jogging back to the admin building. He was smiling.

An hour later, I had finished packing all of Will's personal items into his footlocker. It was a slow process. I studied each picture of his family before wrapping it in paper and carefully positioning it so it wouldn't break during shipment. I had never noticed before, but his oldest daughter, Karen, age seven, had a look about her that was distinctly Will's. Something else needed to be included. Something important. I removed a spiral notebook from my wall locker, sat down at the team table, and began to write.

Dear Mrs. Washington,

I've grown to know you so well through my friendship with Will that I feel as though you are as dear a friend as he was. By now you know of his passing and I want to let you and his family know what I felt for him.

Will was a man rich in everything that is strong and good. From our friendship, I received a greater reward from his strength and insight than I ever could have possibly given back. He taught me, not in words or lectures, but through silent example, how to maintain truth, loyalty, and fidelity, and as he phrased it, "Press on in the face of adversity."

He never deviated from his convictions. My regret is that I never took the moment to tell him how much I loved and respected him. Perhaps he knew it all along, for I truly felt it from him without words.

I once asked Will how he could be loyal to a country that denied him complete freedom. He thought for a moment, then quoted the words of the woman he loved. He always bragged about you being in college, and he was very proud of your insight. He said you told him once, "When a person denies freedom to another, he is actually limiting his own, and I believe that people the world over are waking to that fact." He said the trick was not to let hate and discrimination infect him just because it took time for people to wake up and do right. He told me he would never allow hate to affect him or his family as long as he had the power to prevent it.

I never stopped growing in Will's influence. He helped me get over a Dear John letter I received shortly after he came on the team. He laughed and told me, "Heck, Brett, if that gal back home don't have the good sense to wait on a man like you, chances are she's missin' a few dots on her dominoes in the first place."

I think everything Will ever said has stayed with me, and every experience we shared brought us closer.

I was with Will when he died. He asked me to tell you that he was going across the river, and he would see you and the kids on the other side. Perhaps someday I'll have the privilege of seeing him there also.

Chunky, I've included my parents' address in Fort Worth. If you ever need my assistance in any way, write to them and they will make sure the message gets through to me. I have decided to extend my tour here, so for at least the next six months, my address will be the same. Vietnam.

Love and allegiance,
Brett Yancy

Chapter 12

I placed my letter to Chunky into the footlocker, closed and locked it, and taped the key below the lock. After attaching an address tag to the top, I carried the locker to the mail room.

I didn't like having to tape a key to it, but Army postal regulations required it. They didn't want anyone tempted to load up a footlocker full of marijuana and send it home.

My second task was to see Colonel Kahn and request that Binkowski be released from admin duty early.

As I walked down the narrow plywood-lined hallway toward the colonel's office, the stagnant smell of Da Nang drifted through an open window. At the same time my ears caught the indignant squeal of Rufus Twitty. He emerged from an adjacent office and rolled into my path like a dumpy roadblock barrel. He stood in front of me with his usual hands-on-hips stance.

"What you needin', Yancy?" he blurted.

I restrained the urge to knock him on his fat ass. Self-control seemed easier this time, perhaps because I had something more important on my mind and didn't want a pissing contest with him complicating my effort.

I looked beyond him toward the colonel's office. "I need to see Colonel Kahn for a minute."

Twitty stepped back and looked me up and down with contemptuous eyes. He squealed, "Yancy, you ain't never gonna make it in this army. You're just imperious to the fuckin' regs. You ever hear of a thing called the chain of command? You're supposed to see me with any request to speak to the commanding officer."

Twitty was turning red as he held his hand up to my face, thumb and forefinger pressed tightly together. "Yancy, you're 'bout that far," he shouted while shaking, "about this far from disciplinary action!"

It did my heart good to see Twitty's feathers ruffled. It was almost a compliment.

He stepped back and spoke in a milder tone, as if trying to recover his composure. Looking down at my old scuffed jungle boots, he screeched, "Those boots are crying for some Kiwi, Sergeant."

I really wasn't in any mood for flak from Twitty. "Sergeant Major, the enemy—I assume you've heard of them—can smell boot polish a hundred meters off. That's why no one in recon uses it, including me. I hope someday you'll find it in your heart to forgive me." I paused, blinked twice deliberately, and continued. "And, while I'm here, consider this a formal request to see Colonel Kahn, in compliance with the chain of command."

Twitty leaned back as if half the wind in his bagpipes had leaked out. He glared momentarily into my eyes before letting his own drift downward from my faded beret and unshaven face to my wrinkled fatigues, then fixing on my scuffed boots. While his bitter eyes scrutinized me, I felt a gnawing frustration. I began to wonder why my own sergeant major was so unconcerned with my needs and so disconnected from the ways of a field soldier.

I knew Twitty had never seen combat. He was a garrison soldier, used to spit and polish, rules and regulations. I was a field soldier, more concerned with a clean rifle than clean boots. It was like two different armies on the same side trying to fight the same war, each with a different battle plan.

Twitty blew out onion-laced breath as he dropped his hands from his hips and walked back into his office. "The colonel's in the fuckin' commo bunker. Maybe you can intercept him there. He's been in there all mornin' monitoring that guy Blister, in Forward Air Control. Seems they lost RT Vermont last night."

A chill swept over me. Vermont was our best team. Billy Wald, the One-Zero, was a good friend. We'd been through jump school and most of our Special Forces training together. His team always came back with the bacon. "Walk-on-water" Wald was the type of guy who could stroll through a ghetto at night and someone would throw him a rose.

I hurried out of the building and sprinted toward the commo bunker at the center of camp.

As I neared the half-buried bunker, Colonel Kahn emerged from the sandbag-arched entrance into the crisp morning breeze. His face was drawn and dark half circles sagged beneath his weary eyes. He leaned against the sandbag retainer wall, peering toward the sea.

The grim look on his face told me the likely answer to my question, but I had to ask it. "Sir, I just heard Vermont's in trouble. Are we launching a bright-light force to get them out?"

His angry voice tore into me. "Negative! They got hit in their RON position last night. Moonbeam monitored their last communication during the firefight. Billy's last transmission ended with . . ." His eyes narrowed, restraining a tear. He whispered, "I'm hit." The tear came as Colonel Ivan Kahn repeated Billy Wald's last words; "I'm hit!"

My jaw tightened. Helplessly, I watched my commander weep. My fists clenched. I held back a powerful urge to console him. Then I looked away. The burden of our sorrow remained isolated within each of us. My mind searched to find a way to deny that Billy Wald was dead.

I lunged forward to Colonel Kahn's side, shouting, "Damn it, sir, he could still be alive! So he took a hit. That doesn't mean he's dead! We need to launch a bright-light now, right now. Maybe—"

"Forget it, Yancy!" he shouted back, glaring. "They're beyond being rescued. I just got off the horn with Blister. He was on-station at first light. He got photos of a smoking pile of bodies and rucksacks in a clearing near the RON."

Bewildered and silent, I leaned against the sandbag wall.

Colonel Kahn stood away from the sandbags, wiped his eyes with a quick sweep of his hand, then spoke in a clearly angry tone. "Get down to recon company and tell every fuckin' One-Zero and One-One I want them assembled in the isolation briefing room in ten minutes!" He paused, hearing the distant cracking of rifle fire echo from the camp firing range. "And tell whoever that is on the range to break training and get in there too!"

The tremor in his voice told me it had something to

do with Vermont. It wasn't my place to question him about it. I snapped, "Roger, sir," then ran, full-speed, toward the recon barracks area.

It was unusual for Colonel Kahn to call a mass assembly in the isolation area. The isolation compound was specifically reserved for teams in preparation for a mission. A large cement building, surrounded by a ten-foot-high chain-link fence, it had no windows, and no electronic devices were permitted inside. Once a team entered, they were in total self-contained isolation. Everything they required during mission prep—maps, intelligence updates, photographs of the mission target area, and food—was provided by an assigned area-study technician, usually an NCO.

With the exception of range firing, the team didn't leave isolation until they had completed their preparation requirements and it was time to board the chopper. The isolation concept was simple but important. It prevented any potential leak as to the destination and mission of the team.

About thirty men crowded into the small briefing room. Colonel Kahn was waiting—everyone stood. The dead serious look on Ivan Kahn's face quickly squelched any conversation among us. The shuffling of feet stopped. All attention was on Colonel Kahn.

He took a step forward from the large tactical map behind him and spoke with a loud emphatic voice. "At approximately oh-six-thirty hours yesterday, RT Vermont inserted into target area Hotel-7 with the mission of implanting and activating two sensor devices near an NVA battalion staging-and-training area. At approximately twenty-three-thirty hours last night, while in their RON position, Vermont came up on the emergency freq to Moonbeam. Sergeant Wald informed

Moonbeam using whisper voice mode that his team was under heavy probe by the enemy, and that the enemy was using dogs to locate and flush them out.'' He hesitated for a moment, then resumed speaking while pacing. ''We've had reports from CCS of dogs being used by the NVA in Cambodia to hunt down recon teams.'' He frowned. ''Be goddamn advised! It is now confirmed that they are also using dogs to track us in Laos.

''During Wald's transmission with Moonbeam, the enemy initiated heavy contact with Vermont. Moonbeam directed Wald to detonate his claymores and escape.'' The colonel raised his voice. ''The last intelligible transmission from Billy Wald was, 'We don't have claymores set out,' a pause, then, 'I'm hit.' ''

The colonel halted his words and darted a vicious stare at every face in the room. He screamed. ''No goddamn claymores set out! A seasoned recon team and no fuckin' claymores out in their RON! Why?''

He screamed again. ''Why, goddammit?''

Colonel Kahn stood silent. Angry furrows of skin gathered over his glaring eyes as they shifted across every face in the room. He removed his beret. Sweat rolled over his scowling face like hot lava creeping down a volcano.

He yelled, ''Six good men killed and their fuckin' bodies burned because the goddamn team leader didn't have his defense claymores out! Hear this! Up until now it has been SOP for teams to use claymores in their RON position. It is now a direct order to use them, and any team leader discovered not using them is gonna be fuckin' court-martialed. I don't give a fuck where you are! If an RON site doesn't facilitate the usage of a claymore defense, it's the wrong goddamn site! And, gents, if they bring those fuckin' dogs in on you, you don't stand a snowball's chance in hell of escape without claymores.''

Colonel Kahn's words lingered in the stillness.

He put his beret on, then said softly, ''I need one volunteer team for body recovery on Vermont.''

Every arm in the room went up.

Chapter 13

Swede Jensen insisted on driving me to Da Nang air-field. Before leaving camp, I asked Colonel Kahn if Binkowski could be released from headshed duty early. He compromised, saying he would break Ski loose in the afternoons while I was gone. Binkowski was elated with the news. After my request for Binkowski, I asked the colonel if I could skip the trip to Bangkok and take it some other time, explaining I didn't feel like a vacation.

The colonel gave it some thought, about three seconds' worth, then grinned and said, "Yancy, don't argue with me. You get your ass to Bangkok before I send you in for a psychiatric examination. That's an order."

Jensen revved the jeep and pulled out of camp onto the main road to Da Nang. He gripped a small Clint Eastwood–type cigar in his teeth as we splashed and bounced along the narrow road, dodging potholes and people.

High-noon sun glistened off the black and white clothing and conical straw hats of the Vietnamese scurrying along the broken edges of asphalt roadside. Some carried bamboo poles across their shoulders, suspending swaying buckets of water from each end. Others carried backpack baskets of rice and fruit, and others remnants of garbage pilfered from a nearby dump.

Ahead of us, an old woman drew her pants down and squatted over a pothole. Jensen honked at her as we passed and yelled, "Hey, Mamasan, don't forget to flush!"

She smiled back through black-stained teeth and waved.

Moments later, we reached the big bridge spanning Da Nang Harbor. The high water I'd driven through earlier with Fousi had subsided. Now a young Vietnamese man, standing beside a water-buffalo-drawn cart, blocked the entrance to the bridge.

Jensen honked, then leaned outward from the jeep, and shouted while waving his arm, "Get that fuckin' reindeer outa the way!"

The youth frowned, then turned his back to us while reaching into his apron. I pulled the Beretta from beneath my shirt and flipped it off safety.

"Watch him, Swede," I said softly.

"Don't worry, buddy, I'm— Shit! It's a fuckin' grenade!"

The Vietnamese fumbled to yank the pin free while moving toward us.

Frantically, I leapt from the jeep and centered my aim between his hate-filled eyes. I fired, then fired again. Both wad cutters ripped into his head, jerking him backward. As he collapsed, the M-26 flew from his hand, releasing the detonation spoon. The grenade rolled into the adjacent ditch. The buffalo bolted wildly into the same channel.

"Aw, shit!" Jensen cried out.

I dived into the jeep as Jensen accelerated and the

vehicle lunged straight ahead over the sprawling body in front of us, then onto the bridge road. We both knew the grenade had a six-second delay on it and the clock was running. Forty yards onto the bridge, it exploded. I cringed forward, gripping the dashboard, then quickly looked back and saw pieces of wood and water buffalo showering down into the harbor.

I glanced over at Jensen, replacing the Beretta in my shoulder holster. His eyes were tense. He had bitten through his small cigar. The broken end dangled over his lower lip, suspended by a few shreds of tobacco.

I drew in a deep breath, and grinned. "Need a light there, Swede?"

The roar and vibration of four engines on the C-130 drew us down the runway, then up and westward toward Laos. I checked my watch: 1300 hours. The takeoff was right on time.

After loosening the seat belt, I leaned away from the nylon webbing seat back to look out a small troop window. Da Nang quickly fell away from view, replaced by rich green rice fields laced with small canals.

I turned and surveyed the inside of the aircraft. A faint scent of hydraulic fluid, canvas, and refrigerated air filled the cargo compartment. I had jumped this type of aircraft many times Stateside. I felt comfortable.

In front of me, two new jeeps sat anchored in the center cargo area. Behind them, near the tailgate, a large steel cargo container was strapped down. A heavy-set loadmaster in a gray flight suit busied himself checking the tautness of the cargo straps.

I positioned my travel bag on the end of the long troop seating area and stretched out, resting my head on the lumpy assortment of civilian clothing I had packed. The flight to Nakhon Phanom—NKP—Thailand, was ninety minutes. After a brief layover to off-load cargo, we would continue on to Bangkok.

The only other passenger I had seen board was a stout, mustachioed man wearing civilian clothes and carrying a rifle case. On his right hip hung a black tooled-leather holster with a .357 Magnum in it. CIA en-route to NKP, I guessed.

The Royal Thai Air Force base, located just north of the small town of Nakhon Phanom, looked more like an American base. It housed the headquarters for CIA operations into Laos. It was also the site of an elaborate sensor monitoring facility on a par with something out of *Star Trek*. Task Force Zulu monitored all sensor transmissions coming out of Laos. In addition, NKP also served as an alternate launch site for our recon teams when bad weather prevented low-level chopper penetration into Laos from South Vietnam launch sites. Nakhon Phanom was a busy place.

I glanced at the man sitting on the other side of the troop cabin. He puffed on a long cigar and read *Time* magazine, just another commuter flight for a bored James Bond.

I positioned a seat belt loosely around my waist, slid my beret over my eyes, and let the drone of the engines lull me into sleep.

Chapter 14

"Excuse me . . . excuse me." A soft pleasant voice woke me from my nap.

I tilted my beret back from my eyes and blinked to shake off what I thought might be the tail end of an erotic dream. Emerald eyes smiled at me, and the shapely, fatigue-clad figure spoke again, this time with more apology than urgency in her tone.

"I'm sorry to wake you, but I'm hoping you have a light. You know how it is when you need a cigarette."

"No, I don't, but I can imagine." I unfastened my seat belt and sat up, reaching into my shirt pocket. I handed her an OD match pack as she sat down beside me.

I looked toward the mustachioed man reclining on the far side of the interior. He seemed asleep.

She read my eyes. "I was going to ask him, but . . . well, he has a gun on his hip and I wasn't sure how he'd react to being awakened . . . you know what I mean?"

I nodded with a halfhearted side glance while she lit her cigarette. I withheld the urge to tell her I had a

Beretta under my armpit; she might get the impression all men were basically insecure.

She sat against the webbed seat back and exhaled her first drag. The smoke drifted from her mouth like lazy vapor.

I leaned against my bag and laced my fingers behind my head, studying her. Short, windblown pageboy hair seemed natural in its disarray. A black camera case hung from her slender neck, as though she were a misplaced tourist. Her loose-fitting fatigues did little to conceal the swell of her breasts. No name tag, no makeup, no rings. A Rolex submariner watch encircled her right wrist.

Before speaking, I glanced at my crotch to make sure I wasn't overreacting. Mom had always told me it wasn't polite to point at a person when speaking.

"My name's Yancy. I didn't see you board at Da Nang. Are you Army?"

"I'm Tracy. Tracy Gibbs. No, I'm not Army." She extended her right hand to me. "I'm sort of your local high-risk journalist. I'm over here doing human-interest stories about men at war. I was in the cockpit during takeoff, that's why you didn't see me."

Shaking her hand, I glanced toward the cockpit. "Well, that's probably a good place for a human-interest story."

She grinned. "Yeah, I have several volumes of material on pilots. But they're usually more interested in getting into my pants than into my stories."

Smiling, I said, "Well, you can't blame the guys for trying. We don't see many round-eyed women over here. I've heard your name before. I think it was in Nha Trang about a year ago."

She smiled. "A year ago?"

I watched her eyes roll, thinking back. When they fixed on mine, she said, "Yes, I was in Nha Trang last October. I interviewed a big soldier by the name of . . ."

When she hesitated, I gave her the name. "Rowdy Wagner."

Her eyes brightened. "Yes. That's the one. You've got a pretty good memory, Yancy." She took a draw on her cigarette, then spoke with a casual voice, as though peeking through a curtain. "What do you do over here?"

I got a gut feeling she was sizing me up as a potential story. I assumed a pseudo-serious frown and answered, "Oh, I run the snack bar at Cam Ranh Bay."

She cast me a subtle smile. "How 'bout that. I've never met a Green Beret snack-bar manager before. What MOS is that?"

She glanced at my beret, shifted deliberately down to my scuffed jungle boots, then looked directly back into my eyes and waited.

"Oops!" I said softly. "Well, if you won't believe snack-bar manager, how 'bout combat forklift driver? And while I'm tap-dancing here, allow me to cleverly change the subject. What magazine are you with?"

She turned directly toward me, crossed one leg over the other, then spoke with a slight tilt of her head, "*Personality* magazine . . . and no, I won't believe combat forklift driver, either.

"What I will believe is long-range ground recon working out of Command and Control North, possibly Command and Control Central. That about right, Yancy?"

I sat up and leaned forward, resting my elbows on

my knees. I thought for a moment before answering her question.

"Tracy, if you're as knowledgeable about Command and Control as you imply, then you're also aware that I can't talk about it." I paused and winked. "So, if you're thinking of me as a story, you'll have to get me drunk and seduce me first." I cast a sly grin and added, "I will promise you won't have to spend much on liquor."

I smiled directly into her green eyes, but she wasn't smiling back. Instead, she dropped her cigarette to the floor, snuffed it out with her boot, then picked up the butt and placed it in her pocket.

She stared with clear gentle eyes. "Thanks for the invitation to what I'm sure must be a great ride, Yancy, but I'm not over here to fuck myself to stardom. I'm trying to give the people back home some threads of pride to cling to. About the men serving and dying in a futile goddamn war. Now, if you'll excuse me."

Tracy stood, walked toward the front of the troop section, sat, and lit another cigarette. I watched her. She didn't look back at me.

I'd never met a woman like her, totally without pretense. It was time for an apology. I stood and walked toward her.

Suddenly, a jolting boom hurled me backward, slamming me over the hood of a jeep and into the windshield.

Tracy was thrown sprawling onto the floor.

The plane bucked wildly, then plunged. I landed spread-eagled across the hood and grasped the fender to keep from being thrown upward. I heard the revving strain of the engines and felt the g-force pulling us up.

I scurried from the jeep and searched the floor for

Tracy. She clung to an anchor strap. "Are you okay?"
I shouted above the engine roar.

She raised her head slowly. Blood oozed from a cut
on her neck. I yanked the cravat from my collar, spit
on it, and wiped the blood away to inspect the cut. It
was shallow.

"Don't get up!" I ordered. "Hold this against your
neck and stay put. I'll be back."

I stumbled toward the rear of the plane and grabbed
a first-aid pouch hanging near the troop jump-door. I
glanced out a window. Through thick black smoke I
saw that our altitude was just above the trees.

"Give me a hand over here!" an urgent voice
shouted. It was the mustachioed man, kneeling over the
load master. "Help me put him on the seat."

The loadmaster was dazed, but conscious. We lifted
him onto the long bench seat and lay him supine.

"What the hell hit us? A thirty-seven round?" I
shouted.

"Don't know, but that'd be my guess. How's the
girl?"

"Okay. You got him handled?"

"Roger," he snapped.

Rushing back to Tracy, I saw she was trying to pull
herself up from the floor. She had wrapped the cloth
I'd given her around her neck.

I helped her onto the troop seat and buckled her in.
"Don't ever ask for a job on my RT. You'd never make
it the way you follow orders, Tracer!"

Her voice became exhilarated. "So you are a One-
Zero. I knew it!"

I jerked a gauze pad and some antiseptic from the
pouch, pulled the cravat from her neck, and quickly
treated the wound, then leaned up to a window and

checked our altitude again. We were about fifty feet off the trees. The outboard starboard engine billowed black clouds of smoke.

Tracy ran her fingers casually through her hair, as if the trauma had been little more than a bump in the road.

My adrenaline was still pumping. I knew we were hanging by a thread.

"What did you call me a moment ago? Tracer?"

I ignored her and bounded toward the cockpit ladder, then up and inside. The pilot's voice transmission answered my questions. His words were calm. "Roger, NKP, we're hit. Attempting to extinguish engine fire . . . roger that, we're going to jettison cargo. Stand by."

Minutes later our limping plane crossed the Mekong River and touched down on sweet Thai earth amid fire trucks, ambulances, and cheering spectators.

I still don't know, nor would even try to guess, what they taught combat pilots, but they were all the same; the more perilous a situation became, the calmer they got. It was as though their panic thermostats functioned backward.

Chapter 15

Half an hour later, I sat alone in the base hospital snack bar with a cup of coffee and a tuna sandwich. The doctors examined and released me, but insisted Tracy get an X ray. She promised to meet me for coffee afterward.

A stout figure approached me from the side. It was the same mustachioed man who was on the plane. He sat down at my table and immediately began talking as if we had known each other for years.

He sounded like a radio announcer. "Well, the loadmaster's gonna be okay. He took a hard lick when that thirty-seven knocked the sky out from under us. I'm Calvin."

He didn't offer his hand or wait for a reply from me. "I saw you fly through the air when we took that hit. How you feelin'?"

"I'm Yancy. Still in one piece." I sipped my coffee and decided to ask if he knew anything about local flight schedules. "Any idea when they have another flight out for Bangkok?"

He poured two packets of sugar into his coffee and stirred it. "Not for a couple of days yet. But hell, there's worse places to get stuck than NKP, believe me. I've been assigned here for the last six months. Town's just six miles down the road, and five dollars gets you a woman all night. You ever had any Thai pussy? Man, it's good.''

Calvin's style was irritating, but right now, he was the best source of information I had. I grinned tactfully. ''Yeah, I've heard that. But then, the worst I ever had was wonderful.''

He laughed. ''Well, ain't that the damn truth. But there's different degrees of wonderful. Now, Vietnamese pussy is somewhere around zero on the scale.''

Calvin leaned forward, elbows on the table like he was going to discuss a battle plan, his hands moving as he continued. ''Now, these Thai girls flat get with it, and they're clean. See, the government here registers all bar whores and makes them take a VD test ever' week. All the bars post a list of the diseased numbers and check the IDs of the girls before they let 'em in the bar. Hell, they even announce the damn numbers on the radio like it was an inclement weather report. What I'm sayin' is, Yancy, you don't have to worry about your dick fallin' off over here.''

I decided the best way to get Calvin off what was obviously his favorite subject was to lie. ''Gee, that's great, Calvin, but what I'm really interested in is Buddhist shrines. Are there any temples in the area?''

Calvin sat back abruptly from the table, like someone had just poured cold water on his crotch. He blinked and spoke the first words slowly. ''Buddhist . . . shrines . . . Are you shittin' me?''

I kept a silent poker face staring into his.

He stroked his mustache and studied me before answering. ''Well, if you're serious, Yancy, they do have temples here and there, but I couldn't really tell you if they're Buddhist or Baptist.'' He glanced hurriedly at his watch. "Well, I gotta get going. You enjoy those Baptist shrines, you hear?''

"Roger, Calvin, thanks.''

A moment later Tracy came in. She wore a rigid white neck brace. I stood as she neared the table with her coffee.

"Hi, Yancy. How do you like my new turtleneck?''

"Nice, but didn't they have it in camouflage or OD?''

She turned and checked her reflection in the window. "No, but I rather like the white . . . gives me a bit of the Hepburn look, don't you think?'' She fluttered her eyelids melodramatically, then looked at me. "I really don't need the brace. I'm only wearing it to make the medic happy. I think he wanted an excuse to fondle my neck.''

She lowered her tone. "By the way, thanks for the help up there. Are you okay?''

"Fine,'' I replied. "It looks like I'm stuck here for two of my three days' leave. But Calvin, the fellow wearing the quick-draw rig on the plane, was telling me, just before you came in, that there's worse places to be stuck. He gave me some tips on the culture and nightlife in NKP.''

Tracy smiled warily. "Yeah, I can imagine what he was telling you about NKP nightlife.'' She brightened. "Listen, I'm over here for a brief holiday myself. I'm hopping a flight up to Chiang Mai in about an hour. You want to tag along? We'll be back in a couple of days.''

"Where's Chiang Mai? I never heard of it.''

"Northwestern Thailand, up near the Burma border. It's where ninety percent of Thailand's wood-carving industry is located. This is my second trip up there. This time, I'm going to buy some gifts to send to the family. The prices are unbelievably cheap. What do you think, Yancy? It's really beautiful.''

The thought of wood carvings didn't excite me; the opportunity to get to know Tracy did. But I sensed that with Tracy Gibbs, an invitation to tour a beautiful remote place didn't necessarily include a free pass into her bedroom.

Trying not to sound too eager, I said, "Sounds good to me. Beats sticking around here looking at Baptist shrines.''

"Baptist shrines?'' She gave a puzzled frown.

"Just a joke, Tracer.'' I chuckled.

"There's that word again. Tracer. You still haven't told me why you stuck that tag on me.''

My notion that Tracy Gibbs knew her way around Southeast Asia proved correct. During our two-hour flight to Chiang Mai, I learned she had been here for the past eleven months—traveling, writing, and learning all she could about the war.

I also learned she was a bona fide Connecticut Yankee, Hartford type, and that she had graduated from the University of Ohio, class of '67. Tracy didn't attend her graduation ceremony. When I asked her why, she quoted the words of Henry David Thoreau upon his graduation from Harvard: "Let the sheep keep his skin, I have what I came for.''

A year after graduation, she was working for *Personality* and engaged to a successful CPA. A short time later, she broke the engagement. She then convinced her editor that human-interest stories about men at war would boost circulation. In the same breath she volunteered for the assignment.

Tracy was a patriot, a patriot with an aversion to media and governmental wool pulling.

As we landed, the glowing embers of an orange evening sun filtered through tall teak trees surrounding our rural airfield.

Tracy and I collected our bags, boarded a brightly decorated taxi, and rode westward toward the bustling little town of Chiang Mai.

In the distance, a white cloud hovered above the town, smoke from evening meal fires rising into the dimming windless sky. Ahead of us an elephant lumbered slowly along the roadside, pulling a huge teak log. Our driver honked as we passed through the fog of dust rising from the elephant's path. The dark-skinned man sitting high on the elephant smiled and waved.

Our driver pointed toward the log being pulled through the trail of dust. "There come more work. Today, tree. Tomorrow, maybe table and chair . . ." He grinned back at us, then added with an insinuating tone, "Maybe bed."

I casually took Tracy's hand, interlacing our fingers. She didn't resist.

Soon we arrived at the Chiang Mai Sitrep Hotel and pulled beneath a bright yellow awning at the entrance. The lodge was nestled into a hillside above the town. A large stone Buddha sat on each side of the carpeted steps leading inside.

Entering, I smelled the soft scent of flowers. The fragrance drifted through the spacious, red-tiled lobby. Next to the lobby were rattan tables, chairs, and couches on an expansive outdoor terrace overlooking the town. One section of the terrace served as a restaurant.

Standing at the desk, we were greeted by an elderly Thai man. "Welcome to Chiang Mai. You like a honeymoon suite?"

The question was directed to me. I cast a glance to Tracy, indicating the decision was hers.

Tracy replied through a smile. "No, we'll have separate rooms, please."

I added with mild emphasis, "Adjoining rooms, please."

He blinked.

After checking in, we walked toward the terrace to view the last glimmer of sunset before going to our rooms. A half mile below us, the Ping River wound its way through town. The bustle of the little city seemed to subside with the fading sun. All appeared tranquil and happy in this part of Asia. It was a first for me. I wondered if Vietnam could ever be like that.

We sat, half leaning against the low stone retainer wall around the terrace. The panoramic majesty of an unending beryl-green rain forest blanketed the valley and rose into distant cloud-shrouded mountains. A soft rumble of thunder rolled off the hills and into the valley below.

"Tracy, this is really beautiful. Thank you for inviting me here. I still don't know why me, but I'm not complaining."

"You're welcome, Brett Yancy. I knew you'd like it here. And as far as 'why you?' goes . . . well, it's because you're a gentleman. You've got some rough edges, but you're still a gentleman."

She leaned and lightly kissed my lips as a gusty mist of rain swept across the terrace.

Tracy spoke happily. "We'd better go to our rooms and change out of these fatigues before the locals think they've been invaded. How about a rainy-night dinner on the veranda, *monsieur* . . . say in about an hour?"

I agreed, and slipped my arm over her shoulder while walking toward the lobby. As we walked away, two Thai boys in starched white jackets began drawing a large orange awning out over the terrace. A gentle rain fell.

By the time I got to my room, the rain had become heavier. Large drops pelted against the French patio door as I entered. I got my wish. Tracy's room adjoined mine. And something more, a large bouquet of roses sat on the desk. Next to it was a bottle of champagne with two glasses. Attached to the ice bucket was a note:

> Welcome to land of the smile
> We happy to have you as hour guest.
> Enjoy.

I glanced at the misspelled word and smiled, just as they had invited me to. If the rates were by the hour, I'd better make the most of each one.

I removed my beret and shirt and placed them along with my shoulder holster on the bed. I hastily poured two glasses of champagne, carried them to Tracy's door, and knocked.

"Who's there?"

I dramatized my voice. "A handsome and wind-blown gladiator for the oppressed people of the world. I just happen to be in the area, resting from the Crusades, and giving away free champagne."

Without opening the door, she replied in an amused

tone, "Yancy, two questions. Number one. Are you on drugs?"

"Negative, don't need 'em. Dope is for dopes. Next question."

"Okay. Well . . . I never asked you. Are you married?"

"No, but I did have the ninety-day home trial once. I know how everything works. Open the door or I'll drink your champagne myself."

"Wait a minute. Let me get something on. I was just about to jump in the shower."

A few seconds later Tracy, wrapped in a white towel, opened the door. She'd removed the neck brace. She tried to conceal a smile, but her eyes gave it away.

"Sorry to bother you, *mademoiselle*, but I wanted to share my first taste of champagne in Thailand with you." I handed her a glass then touched mine to hers and lifted it high. "Here's to the land of the smile."

"To the land of the smile," she echoed.

While tilting our glasses back and drinking, my eyes moved over her body. I caught a glimpse of shy pride in her smile as she watched me study her. As the glass left her mouth, champagne glistened on her lips, mirroring a sparkle from her emerald eyes.

Enchanted, I stepped into the room, closed the door with my foot, and pulled her into my arms.

She yielded reluctantly, then embraced me with a full admission of desire.

I dropped my glass to the floor, picked her up in my arms, and carried her to the large crimson silk bed. I gently placed her on the bed, then stood and removed my clothes. Her eyes moved over me. She pulled the towel away and reached out to me.

The tan length of her slender legs parted beneath me as I eased myself over her nakedness.

With one leg still draped over my thighs, she nestled her head against my chest.

She spoke apprehensively. "Can you handle a confession?"

I kissed her forehead. "Sure, honey, just don't tell me I'm too small."

She blinked, then rolled her eyes up to mine. "No, Yancy, no problem there. I need to tell you that I wanted you, too, that it wasn't just you seducing me."

I leaned back to study her face. "Honey, so what's wrong with that? If you think you're just another notch in my gun, you're wrong."

Without answering, she rolled from the bed and paced to the dressing table to light a cigarette. After taking a long drag, she walked back and sat on the edge of the bed facing away from me, as though studying the rain—silent.

After a moment her head tilted downward. She sniffed, quickly brushed a hand to her cheek, and turned to face me with misty eyes. "Brett . . . please don't think I'm some maudlin chick whoring my way through Southeast Asia. I like you. I genuinely like you, and, damn it, that doesn't happen a lot with me! I'm not even sure I like the feeling. It . . . it makes me so damn vulnerable."

I took the cigarette from her hand and cast it into an ashtray. I pulled her down into my arms and brushed her tears away. "Tracer, I like you too. I like all of you."

Chapter 16

As Tracy and I walked into the terrace restaurant a Filipino band played "I Left My Heart in San Francisco." After being seated at a corner table, we smiled as the singer tried to pronounce the words. "I'm lee my ha en saw fra-hes-co."

Tracy recommended the Japanese Kobe steak dinner. After the first bite, I had to admit Texas steaks had serious Japanese competition.

"They feed their cattle beer and play music to them at night." Tracy remarked, "They claim that's why the meat is so tender and tasty."

After another bite I replied, "I wonder if they do that with their women too."

I ate all my steak. Since Tracy could only finish half hers, I volunteered to take care of the rest. After a dessert of ice cream and wafers, we sat back and relaxed. Tracy smoked while I sipped a Beam and coke.

I took another sip of my drink, smiled, and asked, "Why did you break it off with your fiancé? Did he pick his nose in public or something?"

She paused before answering. "No, he was socially impeccable. Perhaps too perfect. Truth is, he wasn't a bad guy at all. Looks, money, status, he had it. But, after a few months with him, I began to realize I didn't fit in.

"Accountants have this closure fixation. Everything has to be finalized, completed, neat, and tidy. I didn't want to live my life in a structured existence like that. I tried for a while, believe me, but I felt like a round peg in a square slot. So, I took my mask off. He's still wearing his."

Tracy crushed her cigarette into the ashtray, then looked back at me. "How about you, Brett Yancy? Ever engaged?"

"Yeah. And she wasn't a bad gal either. But she Dear Johned me a few months after I got to 'Nam. Ironically, she used the same words you used back in the plane. In her last letter she called this a futile goddamn war."

Tracy leaned forward and set her wineglass on the table, then looked directly at me. "She's right, Brett."

I raised my eyebrows and politely rebuked her. "Tracy, do you really think a nation with our arsenal, our strength, and our history of winning is going to let a small country like North Vietnam whip us?"

Her reply was subtle. "It's not North Vietnam that's going to whip us, Brett. It's our whole misconception of the war's winnability.

"The South Vietnamese are not motivated to win. These people have been involved in one war or another for centuries. It's a way of life with them.

"Half their leaders are corrupt, and the ones who aren't are incompetent. The Vietnamese business community isn't beating any drums to end the war. They're back in protected areas getting rich. And the poor peasant out in the hamlets and rice fields doesn't have any political influence. His allegiance is to anyone who's got a gun pointed at him.

"And consider this: Our soldiers come over here to fight an elusive, well-trained, highly motivated, and seasoned enemy for one year. Just when our soldier is beginning to know the enemy, his ways and tactics, our guy goes back home. His replacement comes in only to learn the same hard lessons and make some of the same fatal mistakes. Then, the process repeats itself."

Tracy paused, moved forward to the edge of her chair, and continued, "It doesn't take a brain or a West Point tactician to see our concept is demented. Our generals don't see it, or won't admit it if they do. The Communists are in for the duration. For us, it's a part-time war with full-time fatalities, and damn it, it pisses me off that good men are dying in the process!"

Tracy's voice quivered. She snatched a napkin from the table and looked away. I was impressed with her reasoning. I had to admit she was at least partially right. But she had overlooked one important point about war.

I waited a moment. She turned back and looked at me with red-rimmed eyes. I tried not to sound defensive. "Tracy, no war is fought with a clear set of rules and clear minds. There are screwups, gray areas, errors, and even corruption, but you can't deny the noble purpose of our efforts. If somebody doesn't help beat the Communist thugs off this part of the world, then a lot of people who deserve a chance at freedom are going down the tube and I—"

Tracy placed her hand on my arm and interrupted in a soft voice. "Yes, it is a noble purpose. And valiant men, perhaps America's best, are responding to it. But, Brett, it's an ignoble war, and a no-win situation."

With smiling lips and imploring eyes, she added,

"Honey, let's don't let an argument spoil our splendid moments together. May I have this dance?"

I took a sip of my drink, then glanced into her eyes. She was right, and I wasn't going to let my ego rain on our picnic.

We moved comfortably into each other's arms and danced to "Sittin' on the Dock of the Bay." Her soft fragrance drifted over me like the descent of autumn leaves. My hands roved slowly over her back, caressing the smoothness of her dress. I felt the warmth of her braless breasts press against my chest and the gentle rhythm of her thighs hug mine.

I looked admiringly down at her. "Honey, this dress looks beautiful on you."

"Thank you, *monsieur*," she murmured.

Sliding one hand slowly down to her buttocks, I whispered, "You know, it would also look very nice draped over the nightstand by my bed."

She tilted her face upward and studied my eyes. Smiling, she whispered back, "Well, we won't know unless we try it, will we?"

A warm morning sun yawned through a corner of the patio curtain. I reached one arm slowly toward the nightstand and retrieved a room-service menu, trying not to disturb Tracy.

She stirred, lifted her head, and looked at her watch. "What are you doing up so early, Yancy?"

"Just a habit, darlin'. I always wake at first light. I was thinking about calling down for some breakfast. You hungry?"

Tracy rolled back, frowning. "No, and I don't understand how you could be hungry." She yawned. "You ate over sixteen ounces of steak last night, including mine, not to mention rice, bread, salad, cookies, and ice cream. You're incredible!''

I kept my eyes on the menu and replied, ''It's all this good lovin', honey. Lovin' stimulates my appetite. I have to keep my strength up.''

Playfully, she rolled her naked body over me. Straddling me, she locked her strong thighs around me. Her lips began to shower fleeting kisses over my face and chest.

She brought her head up to my ear and darted her tongue into me, whispering, ''If you're ordering room service, Mr. Gladiator for the Oppressed, I'll have coffee and orange juice. But please tell them to delay it for at least half an hour. I'm going to make sure your appetite is up to it.''

The cool mid-afternoon sun kept its promise. Sparkles of sunlight danced off small pools of water gathered along the road leading into Chiang Mai. Tracy and I had decided to ride a *samlor* into town rather than take a cab.

High water, cascading through roadside ditches, swept leaves, branches, and garbage along in its swift murky pathway. Ahead of us, an old bus toiled slowly through pedestrians and bicycles, leaving a dark trail of diesel smoke in its wake. The little city was alive with activity.

Tracy, using a combination of English, Thai, and sign language, instructed the *samlor* driver to take us to a wood-carving factory. I envisioned it being a large modern complex. Instead, we arrived and walked into what was little more than a big barn. The term ''family gathering place'' would have been more suitable than ''factory.'' Men and women, young and old, sat in circular clusters throughout the barn. Some were carving, some eating from bowls, and others moved about carrying boxes and crates. All seemed to be talking at once. The scents of marijuana, rice, and burning coal swirled through the large noisy room.

After a moment of waiting and watching, we were approached by a young Thai girl wearing a long black skirt.

She spoke through a broad smile. "*Sawadi ka.* Hello, may I helping you, please?" She bowed slightly.

Tracy responded, smiling. "*Sawadi ka.* Yes, we want to see everything you have, please."

"Yes, please, you coming this way, please." The young girl's charmingly disarranged English was redeemed by a happy smile. She escorted us to a large warehouse behind the big barn and began showing us just what Tracy had asked for—everything!

As Tracy's excitement heightened, I sensed, after fifteen minutes, the shopping process was going to take some time. I excused myself and returned to the barn to watch the workers.

I came into the work area and sat myself on a crate at the rear door to watch. Occasionally, a worker walked by and rendered a big smile and a brief bow.

Moments later, two solemn-faced, orange-robed males entered the room. Each carried a large, smooth wooden bowl in his hands. Their naked, clean-shaven heads sparked angry memories of Baldy.

I studied them while they moved slightly through the room. When they approached each worker, the worker would stand, bow, and place a token of money or fruit into the bowl. That done, the worker would bow again and resume his task.

I watched their bald heads as they ambled through

the crowd. I contemplated the bitter memory of Baldy and the gnawing question: Why would a regular North Vietnamese soldier shave his head? I'd seen plenty of the little bastards during the last year. I'd watched them from concealed vantage points so close I could spit on them. I'd searched their dead limp bodies after an ambush. None of them had shaved heads. Not one.

My mind shifted back to the agonizing seconds when I saw Baldy's sniper shot rip into Will's back and slam him down into the grass. I recalled the torment of a split-second decision—whether to pursue and kill the escaping assassin or get to Will's side and try to save him.

I had made the right decision.

I remembered holding Will in my arms and feeling the warmth of his dying blood soak into my chest. I could still hear the tender weakness of his final choking words: "Tell Chunky I'm going across the river, man. I'll see her and the kids over there. Might even see you there, boss."

Contempt flooded into me as I glanced back at the smiling monks moving toward the door to leave. A sixth sense stirred inside me like a wave. Was it possible Baldy played a Jekyll and Hyde role, like the monks inside Marble Mountain? If so, it was an ingenious method of moving into our areas and observing us up close. He could plant mines, booby traps, even make dead-letter drops to other agents.

I shrugged. It was only a guess. Right now, I didn't care if Baldy swung through the trees on vines. In less than two weeks, I'd be back in Hotel-5, stalking him. I wasn't coming out until I cut the last gasping breath of life out of him.

"Brett. Brett, are you okay?"

I looked up to see Tracy's puzzled stare. I stood and forced a smile at her.

She gently touched my shoulder. "You looked like you were peering into a tunnel. Anyhow, I've made all my selections. Would you come help me fill out the address labels? I'm having everything shipped directly to the States."

After departing the factory, we ate at a nearby restaurant, then spent the remainder of the day sightseeing. We visited a Buddhist shrine, took a boat ride on the Ping River, and even found a liquor store that featured American labels.

Tracy insisted on buying me a bottle of Jim Beam. I objected, but she overruled me. "Look, you told me if I wanted a story I'd have to get you drunk and seduce you first. Well, I may be doing it backward, but this evening I'm going to get you drunk. In fact, I may even try some myself."

I grinned. "Okay, but I'll warn you now, Kentucky bourbon opens the cage on all my sexual perversions."

She slipped an arm around me as we walked. Keeping her gaze forward, she mused, "Sexual perversions . . . hmmmm . . . maybe we should take a cab back to the hotel. We could start sooner, if we take a cab!"

Chapter 17

A cool breeze swooped down from the dimming sky and fluttered through the pages of a magazine on our poolside table. I placed the ice bucket on top of the magazine, filled my glass with ice cubes, and poured my third drink. I glanced at Tracy at the adjacent table, poised behind a portable typewriter. Her fingers moved swiftly over the keys, stopping occasionally while she peered upward, as though picking thoughts from an invisible orchard.

"How's your drink, Tracer?"

She took a quick sip from her almost empty glass, and resumed typing. "Fine, thanks. I'll have this finished in a minute, then I'll have another. This is coming out great." Her voice was enthusiastic, but she didn't elaborate on what was so great.

I studied her labored concentration, allowing my eyes to drift over her body. She was beautiful, intelligent, thoughtful, witty, and charming. Not to mention, a wonderful lover. If she got any more perfect I'd have to believe she was a dream.

For my own emotional stability, and hers, I needed to get this fascination into a realistic perspective. Tracy and I were two wayward trails crossing in a jungle. We could enjoy it, but we couldn't let ourselves get bogged down with emotion. She had her target areas and I had mine—Hotel-5.

"I'll have that drink now." She stood holding her glass toward me. She slid her chair near mine and lit a cigarette while I mixed her a Beam and Coke.

"Easy on the bourbon." She smiled. "I still have an interview to do. I can't be getting soused while I'm on the clock."

I handed her the drink. "I hope you're not serious about an interview with me," I said unenthusiastically.

Her voice became defensive. "Yes, I'm serious. And if you need to know why, it's because you're one of the few men I've met in this war who still has his head screwed on straight. You're not a drunkard or a doper, and you're sensitive to the issues affecting the war and the people caught up in it." She paused, sipped her drink, then added, "You're also an intelligent guy, in spite of the fact that you jump out of perfectly good airplanes."

She spoke with a smile that could have charmed an executioner out of his ax. I sympathized with her sense of purpose. But I just didn't want it.

I cast my eyes skyward. "Tracy, thanks for your interest. It's very complimentary, but I'm not a candidate."

She nodded, then snapped, "Fine, Yancy! Forget it! But whatever happened to 'noble purpose,' if I may quote you. Or was that just some fancy rhetoric to drive home a point? I'm trying—"

"I'll tell you what happened to noble purpose! It got ripped apart, splattered with blood, and crushed into hot earth by a Communist bastard. Right now my noble

purpose is fuckin' avenging William Washington. And
I'll tell you this: If I could bring Will back, I'd sell out
this whole fuckin' war in a New York minute!''

I stood, grabbed the bottle from the table, then sat
in back down and looked directly into her eyes. ''You
want a goddamn story? Go talk to Will Washington's
widow! Go home and talk to the amputees, and the
mothers and dads who raised their sons only to have
them shipped off to this fuckin' death trap and brought
home in a fuckin' flag-draped coffin.''

I trembled for a moment, then tried to lower my tone.
''And while you're there, talk to the muddled, thank-
less morons who dare spit on the uniforms of the guard-
ians of their freedom. You can tell 'em Brett Yancy said
their slobber is better directed at the fuckin' pin-striped
politicians who keep us here, not the hollowed-eyed
pawns over here dying for noble fuckin' purpose!''

I poured a stout shot of Beam into my glass and
gulped it. I looked upward and breathed a long sigh of
relief. Tears had come, but they'd been vaporized by
the heat of my rage. Now my rage was purged, but in
the process, I'd spewed it all on Tracy.

I turned to see her staring at me. She tilted her head
down and clasped her hands in front of her. With a soft
tremor in her voice, she said, ''I love you, Brett Yancy.
In two days you'll walk out of my life, and I don't know
if I'll ever see you again. But I want you to know
straight out that I love you.''

I gathered her up in my arms. I had told her about
Will during the flight from NKP, carefully camouflag-
ing my emotion and sorrow. Now she knew how carved
up I was about it, but that didn't justify unloading both
barrels of my bitterness on her.

Tracy tightened her embrace around me. I stroked

her hair and pondered her confession of love. I knew it was no hip shot. She wasn't the kind of woman to throw that word around loosely. My feelings for her ran deep and were getting deeper. But it wasn't love. In another place or time, perhaps she and I might have a chance at love. But not here, not now.

I kissed her forehead. Her tearstained face tilted up to my eyes like she was searching for a response to her confession. She needed and deserved some reflection of my feelings. I tried to smile, but I could feel only about half of it working.

Looking down into her eyes, I said, "Tracer, I'm enchanted with you. I think you're the greatest thing since thirty-round magazines, but right now is not the time for us to be hanging our hearts on the firing line. We don't know where, when, or if we'll ever see each other again and I—"

She backed up abruptly and grabbed a fistful of my shirt. Her green eyes flared. "Damn it, Brett, you need to start listening and stop jousting at windmills! I know we're heading in different directions. I said I love you, and in the same breath I admitted we may never see each other again . . . but I don't care . . . it's the truest, strongest feeling I've ever had for anyone outside my family. So don't you start feeling like you have to comfort me or make explanations just because the other side of my seesaw doesn't have you on it!"

She released my shirt as quickly as she'd grabbed it, then sat down and folded her arms across her lap. As though talking to the wind, she said, "Falling in love with a Green Beret is about as smart as being a stowaway on a kamikaze flight." She paused, picked up her glass, and jabbed it toward me. "I'll have another drink please. A good one!"

I mixed us another stout drink, then pulled a chair up and sat facing her. She immediately propped her legs across my knees and nestled back into the cushion of her chair. Our eyes scanned gently over each other's bodies, then met comfortably eye to eye. We sipped our drinks without talking. The rustling murmur of soft winds stirred through the trees. The scent of lilacs drifted through the air.

She spoke quietly. "You never did tell me why you call me Tracer."

I smiled. "Remember back in the plane when we took that hit and you went sprawling across the floor?"

She nodded.

"Well, when I finally got to you, I saw a small crease of blood along the cut on your neck. It looked like a tracer bullet had grazed your neck and left its glow on you."

She smiled. "Well, it's unique. Thank you for telling me."

Raising my glass into the air, I said, "Unique name for a unique lady."

Tracy lifted her glass high. "Chugalug, Yancy."

We tilted our glasses back and gulped. I finished first, then watched her face squinch at the taste. She handed me her empty glass. "I get the feeling you've had more practice at this than I have."

I stood and mixed us another. "You're right, Tracer. It's part of our training."

She watched the fading sunlight dance through tall teak trees. "You ever been in love, Yancy?" There was a slight slur in her words.

I quipped, "Once, but it turned out to be lust."

"Well, do you have a definition of love, or do you even think about it?"   .

I sipped my drink and thought for a moment. I could feel the amber current of Beam moving through me. "Tracer, I'm not sure. Depends on a lot of variables. But I do know this. Of all the words in the English language, the word *love* is probably the most abused. There's a song out, Led Zeppelin's 'Whole Lotta Love' that talks about a guy wanting to give every inch of his love."

I paused and took a long drink. I tried to remember how many drinks I'd had. My words slurred. "So where does that leave the guy who's hung like a stud field mouse?

Tracy laughed loudly, then she murmured, "Brett Yancy, I do believe you are starting to feel the spirits."

I grinned widely while massaging her foot. "Yeah. I am, Tracer, and the spirit feels good. But how 'bout you? What's your definition of love?"

She placed her drink in her lap and gazed toward the pool. "You know, I came home from college after my first year, thought I was in love with this campus Casanova. One afternoon while having lunch with my dad, I decided to ask him what he thought love was.

"He thought for a while, then said it as plainly as it can be put. He said love was simply two hearts, each fertile to the other's need, each supportive of the other's goals, and each understanding that failure and mistakes are destined to happen in both of you. He said it was like you are each the guardian of the other's balance scale in life." Tracy held out her hands, moving them to simulate the rise and fall, then the balance point, of an imagined scale. "You give freely from the pockets of your time and concern, and place the needed amount on the other's scale to balance it.''

Tracy stopped talking for a second. She tilted her head sideways, smiled, and said, ''You know, I think he's right. Are you hungry? I'm starved.''

Chapter 18

I never made it to Bangkok. Tracy and I decided to stay an extra day in Chiang Mai and take a direct flight to Da Nang.

We laughed, loved, practiced Oriental massage on each other, and, as I should have expected, ended up shopping again. Tracy lured me back to the wood-carving factory. Seeing her enthusiasm I, too, got the shopping bug. I bought half a dozen items, mostly jewelry boxes, and shipped them to my parents for distribution to the family.

Later in the day, Tracy helped me select an umbrella and a fashionable raincoat for Fousi. We also bought crayons, coloring books, and several dresses for Lon and Ming, as well as some gifts for my Montagnards.

When Tracy asked who Fousi was, I told her the whole unabridged story, adding that while my friendship for Fousi and her family was steadfast, I felt it was best for Fousi and me to be Platonic from here on. I wasn't sure how easy that was going to be, particularly if Fousi slipped her warm body into my bed on some rainy monsoon night. But I reasoned I would cross that rice paddy when I came to it.

After telling Tracy I planned to bring Fousi and her sisters back to the States, she recommended I contact a Baptist adoption agency in Dallas that worked to bring orphans of the war to the U.S.

I didn't agree with Tracy's concept of the war. In fact, it quietly pissed me off every time she mounted her soapbox. But I did agree that Fousi, Lon, and Ming would have a much better life in the United States with a far greater chance for a good education. The decision ultimately would have to be Fousi's, and she would have to understand that even if I was able to get all the right strings pulled, I wouldn't be there to hold her hand during the transition.

On the final morning in Chiang Mai, I awoke to the slapping rhythm of typewriter keys. Tracy, robed only in my fatigue shirt, sat at her portable Smith-Corona. After rising and sharing a cup of coffee with her, I showered, dressed, and excused myself, explaining I needed to buy something in town before we left. What I didn't tell her was, there were two important items I planned on buying. One of the items would remain my secret.

I'd completed my private shopping. A soft rain fell gently onto the naked shoulders of my *samlor* driver as he strained to make it up the final hundred-yard incline to the hotel.

Gazing from the canopied cart into the gray misty fog ahead, a chilling thought came to me. Without looking, I reached to touch the two small items on the seat beside me.

One represented love; the other was an instrument of death. My fingers moved to touch the smoothness of a book. Will's book. *The Prophet.* He'd given it to me in friendship. The copy I'd just purchased would be my gift to Tracy when we parted later today in Da Nang.

Next, my fingers moved to slip comfortably around the carved bone handle of a knife. It felt good in my grasp. I pulled the knife slowly from its black sheath.

I had known the first moment that it was the precise instrument I must use to thrust hilt-deep into Baldy. I touched, then lightly drew the end of my thumb across its finely honed edge. The long spangled blade was new, virgin to the stain of blood. When my mission was complete and its bright steel cloaked with warm blood, it must never be wiped clean or used again.

As I touched the blade, a second ripple of conscience came. Killing had been part of duty and survival, kill or be killed. But this killing would be different. It would be personal. A face-to-face premeditated murder. I silently vowed that when I stood over Baldy's carcass, no moral pangs would thwart my satisfaction or degrade the righteousness of my act.

A warm beam of morning sun cut through the fog ahead as we approached the hotel. I gently slid the knife back into its sheath and began to feel comfortable, allied with the malignant spirit in me.

Tracy's grip tightened briefly on my hand when the screech of our C-130's wheels hit the hot asphalt of Da Nang airfield. The roar of the reversing props lunged us forward gently. We were back in 'Nam.

No one, among the dozen or so passengers on board, hurried to peer through the porthole windows at familiar drab surroundings. The Hercules taxied to a large sandbagged revetment and stopped. There was a small Quonset hut that served as a terminal. Above the entrance hung a sign that read: WELCOME TO THE HOBO HILTON. DA NANG AIR FORCE BASE, VIETNAM.

Heat, light, and the fetid odor of the old city rushed over the lowering lip of the tailgate ramp and onto us like flooding water over a spillway. I squinted into bright sunlight and rippling vapors of heat streaming through the cavernous opening at the rear of the aircraft, then glanced at Tracy.

She looked at me with somber eyes. The lower edge of her soft lip was drawn tightly between her teeth.

A half dozen men in varied uniforms filed slowly past us, then out and down the ramp. I pulled my hand from Tracy's soft grip and reached under my seat to remove the small package still wrapped in brown paper. I handed it to her with both hands.

"Here's something I thought you might like, Tracer. William Washington gave me a copy of this on my last birthday. He said it should only be given to someone special."

Tracy smiled and carefully tore away the wrapping paper from the book. She looked down into the gentle face of Kahlil Gibran on the cover.

Her voice quivered. "You know, I first heard of this book in college. I went to several stores trying to find it but none of them had it. Now suddenly it's in my hands, inside a damn airplane in a damn war zone." A tear slid down her cheek. "Thank you, Brett."

Her eyes hurried back to the book while her fingers turned to the first page. She read aloud the words I'd written to her, the same words Will had selected for me. " 'When you part from your friend grieve not, for that which you love most in him may be clearer in his absence, as the mountain to the climber is clearer from the plain.' "

She looked up and leaned, pulling me into her arms. I felt the warm moisture of her tears against my face.

She sniffed quietly and whispered, "Brett, I wasn't going to tell you this, but I have to . . ." A soft urgency lined her words. "Last night I had a dream. It was a very vivid dream. You and I were walking beside a river beneath tall trees. There was a little girl walking between us. She was four or five years old, and we each held her hand as we walked along. In the distance there was a circus or carnival with a Ferris wheel. As we walked nearer to it, we could hear the music of a calliope. The little girl between us skipped to the sound of the music and we swung her up between us and she laughed."

Tracy pulled back from me and glanced at the loadmaster, walking toward the front of the aircraft. She hesitated, then looked directly at me and said, "When we neared the carnival, I looked at you and you were wearing a black patch over your left eye. You weren't wearing it earlier in the dream, only when we neared the carnival."

She halted. I sensed there was more, but she had decided not to tell it. Instead she looked at her hands and pulled a gold ring from her middle finger. I had noticed the ring before, but never asked about it. It looked old and was intricately etched with two hands holding a heart between the extended fingers. Above the heart there was a detailed engraving of a crown.

She held my left hand and carefully pushed the ring onto the small finger with the lower end of the heart pointed inward toward the top of my hand. "Brett, I want you to wear this. It's been in my family for a long time. It's not a good-luck charm but the luck of the

Irish is with it." She smiled and gripped my hand tightly between hers.

I leaned forward, kissed her, then pulled slowly away, and carefully removed the ring. I placed it into her palm and folded her fingers over it.

Easing my hand gently around the back of her neck, I spoke quietly. "Tracer, the ring is beautiful and I feel very honored that you want me to have it, but I can't accept it. Honey, I go places, you know, where the sun don't shine, and if I get zapped this family treasure of yours is likely to end up in some Hanoi hockshop beside a hundred other thieved rings."

I hesitated and smiled, asking for understanding. "I think the spirit of the ring will be with me just as you intended. But you need to understand my feelings, darlin'. When a man's number is up, it's up. No charms, clovers, Buddhas, or prayers are going to stop or change the direction of a high-velocity bullet."

Tracy started to say something but was interrupted by the authoritative voice of the loadmaster. "Sorry to bother you folks, but we're going to be taking off again in about fifteen minutes. Are y'all going on to Saigon with us?"

Looking up, I said, "Negative. I'm getting off here. The lady will go on."

I reached under my seat to retrieve my bag. At the same time, I heard Ski's unmistakable Yankee bray from the rear of the plane. "Anybody left in here named Brett Yancy?"

Tracy and I turned to see Binkowski's Neanderthal frame standing on the lower edge of the tailgate. He wore freshly starched fatigues, and, for the first time since I'd known him, a green beret. Tracy walked with me to the rear of the aircraft. When we came into the light and Binkowski saw her, his face lit up like a child's on Christmas morning.

I shook his hand but I don't think he noticed. He was mesmerized, grinning from ear to ear. "Ski, meet Tracy Gibbs. She's a correspondent with *Personality* magazine."

Ski's mouth gaped while she shook his hand.

"Ski's going to be my new One-One." I paused to give Ski a chance to recover from post-round-eye trauma.

Ski shook her hand like it was the handle of the last water pump on a desert. At the same time he mumbled something that sounded like a contorted version of "Pleased to meet you."

Tracy started to laugh with the pumping jolts from his handshake. Finally, I interrupted. "Ski, I'm sure Tracy would love to stand here and shake hands with you all afternoon, but her plane . . ." I pointed upward toward the tail section of the C-130. "This plane is leaving in about ten minutes."

Ski pulled his hand away abruptly and came to attention. He tried to speak, cleared his voice, and said, "Sorry 'bout that, guess I just got a little carried—"

Tracy interrupted, smiling. "I understand, Ski. It's good to meet you." She looked toward the Hobo Hilton. "If you gentlemen will excuse me I'm going to take advantage of the facilities."

Ski watched Tracy's tightly clad buttocks as she jogged toward the building. "Sergeant Yancy . . . I mean, Brett, she is an absolute fox. Where did you . . . never mind. It's none of my business."

He started to light a cigarette, then noticed the refueling truck near the wing of the plane, and shoved the pack back into his pocket.

I looked at his new beret and gestured. "Where'd you get that? Looks good on you."

Ski smiled proudly. "Colonel Kahn gave it to me day before yesterday. I was out on the firing range. He pulled up in the jeep, got out, and put it on me himself. He said if I was going to run with the big dogs and piss on tall trees, I might as well be wearing the same collar. He also told me that after ninety days with Texas, he would award me an *S*." Ski lowered his voice and added modestly, "Of course it would need to have your endorsement."

An *S* was a Department of the Army administrative designator that signified Special Forces qualification. Ordinarily it was awarded only after graduation from Special Forces training. However, an SF commander had the authority to award it in the field.

I didn't agree with giving a man the green beret before the fact, but that was Colonel Kahn's decision, and evidently he felt Binkowski deserved it.

The colonel knew where RT Texas was heading in a few days. Perhaps he felt if Binkowski didn't make it back from Hotel-5, at least he would have stood, however briefly, under what President John F. Kennedy called "A mark of distinction, a badge of courage, a symbol of excellence in the fight for freedom."

Standing in front of Binkowski, you'd think you were looking at someone who just stepped out of a recruiting poster. The deep green color of his new beret, his starched fatigues, his shined boots, all complimented by his tall muscular frame, made him look like Mr. Special Forces. He glowed with a new sense of pride.

But I wondered how much of it would be left once the wrapper was torn away and we got down to the real nitty-gritty of war. When the band stops playing and

the tingle of pride that gathers in your nose dissipates
and it's time to face the enemy, then, and only then, do
you know how deep a man's true grit runs.

"Well, Ski, you're going to get a chance to piss on
tall trees." I grinned and added, "If you don't shit in
your pants first."

I looked around and saw Tracy approaching, half
jogging toward us. She noticed the refueling truck pulling away from beneath the wing of the Hercules.

Her voice was falsely cheerful. "Well, I hate to leave
you two handsome gladiators, but it looks like I'd better
get on this flying boxcar before they leave me." Suddenly she infused her voice with drama. "Oh, Brett,
would you get my book from the plane? You forgot to
sign it. Hurry please. I'll wait here."

I didn't understand the sudden importance of my sig-
nature. Nonetheless, I jumped inside the plane to retrieve the book and hurriedly signed it just as the first
prop of the C-130 began its slow whining start. Within
seconds, its groan burst into power, sending a flood of
hot air over us. The loadmaster stood at the edge of the
tailgate waving Tracy to board.

I took her into my arms and felt all her strength lace
around me. Her tear-wet lips found mine as hot winds
from the props streamed over us.

She broke away. Above the roar of the engines, she
shouted, "I love you, Brett Yancy. Thank you for three
wonderful days. You take special care of yourself, and
try to answer my letters. Okay?"

I brought the raveled end of my cravat up to wipe
her face. "That's a promise, Tracer."

She sniffed, then turned to Binkowski, who had one
hand gripping my bag and the other holding his beret
on. "Good to have met you, Ski, and thank you."

Ski nodded enthusiastically while smiling. Tracy turned, kissed me, then hurried up the long ramp into the dark cavernous hollow of the plane. A second later the tailgate began to rise as though slowly closing and obscuring what could have been a dream.

Ski and I walked to the jeep without speaking. We leaned against the fenders to watch the huge camouflaged plane slowly taxi away. Moments later it streaked smoothly down the runway and rose into a cloudless southern sky.

Ski lit a cigarette after we got into the jeep. "That's some woman, Brett. She seems like the type of lady a man could fall in love with real easy if he's not careful."

I found his comment irritating, perhaps because I was silently reliving some wonderful moments. And perhaps it was because he was hitting a little too close to the truth.

I pulled my beret from my cargo pants pocket and put it on. I touched my left index finger first to the unit emblem, then brought my finger straight down to my eyebrow to ensure it was in line.

Ski still hadn't started the jeep. He was watching Tracy's plane fade into the distance. I looked skyward toward the disappearing speck and said, "Yeah, she's quite a gal." I turned toward Ski. "Tracy said thank you directly to you when she left. Any idea why she would say that?" I questioned.

Ski grinned and reached into his shirt pocket. "No, but it just may have something to do with this." He passed me a small makeshift envelope sealed with tape.

I opened the envelope and found the ring Tracy had tried to give me. A note was enclosed. My eyes moved slowly over her words.

Dear Brett,

You once told me I didn't follow instructions very
well. Maybe my insistence that you have this ring
is just another example. Try to forgive me, and
please, for me, accept this and wear it.

                                        Love,
                                        Tracer

I slipped the ring on my small left finger, whispering, "Damn her!"

Binkowski was still watching me. "What'd you say?"

"Nothing!"

He grinned. "That's a nice Claddagh ring. A good
Irish girl doesn't give that to just anybody."

"What'd you call it? A clotter ring?"

Ski started the jeep and began to drive. "Not clotter,
Claddagh," he said authoritatively. "You see, it's an
old Irish custom to give a Claddagh ring to the one you
love. I went to school with a lot of Irish in Boston. A
girl once gave me one at college, but she snatched it
back when she caught me with another girl. Damn near
ripped my finger off. Talk about Irish temp—"

Binkowski was the type who, if you ask him the time,
he'd start telling you how to build a watch.

I raised my voice and broke in. "Damn it, Ski, skip
the colorful details. Just tell me about the ring! Okay?"

He blinked and lowered his voice a notch, but maintained his authoritative tone. "The ring. Roger. Well,
you see, the fingers holding the heart symbolize the
love the giver holds for the one they give it to. And the
crown above the heart symbolizes their loyalty. I'd say
the lady loves you. Yeah, no doubt about it, she's in
love with you." He nodded smartly as though he were

talking to a reflection in the windshield, then glanced at me with a half-smirking grin. "You love her?"

Binkowski was irritating me again. It was his damn schoolboy charm that was doing it. The kind I couldn't get really pissed off at because it seemed so sincere.

I pulled a small box of C-ration chewing gum from my pocket and opened it while deliberately ignoring his question. I reminded myself I needed Binkowski. I flipped the two hard-shell pieces of gum into my mouth and bit into them. "Specialist Binkowski, you have a tendency to be easily diverted from the subject at hand. You need to work on that. But to answer your question, no, I don't love her. I don't have time for any long-term love affairs right now. Vietnam isn't the place. I don't need to be daydreamin' about some woman when I . . . we both need to be keeping our minds on the mission."

He retorted immediately, "I don't think you understand the significance of that ring. This woman—"

It was time to change magazines on this conversation. I butted in. "Did you get that map study done on Hotel-5 like I asked you to?"

"Roger. I know the place inside out. By the way, Blister was working a team north of there a couple of days ago. He got some aerial photos of what looks like a battalion staging area just north of target area about eight klicks. And, get this, one of the photos shows what looks like a Soviet amphibious tank. All you can see is the turret, but it damn sure looks like a Soviet PT-76."

It was evident Ski had been doing a lot more than studying the target area. "You've been doing some homework, haven't you, Binkowski?"

Ski smiled broadly. "Roger that. They say it pays to know the enemy. Right?"

"Well, Ski, I'm not sure it pays anymore, but it does sometimes help us stick around till the next payday."

I wasn't surprised to hear about the Soviet tank. Soviet advisers, as they were called, had been sighted by several of our teams in the past. So far, no team had been able to capture one of them. If we were able to snatch a Soviet soldier on this mission, it would damn sure blow the doors off the official Russian claim that no Soviet troops were in Laos.

Chapter 19

It was mid-afternoon when Ski and I arrived back at camp. A strong ocean breeze lapped hard at the United States and Vietnamese flags hanging outside the admin building. Both flags were faded and badly frayed at the ends. It surprised me that Sergeant Major Spit-and-shine Twitty would allow that.

Ski pulled the jeep into its designated parking spot. High winds swirled a thick gust of stinging sand across my face when we stepped out of the jeep. I was squinting as I walked through the sandy cloud and into the office. Binkowski followed.

Once inside, I turned to SKi. "Check my mail, would you? I need to see Colonel Kahn for a minute."

I strode quickly down the dark narrow hallway, anxious to get the answer to an important question. I glanced into Twitty's office. He was gone. The colonel's door was open. I started to knock, but he looked up from his desk, saying, "Come in, Sergeant Yancy. Glad to see you back. How was Bangkok?"

I removed my beret and saluted before replying. "Never made it that far, sir. We took a hit over Laos.

To make a long story short, and less colorful, I ended up in Chiang Mai the whole time.''

The colonel cocked his hands on his hips and grimaced. ''Chiang Mai. That's too bad.'' He gestured for me to take a seat. ''That's one helluva place to get stuck for four days.''

''Well, sir . . .'' I paused to crack a grin. ''It really wasn't that bad. I met a round-eyed American journalist on the flight. She sort of insisted on showing me the cultural highlights.''

He grinned back. ''I'll *bet* she showed you some cultural highlights. Anyhow, I'm glad you enjoyed your leave.''

He lit a cigarette and leaned back in his chair. ''I've been monitoring Binkowski's headway the last few days. I think he's going to make a good One-One for you.''

''Roger, sir, I think so too.'' I paused before coming out with my main reason for being there. Colonel Kahn waited silently, as if he knew what I was about to ask. I could hear anticipation in my voice. ''Sir, have we got any word back on my request for Will's Medal of Honor?''

He avoided my eyes momentarily. Finally, he leaned forward and quietly lowered his muscular forearms to the desk. ''Brett,'' he began, tilting his head toward the desk, ''Headquarters has downgraded it to a Silver Star.'' He brought his head up with a hard frown. ''Officially, they're saying the regs require you to have five witnesses to authenticate the valorous incident before it can even be considered, and—''

A rush of heat gripped my head. I jerked upward from my chair. ''Damn it, sir, I've got five witnesses! Me and four Montagnards.'' I jabbed a hand forward, fingers spread. ''Those fuckin' pencil-pushin' bureau-

crats aren't stealing what's rightfully Will's. He earned
. . . shit, died for—''

"Sit down, Yancy!" he commanded. "I don't like it
any better than you do, but we're not licked yet.''

I sank back into my chair while he moved to close
the door. He returned and sat on the edge of his desk
near me. "I haven't given up on this. I still have two
other avenues I'm going to pursue.'' Determination
steeled his voice. "Now, the official reason they kicked
this down is by citing the witness requirement. But that's
just whitewash. Unofficially, I believe it's because the
action occurred in Laos, a denied area. So, reading
between the lines, I think the real reason is, they don't
want any public notoriety attached to our involvement
in Laos. The Medal of Honor makes front-page news
back home.''

He emphasized his last words as he stood. He paced
to a large wall map of Southeast Asia and ran his hand
over the area near Hotel-5. He looked back at me.
"Now, the Ashau Valley isn't that far from your target
area. If I have to, I'll change the grid coordinates of
where the action took place. That should satisfy any
Headquarters paranoia about public attention.''

I didn't like having to falsify anything about Will's
valor. On the other hand, I understood Colonel Kahn's
reasoning. Moving the coordinates into the Ashau
meant we were on legal real estate. My tension began
to ease. I was confident that, one way or the other, he
would get the award through—if anybody could.

"Sir, you mentioned you had two avenues to pursue.
May I ask what the other one is?''

He went on to explain that if push came to shove,
he felt he could rally the support of several friends in the
Pentagon and apply some up-the-line pressure to get the

award through. If that method had to be used, I was well aware of what it could mean to Colonel Kahn's career. It was career suicide for an officer to go above the heads of the superiors who wrote his efficiency report.

He would use his silver bullet if he had to. I stood, remorseful for having let my temper flare. I rendered the most genuine salute I'd ever given an officer. "Thank you, sir. Now, I'll get out of your hair and get back to earning my pay."

He walked to the door with me. Opening the door, he stopped, then smiled. "Speaking of pay. As a staff sergeant, you earn about six hundred and fifty dollars a month over here. Give or take a dollar. Do you realize that most of our troops here aren't even making minimum wage?"

I stopped in the doorway, donned my beret, turned to him, and grinned. "Yes, sir, I guess that's right. If it weren't so damn much fun, we couldn't stand it."

Ski waited outside the building when I stepped out into the afternoon sun. He handed me three letters and we began trudging through the loose sand toward the mess hall.

"One of those letters smells like a flower garden. The one with the Australian postmark. Just how many women do you have?"

"Not many, Arnold," I said without breaking stride.

Binkowski hated being called by his first name. I used it deliberately. I hoped eventually he would catch on and think before putting his mouth in gear.

We arrived at the mess hall two hours late for chow. We sat in the empty dining room eating cold meat loaf and rice. While we ate, I talked to him about the team Yards. I let him know it was important they liked him.

I told him he was going to have to work hard to win their confidence.

Ski was going to be second in command of Texas. That meant he was just one well-directed 7.62-mm round away from inheriting team leader. If that occurred, he'd better have their confidence in him well established before he started barking orders. If he didn't, his shit was going to get weak and runny real fast.

I told him he was going to have to listen and learn at the speed of light for the next week. Then I explained the social differences between the Vietnamese and Montagnards. The VN looked down on the Montagnards as second-class citizens, primitives. I emphasized what his position had to be if the Yards got into a hassle with any of the Vietnamese in camp. I dramatized my point by raising a full scoop of rice on my fork and holding it level in front of me.

I looked at the rice while speaking. "The first time you show any favoritism to the Vietnamese over the Yards"—I paused, tilted the fork, and watched the loose rice fall into my plate—"you got about that much team left, amigo."

Ski looked at the empty fork with a serious frown, then leveled his eyes back into mine.

"My point is, Ski, you'd better make damn sure the Cowboys know they're number-one with you at all times. That doesn't mean you can't correct them if they fuck up. Just do it with a smile and remember this: These brave little social outcasts work, sweat, and die for us, not the war or what it means to Vietnam. If this war ends tomorrow and we leave, the Yards know damn well they'll be back pickin' cotton the next day."

Ski frowned into my eyes. His reply was serious. "Roger, Brett. I understand."

I stood and picked up my bag while he lit a cigarette. I wanted to give him some private time to think about what I'd said. "You finish your smoke, Ski. I'm going over to the hooch and let the Cowboys know we have a new man coming aboard. Be at the team hooch, bag and baggage, in one hour."

When I turned and walked toward the door, he raised his voice and asked, "Brett, why do you call them Cowboys?"

"You'll know as soon as you see their bush hats."

En route to the hooch, I stopped by the club and picked up some Cokes. I figures the best way to welcome Ski to the team was to break out the Beam and informally introduce him around the team table.

At the club, I gave Fousi the presents I'd bought. She appeared happy with the gifts. But her joy was subdued, as though she could smell the scent of another woman on me. Her eyes noticed the Claddagh ring on my finger, but she didn't comment on it. The appearance of the ring probably confirmed her suspicions about another woman. I decided this was not the time to bring up her possible immigration to the United States.

A few steps outside the club, I heard the familiar voice of Swede Jensen bellow, "Hey, Yancy, it's about fuckin' time you got back!"

I turned and saw Jensen's blond head peering over the sandbagged edge of a nearby mortar pit. I walked toward him. "Howdy, Swede. I thought you were in the field."

Jensen swung himself up and out of the pit. "Bad

weather in the target area. We couldn't get in. Weather permitting, we'll try another insert later this week.'' He pulled a small cigar from his pocket and lit it before reaching into a side pocket on his pants, withdrawing a large brown envelope.

"Probably just as good I didn't get in," he mused. "Gave me more time for fund-raising here in camp."

Dark furrows of skin gathered on his tanned face when he smiled and handed me the envelope. "Three thousand, six hundred, and fifty-seven dollars. And I'm proud to say there wasn't an American in camp who didn't contribute. Even Johnson, the guy you clobbered in the club, he gave a hundred dollars. I had to go solicit from him down at the hospital." Jensen pulled the cigar from his mouth and flipped his ashes, casting a sarcastic smile skyward. "Somehow I just knew Johnson wouldn't want to be left out."

I was speechless. I hadn't expected Jensen to raise half this much for Will's family. Emotion rippled through me like the opening jerk of a parachute canopy. "Swede, I don't know how to say—"

"You don't have to say nothing. It was the right thing." He paused, then looked back up at me. "Will Washington was a helluva good man and every pendulating Richard in this camp knew it. Now, I gotta get back to cleaning the fuckin' sand outa this mortar so the son of a bitch don't blow up in somebody's face. See ya later, Yancy."

For a moment I stood watching him go about his task, then tucked the envelope into my pocket. Walking away, I heard Jensen whistling while he worked. The tune sounded like the *Blue Danube* waltz.''

A few moments later, I neared the corner of the hooch and heard the Yards' chatter and a song in the background. My guess was they were playing chess. I was right. I stood at the lower edge of the cement steps, unnoticed, watching them huddled around the team picnic table. "Galveston" was playing on the radio.

Chess was the unofficial team game. However, among the Yards it was more like a cross between a heated political debate and a martial-arts match.

Tuong acted as second for Rham, who was playing Phan. Lok was in Phan's corner. I'd heard quieter spectators at Super Bowl games. They shouted, argued about moves, and punched each other. Occasionally one would hurl a playful roundhouse kick at the opponents. It was all in fun and all part of the Montagnard contact sport of chess.

Standing there, I felt like a proud dad must feel watching his children at play. The youngest was Lok, fifteen. The oldest, Phan, eighteen. They were all teenagers by American standards but here they were seasoned fighters. All had killed, but somehow, even in war, they still clung to adolescence.

I smiled and picked up a broken chunk of cement near the steps. I bowled it through the door and down the aisle toward the gathering. "One grenade got you all!" I shouted, entering.

They all looked up with quick-reflex surprise, leapt from the table, and surrounded me with smiles and hugs. You'd think I'd just scored the winning touchdown at the district champs game.

Tuong grabbed my bag and hurried to the table with it. "What you bring us, Sar Brett?" he demanded, digging through the bag.

The question was only pro forma; he planned on answering it himself. Phan and Lok took me by the arms and ushered me toward the table like I didn't know my way around the hooch.

I sat at the big table while all of them continued talking. Rham was the loudest. "We miss you, Sar Brett. You go Bangkok, you get boom-boom, now you go pinsery, get pen-sill."

Everyone laughed but me.

I grinned, and snapped back, "I no go Bangkok. I go Chiang Mai."

"Chiang Mai?" they all said in disbelief. "Why no Bangkok?"

I didn't have to answer the why. Tuong had found the gloves I'd bought for them and announced loudly while opening the sack, "Number fuckin' one!"

They hurried around Tuong as he began distributing the black leather gloves. They began putting them on immediately.

I'd bought them gloves because it was something they all needed to protect their hands while moving through the bush. U.S.-issue gloves were too big and hindered their weapons handling.

Phan removed his right-hand glove, and withdrew a pocketknife. He glanced at me for approval before slicing into the glove. I nodded. He carefully cut off several inches of the index finger and slid his hand back into the glove. The others did likewise. Phan turned and removed his CAR-15 from the rack above his bunk. My eyes instinctively scanned the selector switch to make sure it was on safety. Gripping the weapon, he positioned his exposed finger around the trigger and pulled it several times. Satisfied with the feel of it, he smiled at me. "It okay, Sar Brett. Number-one."

Before long they had all altered their gloves to free the trigger finger as Will and I had taught them.

Lok reached for one of the Cokes I'd brought in and started to open it. I halted him. "Hold on, Babysan. We save for later." I glanced at my watch.

All of them reacted with undisguised surprise. It was the first time any of them had heard me be opposed simply to opening a can of Coke. Their antennas went up immediately.

Tuong stood and walked slowly toward me with a slight tilt of his head. "Why we no drink Cokes now?"

Tuong always worked harder than the others to improve his English. I sometimes thought his motive was so he could ask me more questions than anybody else. He added, "I think maybe something up."

Lok sat the Coke back on the table and repeated Tuong's statement, "I think maybe something up."

They stared at me. I know it was likely they'd heard rumors of a new One-One. It was also likely they knew who the new man was. It was time they heard it from me. They squatted near my feet rather than sat at the table. Their eyes were patient, but serious. I knew how much each of them worshiped Will. I knew how deep their allegiance to him was. They'd sooner go into combat without a One-One than have somebody, anybody, take his place.

I remained seated at the table while they all lit cigarettes. I chose my words carefully, kept my expression objective, and lied, "Soon, new man come. He is good man. Name Ski. He wants to kill Communist who kill Papasan Will. In one week we go back Hotel-5. I need you to help Ski, so we can kill Communist who kill Will." I continued while shifting my eyes slowly to each man. "If you help Ski, you will help me, for Will. Okay?"

I studied them while they pondered my words and

made their silent decision. Their eyes moved around their circle. Occasionally, one of them glanced toward Will's empty bed.

During the waiting moments, I rationalized my lie. It was vital they accept Ski immediately. But, without a reason and purpose, that acceptance could take months if it even happened at all. Time I did not have. I'd given them a reason to accept Ski; I was counting on a mutual goal to create a sense of solidarity.

I had already instilled Ski with reason and purpose. Now, I was attempting to position another spoke in our wheel. I wasn't taking any chances on that wheel coming apart when we rolled back into Hotel-5. When we hit the ground again, we had to be a well-lubricated fighting element, a team, in the fullest sense of the word.

Tuong was the first to rise from his hunkered position. He walked silently over to Will's bunk and squatted beside it. The others didn't stand. He flipped his cigarette into a can, then rested his forearms across his knees and looked up at me. "Sar Brett, you say we go Ho-tel-fi kill *beaucoup* Chuck."

I nodded. "Roger. *Beaucoup*."

I anticipated the next question. Tuong was well aware, as were the others, that just killing Communists wasn't a normal mission. They knew there had to be more.

"What else we do?" he said, looking with dead seriousness into my face.

I rotated my eyes to all of them as I spoke. "We ambush Chuck. Take one prisoner, bring here."

After a moment, Tuong stood and looked at the gloves he was still wearing. He grinned. Suddenly, he jerked his body into a rigid Tae-kwon-do stance, fingers spread and contorted into lethal claws. He strained his voice into a hideous squealing pitch and looked down as though yelling at a fallen victim. "Okay, fuckin' Chuck, we coming for you!"

He snapped two quick scissor kicks high into the air, then dropped swiftly to one knee and thrust his claw-rigged hand into the face of his phantom victim. Slowly he rose and stood, legs spread. He gracefully folded his arms across his chest and smiled at me.

Lok, Phan, and Rham stood, smiling first at Tuong, then at me. It was apparent that reason, purpose, and motivation were strong in the Yards.

Chapter 20

A timid voice came from the doorway. "Knock, knock."

We looked and saw Arnold Binkowski standing outside the hooch, laden with two duffel bags, a rucksack, a guitar, and a fan. It was the first time I'd heard Ski's voice sound apprehensive. I supposed that he had just seen Tuong's martial-arts demonstration and probably thought to himself, "Just what the hell am I getting into here?"

I motioned to him. "Come on in, Ski. You're just in time for some Tae-kwon-do training." I laughed.

"Yeah, I . . . ah, was noticing that," he said, edging his six-foot three-inch frame through the door. He dragged his gear behind him. The little people quickly gathered around, smiling and helping with his gear. It looked like a squad of dwarfs helping the Jolly Green Giant.

"Mercy bo-koo," he said, then bowed.

I laughed. "Ski, you can skip formalities with the Cowboys. This ain't *The Teahouse of the August Moon*." Glancing at Lok, I winked and said, "Jim Beam, Lok."

Lok was our self-appointed bartender. We sat at the table while he hurriedly opened Cokes, blew sand out of cups, then served a round of Beam and Coke. Phan had already taken an interest in Ski's guitar. He strummed it, still wearing his gloves.

I introduced the team members by name while Lok passed out drinks. After everyone had a cup, I held mine high in the air. I had to wait a moment for Phan to set the guitar down and join us.

"Welcome to RT Texas, Ski. We ain't bad, but the bad don't fuck with us!" I'd no sooner gotten the words out of my mouth and began to drink, when a loud bark came from just outside the hooch.

Binkowski turned and looked at a large panting dog sitting in the doorway. "Oh, Brett, I forgot. I hope you don't mind. I, ah, well—"

"He's hot, Ski. Call him in. Lok, get some water."

Ski tapped the side of his pants. "*Lai-day*, Trung-uy."

The Yards burst into laughter, hearing Ski call the dog the Vietnamese word for *lieutenant*. Obediently, Trung-uy ambled into the room and sat beside Ski. The Cowboys quickly surrounded our new dog, petting and stroking him. He reciprocated by licking anybody who got within tongue range.

Trung-uy was a good-sized dog. His breeding appeared to be a combination of Saint Bernard and German shepherd, with his disposition leaning more toward Saint Bernard. He was the biggest dog I'd seen in Vietnam. That was probably because a dog of any size over here was a candidate for the supper table.

I leaned and patted the dog. "Where'd you find this refugee, Ski?"

Ski sipped his Beam before answering, "Down by

the docks in Da Nang. He was just a scared little pup wandering along the roadside. I think someone kicked him off one of those freighters in port. He has a real problem with the heat, wears him out quick. I usually keep a fan near his bed.'' Ski turned and made a survey of the room as if looking for his and Trung-uy's sleeping area.

I sipped my drink. It didn't bother me that Ski had a dog. But it did bother me he'd brought everything with him except his rifle. I figured he'd either forgotten it or had opted to get it later. Either reason was unacceptable.

I didn't intend to rain on Ski's welcome, but my custom is to nip problems in the bud. Besides, I knew the yards had noticed the absence of his rifle. If I ignored it for long, my policy of strict weapons accountability would be weakened.

Keeping my voice casual, I said, ''Ski, where's your rifle?''

He seemed surprised. ''Oh, I left it in my room. I'll get it after evening chow.''

I glanced at the Yards playing with Trung-uy before looking back at Binkowski. I avoided sounding critical. ''I realize that up until now a typewriter's been your primary tool. The primary tool in recon is your rifle. It's more important than fans, guitars''—I turned and looked toward Trung-uy—''and dogs.'' I stood, walked over to Lok's bunk, and removed his CAR-15 from the wall rack. After clearing the weapon, I walked back and handed it to Ski. Sitting down, I said, ''Check it out.'' The Montagnards kept their rifles impeccable. Now was as good a time as any to let him know what was expected of him.

Ski ran his fingers over the receiver and around the

magazine well. "The M-16 and CAR-15 are great rifles," I said. "Their ranges and muzzle velocities are awesome, and they lightweight. One problem. They don't function well if they're dirty." I paused to sip my drink, then added, "They don't function at all if you don't have them with you."

Ski grinned and nodded modestly. "Roger. Understand."

"On the other hand, the enemy's rifle, the AK-47, doesn't have to be real clean to work well. And it's cyclic rate of fire on full automatic is about half that of ours, not to mention that the weapon comes standard with thirty-round magazines and we've only got twenty rounds in ours.

"What that boils down to is, if we're in a runnin' gun battle with Chuck, chances are we're going to be changing magazines twice as often. The time it takes to change magazines can be too long no matter how fast you are.

"The solution is trigger discipline. If you're on rock and roll, fire three- and four-round bursts, because if you bear down on that trigger you'll be up shit creek in about six seconds. Empty."

I paused and took a gulp of my drink to give Ski a chance for questions. I'd instructed him to practice burst firing on the range while I was gone, but wanted to stress the point. In a firefight, trigger control was more critical than aim. Half the time you couldn't see what you were shooting at anyhow. Trigger control was sometimes easily preempted by an adrenaline process called "scared shitless." It made a man want to grip his trigger like it was his last finger hold on the side of a cliff. But, when the magazine empties, that finger hold turns into sand.

Ski remained serious-faced and silent. He hadn't touched his drink or lit a cigarette while I spoke. I continued. ''The only exception to what I've just told you is during an IA emergency.''

''What's IA emergency?'' he asked.

''Immediate action. We use a preplanned maneuver to spit a lot of lead at the enemy during unexpected contact. I'll show you what I mean later.''

Ski stood and squeezed the trigger intermittently, then replaced the rifle on Lok's wall rack. He returned to the table and quickly finished his drink while standing. ''I'll be right back. I'm going to get my rifle and the rest of my gear. Okay?''

I smiled. ''Roger. I'll order us another round while you're gone.'' I turned to the Yards gathered around Trung-uy. ''Phan, you go with Ski, help him bring gear. Lok, *hai* Beam and Coke, please.''

When Ski and Phan returned, I decided to move the team to the beach and incorporate some training into Ski's initiation. The beach was just a grenade's throw from our front porch. It was common practice for recon to use the beach to test-fire weapons since the firing range was way over at the base of Marble Mountain.

I told everyone to bring their weapon and one full magazine. We left Trung-uy and Jim Beam in the hooch.

As we moved to the beach, I put the team in a tactical file to let Ski know where his position was and how we moved. The point man was Rham. Ski's position was behind him, followed by Lok, me, and Phan. Tuong was tail gunner.

I always occupied the center position for greater control, unless we had to run. If that occurred, I immediately took over lead, primarily so Rham wouldn't have to keep looking back at me for directions. And, secondly, if I fucked up and ran us into an ambush, I'd be the first to know about it, the hard way. "A sucking chest wound is nature's way of letting you know you just walked into an ambush," as Swede put it.

During movement to the beach each man stepped cautiously, carefully studying his side of the imagined trail and keeping his rifle pointed in his direction of observation.

Ski was a little awkward at first. After watching the rest of us for a while he began to imitate our procedure almost perfectly. I was impressed with his smooth easy steps and sense of stealth.

As we came onto the beach my nostrils filled with the strong salt-scented freshness of the China Sea. For a moment my mind drifted to Galveston, but the memory faded as Rham opened the concertina-wire gate.

I halted the team and scanned the vast empty area for telltale signs of booby traps. There were none. The low tide had left the sand moist and hard-packed. A hundred meters to the south, two Vietnamese soldiers were wading the tide pools, trying to grab fish caught in low-tide rifts.

I motioned the team around me and began a class on IA drills. I used a stick to scrawl illustrations in the sand, pleased that the little people watched and listened intently to the class. They were aware the class was for Ski's benefit, but their attention added a sense of urgency to a very difficult and critical team maneuver.

An immediate action maneuver was essentially a pre-planned method of withdrawal from an enemy-initiated ambush, something a lot easier said than done. If the ax came down, each man had to know what to do, and to do it instantly. When the fire hit, usually from the side, the first, third, and fifth men had to turn and fire rock and roll into the face of the ambush. When their magazines emptied, they were to sprint back approximately thirty meters in the direction from which we had just come, and take up a defensive position. The remaining team members would then cover the other's escape by continuing fire until empty. Afterward, they beat feet back to join the others.

I had the team demonstrate a "dry-fire" run-through for Ski.

Ski watched the demo, and doubtfully asked, "Brett, I don't want to sound skeptical, but it seems to me that if we get hit, ambushed, the best thing to do is drop flat on the trail and get our asses outa the line of fire."

He was dead wrong. It was important for him to know just why he was being told to face into the teeth of a tiger. I called a smoke break and we sat down. I spoke while everyone but me lit up. "Ski, your point's well taken. In fact, it sounds close to the same idea I had before I learned better.

"Understand this. In a well-executed ambush the enemy is in absolute control. They have the element of surprise with them. It's like a coiled snake striking at you when you open your footlocker. I'm not going to say the enemy has thought of everything, like booby-trapping the opposite side of the trail to prevent our withdrawal into cover, or mining the forward portion of the trail to blow us away if we try and run through the ambush. But we have to assume they have thought of all of that and done it right.

"If we drop to the ground, they've got us by the balls. All they have to do is lob grenades in on us, then stroll in and put a final bullet in our heads. Our options boil down to one: Return high-volume fire and get the fuck outa there fast!''

Ski's face was somber. "I think I see what you mean. It's a tough situation.''

I looked toward a nearby tide pool and saw the ominous brown head of a sea snake bobbing like a cork, eyes leering. I pointed at it as I spoke. "An ambush is kinda like that snake. The best approach is to maintain vigilance, and don't let the bastard get it's fangs into you in the first place.''

I winked, and looked at Phan. He watched the snake move through the water like a cat watches a canary in a cage. I knew he wanted it, but he wasn't going to break away from the meeting unless I told him to. Phan glanced at me with eager eyes.

"Okay, Phan, go.'' He stood and quickly chambered a round. We watched him walk slowly to the water's edge and take careful aim. He fired. The round cracked into the serpent's head. It spasmed and jerked for a moment, went limp, then floated with its scaled yellow belly up. Phan waded into the tide pool and dipped the muzzle of his weapon beneath the snake and raised it out of the water. He turned back with a broad smile and walked proudly toward us with the blood-dripping reptile draped over his rifle barrel.

The yards considered sea snake a delicacy and always insisted Will and I join their feast after they killed one. I knew what Phan was about to say.

"*Beaucoup* snake. I cook. Plenty for everyone.''

I didn't particularly like snake, but when the Yards cooked, or made rice wine, it was a violation of Montagnard manners not to accept. Telling them you weren't hungry didn't work. I'd gotten used to rice wine after I learned to sip it in moderation and accept the inevitable two or three days of diarrhea that went with it.

Phan dropped the snake to the ground at our feet, knelt, and began cutting the head off.

Binkowski's eyes squinted as he watched Phan cut.

"Ski, you like snake?" I asked casually.

His response was reluctant. "Well, uh . . . I'm not, I don't think—"

I broke in. "That's okay, you'll get a chance to find out tonight. Don't worry, they cut it up and boil it. Tastes kinda like kielbasa frog meat, only not as chewy." I strained to keep myself from grinning.

Ski's eyes widened. "Kielbasa frog meat?" he said, dropping the cigarette from his mouth as he spoke. "Are you shittin' me?"

I burst into laughter. His face went blank when the Yards joined my laughter. The Yards, of course, didn't have the slightest idea why I was laughing. Generally, if it was good enough for me to laugh at, they would join in as a courtesy.

Ski shook his head, breaking into a smile. "Okay, Yancy. 'Kielbasa frog meat'—you got me on that one."

Suddenly, a thunderous concussion jarred the beach beneath us. I grasped my rifle and jerked my eyes toward the agonized screams that followed the blast. The two Vietnamese south of us lay sprawled near the water's edge, twisting and clutching at their bloody torsos.

I yelled at Lok while jumping to my feet. "Go doctor! Tell we come with emergency!"

Lok leapt up and bounded toward camp while the rest of us sprinted toward the Vietnamese. I knew they'd hit a booby trap of some kind, but the noise had sounded like a grenade explosion.

Nearing the bodies, I saw one man clutching his

stomach. His quivering legs were drawn up into a fetal position. Blood streamed through his fingers and over his legs. The other man was facedown, shaking violently. Their cries faded into piercing groans.

Binkowski was right beside me when we finally got to them. The yards were hurrying behind. "Take him!" I yelled to Ski, quickly pointing to the man lying belly-down.

I dropped to my knees beside the other man and began yanking my shirt off. I tried to console him while hurriedly folding my shirt into a pad. I pried his bloody fingers away from his gashed stomach, saying "It's okay. We go doctor."

After positioning the pad over his bleeding wound, I swiftly slipped my arms under his back and legs and lifted him.

I glanced around toward Ski. He stood petrified above the shaking man. Horror gripped his face. "Damn it, Binkowski, pick him up!" I yelled.

Tears rolled off Binkowski's face. His voice trembled. "He's fuckin' dead, man. He's fuckin' dead!"

I screamed, "He's not fuckin' dead, goddammit! Now pick him the fuck up and follow me . . . *now*!"

Binkowski shook himself from his trance and leaned over the shaking man. He rolled him over, slid his arms under him, and lifted.

"Let's go!" I shouted. I ran with all the strength I had. The lives we held in our arms depended on how fast we could get them to the dispensary. It was an all-out two-hundred-yard sprint to save them.

A heavy labored breath bellowed at my back. "I'm right behind you, Brett. I'm right behind you, partner."

Chapter 21

Lok had gotten my message to the dispensary. The camp doctor, Captain McRae, and two medics were waiting when we trudged wearily up the sandy hill to the dispensary. They took the bloody, limp burdens from our arms and hurried inside with them. I followed them in and helped cut away the torn, blood-soaked clothing from the bodies. Ski stayed outside.

I was still breathing heavily as I bent over the sink washing the blood off my arms and hands. I heard the field phone ring in the adjacent room. A second later a young Vietnamese girl spoke to me in a soft but hurried voice.

"Sar Yancy, Sar May Twitty want talk with you."

I toweled my hands and stepped into the small office and lifted the receiver. "This is Yancy. Over."

Twitty's excited voice squealed into my ear, "Yancy, what the hell's goin' on? Somebody said we took a mortar round on the eastern perimeter, then I hear you done brought two wounded in. I got the whole camp fallin' out for full alert!"

When he paused to catch his breath, I broke in. "This is Yancy. Negative on incoming. Two Vietnamese det-

175

onated a booby trap on the beach. Binkowski and I just got them to the dispensary. No need for alert status, but they're going to need a medevac chopper in here quick. Over.''

Twitty's voice calmed. "How bad are they hit? Over?''

"Bad. Over.''

"Roger. Understand. Tell Doc McRae I'll have a slick on the way in 'bout two shakes. Out.''

Twitty's response to the situation was unusual. His style was to check with someone else before he made a decision.

After telling the girl to inform Doc McRae about the medevac, I left the dispensary and saw Binkowski leaning against the building. His head was bowed. He held an unlit cigarette at his side. The yards squatted in a circle nearby.

Ski looked up when he heard the screen door slam shut behind me. Tears glossed his face. "Are they gonna be all right?'' he asked, pleading.

"I don't know. How you doing?''

His voice whimpered, then quickly straightened, as he stood away from the wall. "Me? Oh, I'm fuckin' fine! Except I don't think I'm gonna be worth a damn as your One-One. Shit!'' he shouted, looking skyward. "I can't even handle a simple emergency situation without coming unglued.'' His voice began to quiver as he bowed his head again.

I glanced at the yards. I didn't want them to see Ski like this, not that there was anything wrong with Ski's reaction. I just didn't want him to feel any inhibition about pouring out his feelings.

Catching the watchful eyes of the yards, I cast a

glance in the direction of the team hooch. They turned and left.

I looked back at Ski and nudged his shoulder. "Look, partner, don't get down on yourself for getting a little shook up out there. It's normal. The important thing is, you overcame fear and reacted. You ran some two hundred yards carrying more than a hundred pounds. Now, as far as I'm concerned, that deserves more than a hearty handshake and a smile." I glanced at my watch: 1645 hours. "Come on, I'll buy us a beer before chow."

Binkowski looked up and returned a meek smile. "Thanks, Brett. What you're saying means a lot, but I should of done better. A lot better. I wasted time and—"

I broadened my smile and interrupted him. "Hell's bells, partner, this is only your first day on the team. Nobody expects you to be perfect right off the fuckin' bat. Now let's go have that beer."

We turned and began moving toward the camp club. After walking just a few steps, Ski stopped abruptly in his tracks and jerked his head back toward the beach. "Shit! Where's my rifle? he shouted. "I don't know where . . ."

I laughed. "Calm down, partner, the Yards collected our weapons. They're in the hooch."

It was sometime after chow before I was able to learn the status on the two Vietnamese we'd brought in. One had died in the dispensary. The other one, the one Ski had carried, was going to live. After regaining consciousness, he told the medic what happened. He said they'd found a M-26 fragmentation grenade on the beach and decided to throw it into a tide pool to kill fish, a common method of fishing when the sergeant major wasn't looking. An M-26 has a timed delay, but when they pulled the pin and threw it, the grenade exploded instantly.

Later, at the club, Swede Jensen enlightened me as to how Charlie had rigged the grenade to explode immediately. It was simple genius. He said a smoke-grenade fuse and an M-26 fuse both had compatible threads on the screw-in detonators, the difference being that the M-26 has a six-second delay on the fuse and the smoke bomb requires none. Charlie simply had removed the M-26 fuse, screwed in a smoke fuse, and replaced the pin. Knowing the fishing habits of Vietnamese soldiers, he then placed the grenade on the beach for some unwitting victim to discover and use.

Hours later, I lay on my bunk, reading Vonnie's letter. Something dawned on me like a muzzle flash when I read her P.S.:

Darling, an Australian soldier, recently returned from Vietnam, said in a newspaper interview that VC booby traps were everywhere. I know you are probably aware of this. Please be careful.

The possibility that our grenades could have been altered hit me. I immediately stood and told the Yards to assemble all of their grenades on the team table. Why not? It was well known we had VC sympathizers working in camp. I reasoned they could easily enter our hooch while we were at chow or training and make the same fuse switch. We rarely locked the hooch unless we were on a mission.

Using pliers to free the threaded tension, I unscrewed a fuse and removed it. I compared the appearance of the one removed to a smoke-bomb fuse. The team watched.

Naturally, it was Tuong who spoke first. "Sar Brett, what you do?"

I winked at him. "I make sure Charlie no switch fuses on us."

Half an hour later I'd examined all the grenades and hadn't discovered any to have been altered. While the team began replacing their grenades in their ammo pouches, Tuong pulled Will's web gear from beneath his bunk and placed it on the table before me.

"Sar Brett, you no checkee here."

Inspecting Will's grenades, I discovered that two of his four M-26s had been altered with smoke fuses. A chill ran through me. I thought back to the scorching moments in Hotel-5. If Will had used his grenades there was at least a fifty-fifty chance he would have been blown apart. It seemed the cards were stacked against him from the beginning of the mission.

Ironically, Will's field gear was destined to be inherited by Binkowski. I gave Ski one of the smoke fuses I'd removed as a souvenir.

The next morning, I took my evidence to Colonel Kahn. After checking it, he issued a camp directive for all personnel to check their grenades. By evening, a total of thirty-six booby-trapped grenades were found. Colonel Kahn said, "It looks like we've discovered a vaccine before the plague hit."

As far as who was doing the switches, we'd never know. We had approximately sixty Vietnamese soldiers and civilians in camp. We'd have to impose a higher level of security on our gear. I picked up a combination lock from Supply and installed a hasp on the hooch door. I told the team that from now on the last man out of the hooch was responsible for locking up, and under no circumstances was a house girl to be allowed to sweep the hooch without one of us being there with her. I didn't think the new security measures were going to eliminate the threat completely, but I was sure of one thing. I'd never be able to throw an M-26 again without my ass puckering up.

The next six days were hard, crash-course training days for Ski. I cut no slack on morning PT, three-mile runs, rain or shine, with full field gear. After the second day, I noticed a significant decrease in Ski's smoking habit.

I had each of the yards prepare and present a class on a pertinent subject. During the classes, I frequently had to make an additional comment or act as interpreter when one of them stumbled on a word or phrase. The classes went well, though, and they gave the Yards a chance to feel they were contributing to Ski's combat education. I had "Puck-you" Phan give the class on the safe-sleep SOP.

Slowly, my evaluation of Ski was improving. He was quick to learn. He never held back on a question and never complained about the heavy schedule. Often I would sharpshoot him about technical aspects of the training he'd received days before. He always shot the correct answer back.

He was also beginning to look like a field soldier. He'd lost the starched, spit-shined appearance and taken on that wrinkled, weathered recon look. After learning about the multiusages of the cravat as a sling, bandage, or tourniquet, he made it a standard part of his uniform. He wore it loose around his neck like a desert sheikh wears a scarf. His boots hadn't seen polish since he came on the team, and he didn't seem to mind wearing faded, torn fatigues. He was elated when I gave him a watchband wrist compass and taught him how to read it on the run.

He was gradually beginning to "think" recon too. His eyes moved over an area when we walked, checking for danger areas. And the way he walked. His gait had a new kind of purposeful determination about it.

I didn't have to compliment him to build his confidence. He'd learned to be his own silent critic, accept his occasional mistakes, and correct them himself. His pride and confidence were building, but he never got cocky. He listened, asked questions, and studied. He was damn serious about what he called "Introduction to Combat Recon 101."

The Cowboys noticed the changes too. They liked his stick-to-it attitude, and his Yankee "what-the-hell" sense of humor. They shifted between admiration and amusement at his dogged concentration on cleaning his rifle. Ski cleaned his weapon with such meticulous care that it finally became a team joke.

Late one hot afternoon we'd just returned from live-fire IA drills and were cleaning our weapons. We sat cross-legged on the shady side of the hooch with a poncho spread in the middle of our circle. Ski zealously rammed a cleaning rod back and forth into the barrel of his rifle when Rham looked over at him and grinned. "Ski, you something else. You do same-same way to girlfriend, you have *beaucoup* babysans."

Ski glared at Rham with an amused half grin. "Oh, yeah, well, maybe I no have girlfriend."

Rham quipped, "Oh, maybe then you have boyfriend."

Everyone burst into laughter. Ski grinned and said emphatically, "No, I'm not queer."

He removed his cleaning rod and inserted another

bore patch onto the tip. Glancing at me, he said, "By the way, speaking of homos, I got a letter from a buddy back at Fort Bragg. He said a duty officer discovered two leg homos going at it the other night over by the parade grounds. The post commander launched a big investigation about homosexuality. My buddy said it's almost hilarious now when you look around in the PX snack bar. Everyone is so paranoid that nobody will even use a straw anymore. And if anyone dares have a hot dog, they eat it sideways."

I laughed out loud, quickly avoiding Tuong's eyes, so as not to invite a question. Fortunately, he didn't ask.

Ski continued while reassembling his rifle, "As for me, I don't have anything against homos. It probably sounds selfish, but the way I see it is, for every homo, it means there's one more girl for me. Kinda cuts down on the competition."

"Makes sense to me, Ski. You got a steady girl back home?"

Binkowski looked up as though stirred by my question. He was silent for a moment. He looked down at Trung-uy, lying beside him, and petted the dog as he answered. "No, not anymore. About a month ago I got the coup de grace from her. She's a liberal arts student at Boston College.

"Anyhow, they had this big antiwar rally there and a day later she sends me a short and sweet letter essentially tellin' me to take a long walk on a short pier. She included a bumper sticker in the envelope, which said, 'If there were no soldiers there would be no wars.' "

He glanced at me, grinned, and said, "I thought about putting it on Sergeant Major Twitty's jeep bumper." Ski paused. "She's been sucked into the antiwar movement. It's the new hot thing back home."

"Yeah, I know the feeling, buddy. I got one of those not long ago. But you know, your girlfriend's bumper sticker is right."

Ski turned his head toward me with a frown. "What do you mean by that?"

"Well, it's true. If there were no soldiers there'd be no wars." I grinned slyly and added, "Why don't you make up a bumper sticker that says, 'If there were no soldiers there would be no protection'? Send that back to her, but don't expect a reply."

The Cowboys finished cleaning their weapons and one by one went into the hooch.

Ski looked back at me. "You know, that's not a bad idea sending her a bumper sticker back like that. Actually I'd rather lob a couple of frag grenades into that fucking gang of protesting pukes." His voice was bitter.

"Was the demonstration peaceful?" I asked.

Ski's response was vehement. "Yeah, if you can call fifteen thousand people shoutin', carrying signs, and struttin' around peaceful!"

"What I'm asking is, did they get destructive, tear anything up, kill anybody?"

He sounded frustrated. "No, they didn't, not according to the paper my mom sent me. But damn it—"

I broke in, still keeping my voice calm. "Good, then it's their right to protest. As long as a person isn't destructive about it or malicious, the First Article of the Constitution authorizes it."

Ski glared at me. I knew I'd taken some of the wind out of his sails, but it was for his own good. If he started letting bitterness infect him, eventually that all-important thing called a "positive mental attitude" would be lost.

PMA alone didn't necessarily keep a man alive, but the absence of it hampered his ability to think clearly. It was important for Binkowski to be playing with as full a deck as possible when dealing with the NVA.

After a moment of silence, he slammed the bolt shut on his rifle and took a contemplative draw on his cigarette. His eyes narrowed to a near frown while he looked at me. His voice was adamant. "You know, after hearing what you just said, I'm starting to get the impression you like these anti-patriot protesting pukes, and frankly that surprises me. How can you—"

I broke into his heat. I didn't like what was being said and I didn't like the way it was being said. "Look, Binkowski, don't try and fuckin' analyze me or put words in my mouth. Pure and simple, mister, you and I are out here on this jagged edge of freedom, essentially defending the protester's right to disagree with us about anything, and to voice that disagreement peacefully.

"No, I don't fuckin' particularly like war protesters. I damn sure don't like them sneering at me and asking how many women and children I've killed when I walk through an airport with my uniform on. But the fact is, it's their privilege and it's a privilege bought and paid for by a long line of hard-fisted American patriots."

I paused and felt my jaw tighten. "My dad died for it! So just because you don't happen to agree with a protester's ideas about this goddamn war doesn't give you or me the fuckin' right to lob a damn grenade into them. Calling them anti-patriots doesn't get it either, because believe it or not, some of them are just as patriotic as you and I.

"Hell, no, I don't like the fact that an American actress is up in North Vietnam hugging and giving the NVA a verbal blow job. But it's her fuckin' privilege. If we start censoring and limiting why, what, and how people express their disagreement, then we're no fuckin' better than the Communist bastards were over here fighting!"

I'd felt a tear gathering in my eye when mentioning my dad. I ignored it but it persisted, and with its sting it brought back vivid memories of stories my mom had told me about him. Now I felt a need to be alone with those memories.

I avoided Ski's eyes and spoke while standing. "I'm going for a walk. How about taking the Cowboys to the ammo dump and drawing another basic load of ammo for the team. You'll need to sign for it."

"Roger, Brett," he replied weakly.

Walking away, I felt a need to say something to pick Ski's spirits up off the ground and let him know I didn't have terminal heartburn about our argument. I turned and said, "By the way, partner, you did well on those IAs today. I think you're about ready to check into Hotel-5."

Chapter 22

The next morning I was directed to report to the command-bunker war room at 1300 hours to receive our mission briefing. Ski accompanied me.

Major Medcalf, our operations officer, delivered the bulk of the briefing. Having received POW snatch briefings in the past, I knew what to expect. Ski however, took copious notes.

I did learn two good things. One, the air assets we'd had on the body recovery, Hector Gomez and company, would be handling our insert into Hotel-5. And two, recent aerial photo intelligence revealed the NVA battalion located near the target had stabilized. It was believed they had set up what appeared to be a permanent headquarters. If this was true, it relieved my concern that Baldy might not still be there when I came to visit. The presence of a headquarters meant he was still in the area. Of course, it also meant the place would be crawling with NVA.

Colonel Kahn delivered the last part of the briefing, telling us to avoid contact with the enemy until we initiated our snatch ambush. He also advised me to conduct a Stabo-rig rehearsal extract just in case we had to run hard and couldn't get to a suitable sit down LZ for a chopper.

The Stabo rehearsal was a good idea since Ski had no experience in, or concept of, what it felt like to dangle sixty feet below a chopper doing eighty knots.

Colonel Kahn's final words were his usual injunction. "Remember, gents, it always takes longer than you expect, it always costs more than you anticipate, and just to be safe, don't forget to take a good healthy piss afterward. Press on."

The next morning after PT and chow, RT Texas locked up the team hooch and moved into the isolation building to begin mission prep. Colonel Kahn volunteered to take care of Trung-uy while we were gone.

After unpacking our gear, I briefed the Cowboys on the concept of operation. It wasn't important for them to know any details until I developed the ambush plan and we began rehearsal.

Upon receiving a target folder filled with maps, intel updates, and photos, I requested a chopper rigged for Stabo training. I was told it would be on-station at 1400 hours.

My request called for some additional on-the-ground training time at a safe training area called Monkey Mountain, a ten-minute chopper ride northeast of Da Nang. Once there, the chopper would set us down on the coastal edge of the mountain. They were instructed to pick us up at 1600 hours, again via Stabo, and return us to camp. I planned on using the area to give Ski some in-the-jungle training time.

By 1330, I had the team assembled and ready on the chopper pad. As we waited, the Asian sun bounced its glaring heat off the bright cement surface of the pad. I used the extra time to give Ski some information on the what, why, and how of Stabo exfiltration.

"Stabo." It was little more than a sixty- to seventy-foot length of nylon rope hanging from a chopper. The end of the rope was rigged with a small canvas-type sail onto which a man attached himself using regular mountain climber's carabiners. Each man was equipped with a hookup Stabo harness sewn into his web gear. The sail helped give aerodynamic stability to the man dangling below the chopper and kept him from spinning during flight.

The Stabo method was new. However, it had one big advantage over previous versions of rope exfiltration. It allowed a man's hands and arms the freedom to return fire during lift-off. Stabo was an absolute last-resort way of getting out of a hot area. Generally, if a team had to use it for exfiltration, the situation was in a maximized condition of weak-and-flaky.

Chopper crews didn't like the method any more than we did. The method required a chopper to hover, like a sitting duck, over what was usually a heavy firefight, while waiting for a team to get hooked up. On the one occasion the team was forced to use Stabo, the chopper took several hits while hovering. He stayed with us till we got hooked up, but taking off, he neglected to get enough altitude to clear the trees before heading forward. The chopper dragged us through half a mile of trees before rising. Rham suffered a broken leg. The rest of us had so many bruises and cuts we looked like we'd been in a brick fight, and our side hadn't had any bricks.

Ski listened intently to my explanation of Stabo. I could tell he was reluctant about it. Finally he scratched his head and tossed out a question. "You say it's likely we'll be taking fire if we have to come out on Stabo. What—what happens if a bullet, a round, hits my rope?''

I looked at him in disbelief. ''Arnold,'' I said slowly, ''if a round hits your rope, buddy, gravity is going to take over instantly. You don't have to worry about a thing.'' I grinned, winked, and added, ''Just be prepared to do an Academy Award–winning parachute-landing fall when you hit the ground.''

I got the idea that part of Colonel Kahn's reason for recommending the Stabo rehearsal was that, in a discreet way, he was telling me Hotel-5 was ultra-hot.

Soon, the dull thudding noise of a chopper echoed from the westward horizon. I looked toward the slick, yanked my bush hat off, and stuffed it inside my shirt. I signaled for the team to position themselves on the pad. A moment later, I spotted the smiling face of Hector Gomez peering out the starboard door as the slick's drafty shadow hovered and centered above us. A warm gust of sand washed over the chopper pad.

I squinted my eyes up into the rotor draft toward Hector and exaggeratedly tapped my chest with both hands, a signal for him to drop the ropes.

One by one, Hector dropped six thick green cords to us, three out each door. I hurriedly helped the team hook up, made a quick inspection of each man, and hooked myself in. I glanced at Binkowski. He gripped his rifle across his chest like it was the safety bar on a roller coaster.

I yelled over the thudding racket above us, ''You ready for a ride, Ski?''

His eyes were wide as he nodded a reluctant affirmation.

I thrust my arms above my head to signal lift-off.

The whining turbine swiftly accelerated, jerking us up into hot wind. The slick quickly ascended, pulling our strained, dangling bodies forward over the camp and toward the ocean. I felt the leg straps bite into my groin as I scanned the sandy landscape falling away from us. Seconds later, we swayed headlong into high winds a thousand feet above the shimmering jade expanse of the South China Sea.

The chopper turned northward toward the dark green silhouette of Monkey Mountain. The mountain, located just east of Da Nang, was a huge geographical doorknob on the northern edge of the city's harbor. It got the Americanized name because it had a large rock-ape population.

The rock ape, actually a displaced species of orangutan, got its American name because they frequently threw rocks at anyone who intruded into their jungle habitat. The first time I was ambushed by rock apes was a little unnerving. I soon learned a warning shot fired into the air sent them scurrying.

The proximity of Monkey Mountain made it an ideal location for team training. The 3rd Amtrac Marines ran continuous patrols on the mountain to keep the VC out. With the exception of rock apes and Marine patrols, who had a habit of shooting first and asking questions later, the mountain was about as safe as anyplace in South Vietnam.

Our ride to the eastern coastal edge of the mountain was short. The chopper lowered us onto the narrow stretch of beach and departed swiftly after we unhooked. A brief radio contact with the pilot confirmed they would return at 1600 hours for exfil.

I held my finger to my lips to signal absolute noise

discipline. For Ski's benefit, I wanted to keep the training as close to realistic as possible.

Silently, we moved into the shadowy damp mouth of the jungle and took up a close-quarter defensive position. The first moments in a target area were always critical, vulnerable moments. We waited and listened. I focused my mind to search for unusual sounds or, more importantly, the absence of sounds that were supposed to be there. All was quiet except for the normal treetop rustle of the cockatoos and an occasional lizard scurrying through the tangled undergrowth.

Ski slapped at mosquitoes swarming around his neck. Lok quietly took a small vial of insect repellent from his pocket and passed it to him.

In the silent waiting moments, I felt a strange emptiness. This was the first time in almost eight months I'd been in the bush without Will. I missed the confidence his presence gave me. And, I missed the certainty of knowing I could depend on him. I felt a gnawing loneliness, as though a vital part of me were suddenly gone.

The loneliness brought a chill, but memories of our times together quickly cast it off. Times together when even high-volume enemy fire and the intense adrenal fear that accompanied it seemed lessened. Lessened because my partner was right there beside me. I recalled Will saying once, after we'd escaped an ambush, ''Whew, man, I'm sure glad one of us is livin' right or we'd never got outa that.''

Even though he joked about it, it was Will who was living right. There was something about him that let a person know he was always going to do the right thing. Once, when I asked him to go into town with me and check out some commercial affection, he grinned and said, ''Thanks for the invite, but I got a woman back home who's as true as the day is long. She told me when we got married that what Moses brought down from the mountain was not the Ten Suggestions. She lives by 'em, so I sort of try and stay on the same sheet of music.''

Chapter 23

The afternoon training went well and without incident. We didn't encounter any apes or Marine patrols, although at times, I could hear a rustling movement near us and occasional grunts. The noises sounded more like rock apes than Marines.

During our tactical movement up the dark side of the mountain, I deliberately kept us off trails, and in the thicket. The Cowboys didn't like it, but it was the best way to introduce Ski to what bush movement was like. I put him on point and told him to take us due west. He used his wrist compass well. Monitoring his course on my lensatic compass, I only had to correct his direction once.

The first hundred meters of the trek, Ski sounded like a bull charging through a china shop. After a couple of reminders about noise discipline, he quieted his movement. Slowly, he began to learn how difficult clandestine movement through thick vegetation was. He also learned about biting bats, leaping lizards, tree snakes, and wait-a-minute vines.

Thirty minutes into the mountain, I called a rest break. Ski crawled slowly back to my side. Sweat poured off his tired face. He whispered in an exasperated voice, "Brett, seems to me if I had a machete it would be a whole lot easier to get through this shit!"

I took a short sip from my canteen, looked at him, and whispered, "Well, why didn't you bring one, Arnold?" I glanced at my watch. "Let's move out."

A brief flicker of anger flared as he turned and crawled back to his lead position. I didn't feel like telling him at the time that a machette whacking through the vines made too much noise, and even if the noise level was acceptable, there wasn't a machete made that wouldn't dull down to a blunt edge after a half mile of jungle hacking. Critique and questions could wait until we got back to camp and sat down with a cold beer.

As we approached the crest of the mountain, bright, dusty rays of afternoon sun lanced through the tangled branches of the trees. Except for the occasional distant thunder of artillery fire, all was quiet.

We found a small clearing and rested. Ski and I leaned our backs against a tree. The Yards, true to form, squatted and opened small plastic bags of rice. They ate their snack finger-style.

Ski took a long drink from his canteen and whispered, "You know, I noticed several trails on the way up here. They looked like they led to the top. Wouldn't it have been easier—"

" 'Easier' isn't what keeps you alive out here, Ski. The surest way to walk into an ambush or a booby trap is to use trails. There's lots of trails in Hotel-5. You probably noticed that during your map study of the target. And, there'll be times we have to use 'em. Only if we have to."

I paused, then continued while wiping my face with a cravat. "On the other hand, Chuck likes trails. He knows where he's planted booby traps, so he ambles along trails like he was king of the road. I'll guarantee you one thing, though. When we hit him with our ambush, he'll wish he'd never seen a trail."

I winked at Ski. "Look, partner, with or without me, get used to staying off trails, unless the defecation has already hit the cooling apparatus and you're running for all you're worth. Roger that?"

"Roger, Brett."

Our trip down the mountain was much quicker than the one going up. For training purposes, I put the team on a path during a portion of the descent. It gave me an opportunity to point out some of the common terrain danger areas inherent to jungle-trail movement. Ski took hurried notes on everything I showed him.

When we arrived back at the exfil point, our chopper was already circling overhead. The Stabo pickup went smoothly. We were back at camp and on the ground by 1630 hours.

While we waved Hector and company off, I made brief radio contact with the pilot. "Thanks for the ride. We'll see ya'll again in a few days. Tell Hector he might want to bring a four-leaf clover with him on this next trip. Over."

After a brief pause, the pilot responded, "Roger, four-leaf clover, Texas. But Hector says that won't get it. He's gettin' 'short' and not takin' any chances. Says he's bringing a footlocker full of crucifixes for this next show."

The slick faded west into the bright yellow evening sun hovering beyond Da Nang airfield. I hoisted the radio strap over my shoulder and began moving toward the isolation compound. The team followed. A hard southerly wind pressed its warm sandy breath against our sweaty backs as we walked.

I placed my hand over Tuong's shoulder and looked back at the rest of the team following us. "Who all in this motley crew could use a cold beer?" The vote was unanimous.

Tuong immediately looked up at me. "What do 'motley' mean?"

I looked down at him and smiled. "It means 'handsome.'"

As soon as we returned to our large windowless isolation room and put our gear down Major Medcalf entered. He was accompanied by a tall slender sergeant first-class.

The major smiled and handed me a small stack of mail. "How'd your Stabo training go, Sergeant Yancy?"

I glanced at the letters, then tossed them and my bush hat onto my bunk. "Good, sir. A little tough on the family jewels as usual, but the training went well."

He laughed. "Yeah, I know the feeling." He turned his attention to the sergeant standing beside him. The man was so skinny his shirt looked like it was still on a coat hanger. It appeared he'd either just gotten out of a POW camp or was suffering from malaria. He wore a faded green beret.

"Good news and bad news, Sergeant Yancy." The major dramatized his voice to sound cheerful. "This here is Sergeant Longstreath. He's the good news. Longstreath's just been assigned to us from CCC out of Kontum. He'll be your area-study team, all by himself, for the next two days. He's run targets in Laos as One-Zero of RT Alabama, so he'll be a big help with your planning."

I was puzzled as to why a veteran One-Zero was being assigned as an AST. I extended my hand. "Glad to meet you, Sergeant Longstreath."

His handshake was strong but without enthusiasm. As a seasoned field soldier, it was understandable he wasn't happy to be stuck as an adviser and gofer.

"Call me Denver." His voice was soft, but confident.

I introduced the team, then turned my attention back to the major. "Sir, you mentioned that Denver would be with us two days. I understood Colonel Kahn had scheduled us for three days of prep time. We're due to launch on the fourteenth."

The major looked down at his well-shined boots and rocked back and forth on his heels, as though considering an answer. He spoke in a distinctly authoritative voice. "That's the bad news, Sergeant Yancy. Long-range weather reports are sayin' a storm is moving into the target area on or about the fourteenth or fifteenth. We can't chance the target being socked in and preventing infiltration. So, we had to move your insert to the thirteenth. This cuts you short on prep time, but we don't have much choice. We can't scrub this mission."

I didn't like having my prep time shortened. This meant I'd have to hurry everything I'd planned. But the forecast of a storm in the area sweetened the situation a little. Heavy rains meant we'd have better conceal-ment during movement. It would also make it tougher for Chuck to track us. Colonel Kahn's report about the NVA using dogs to track recon teams worried me. Now, if I could count on the weather report being right, the rain would obscure our scent, even if they put the hounds on us. On the other hand, I'd learned Air Force weather reports were little more than "definite maybes."

The major didn't wait for a response to his comment. He changed his tone back to cheerful. "I'll get out of here and let you guys get started. Sergeant Longstreath has already familiarized himself with the target area, so you're in good hands." Before departing, he cast a smart nod toward us and echoed Colonel Kahn. "Press on, gents."

After the major left, Denver lit a cigarette, then spoke with a cynical half smile. "That's the first time in my military career I've ever been referred to as 'good news.'" He pointed to the large wall map of Laos at the end of the room, and continued to speak while we walked slowly toward it. "But, it seems the 'good-news major' neglected to tell you all the bad news about this potential cluster-fuck snatch mission." He glanced at me. "By the way, you ever run a snatch before?"

"Roger. Two."

He ran his fingers over the map area depicting Hotel-5. "Well, this one is likely to be different from anything you've encountered before. To start with, Uncle Ho Chi Minh's Trail runs right along the eastern boundary of your target. That, combined with this battalion headquarters located about here, makes Chuck as strong as ten acres of garlic in that area." He grinned slyly. "It won't be hard to find the NVA, but gettin' a prisoner outa there is gonna be like trying to pull a tooth on an unsedated Bengal tiger." He took a quick draw on his cigarette while keeping his attention focused on the map. "But, then, I guess that's what makes it fun."

I was fortunate to have Denver as my AST. I'd had some in the past who didn't even know how to read a map. Although Denver wasn't particularly elated about being in an administrative capacity, he didn't let it impair his professionalism.

Denver Longstreath seemed to be a double-edged sword. His wry, rough-cut humor was one side of the blade. It reminded me of Swede Jensen's. The other edge was honed razor-sharp by combat. I got the impression he'd left Chuck with bleeding hemorrhoids.

I pointed to the area where we'd conducted the body recovery. "You're right about him being strong in there. I found out the hard way less than two weeks ago."

He turned his head toward me. "Yeah, I know. I read your AAR on that mission." He fell silent for a second, then added, "Sorry about your partner."

I glanced at the floor. "It happens."

Looking up, I followed his eyes toward Binkowski. Ski sat at a large table with the yards, cleaning his rifle. In a lowered voice, Denver asked, "Does this new One-One have any ground time?"

"No. This'll be his first mission."

Denver's eyes squinted as if he'd just bitten into a lemon. "That's great," he said in a low cynical tone. "How 'bout the Yards?"

"Top-shelf. Twelve missions with me." I suddenly remembered the beer I'd promised them. "By the way, I almost forgot. I promised the team a cold beer. Would you mind dropping into the club and picking up a six-pack for us?"

He shrugged. "Don't see why not. That's what I'm here for. To assist and advise. Think I'll make it seven beers. I could handle one myself."

Handing him five dollars, I said, "Why don't you make it an even fourteen. Nothing worse than just one beer." I grinned.

His voice was energetic. "Roger, sounds good. How

'bout if we go over a terrain study when I get back. I've already selected some good ambush sites. I'd like to show them to you and see what you think. By the way, you ever use chemical sulfide, CS gas powder, in an ambush?''

''No.'' I knew we had CS available, but I'd avoided using it because it required the team to carry cumbersome gas masks.

''Works great. Of course, it's against the Rules of Ground Warfare. But shit, so's everything else we do. I'll tell ya 'bout it when I get back.''

He turned and strode briskly out of the smoky room.

Denver wasn't gone long. He returned carrying a rucksack and a paper bag full of beer. He quickly passed out the beer and motioned all of us around the big table. He stood at one end of the table and removed a claymore mine, a plastic canteen, and a roll of black electrical tape from the rucksack.

He kept his cigarette between his lips, talking around it while he pried the rigid face off the mine.

''What I plan to show you guys is how to use CS in a snatch ambush. Believe me, it's the greatest thing since flavored douches.'' He glanced up to emphasize his point.

After removing the claymore face housing, he carefully extracted the wide layer of steel balls meshed into the C-4 plastic explosive backing.

We watched him go about his task. The expression on the Cowboys' faces was mystified.

The claymore is an above-surface mine, about the size of a paperback book. It's command-detonated by means of an electronic hand generator. The mine is awesome in its total configuration. But, for some reason, Denver was removing its fangs.

Ski leaned toward me and whispered a question. "Shouldn't we tell him to put his cigarette out? I mean, isn't that C-4 he's working with?"

"Roger, it's C-4. But it requires electronic detonation. You can throw a block of C-4 in a campfire and all it'll do is burn. The little people even cook with it sometimes, but I don't recommend it. The vapors can be toxic if you don't have a well-ventilated area."

After removing the shrapnel-producing steel from the mine, Denver replaced the plastic cover over the face. He had effectively castrated the mine.

He picked up the green plastic canteen and placed it horizontally across the face of the mine, which read, FACE TOWARD ENEMY. He then began taping it to the mine and explained, "Now let's assume I've already filled this canteen with CS powder." He completed his taping and held the mine in front of him. "Once the canteen is attached to the claymore, like so, you place this mine in the capture zone of your ambush, preferably the center. You then place your unaltered claymores on both sides of this one at ten-meter intervals.

"When Chuck and the gang come strolling into your ambush, you simultaneously detonate all of your mines and, gents, the show is fan-fuckin'-tastic!"

His voice rose in excitement. "You got this huge yellow cloud of gagging CS dust raining through the jungle, and, man, the ones that aren't dead are wishin' they were. You rush them immediately. Chances are you'll still have two or three alive in your capture zone. But they'll be staggering around and puking, like Saturday-night winos in an alley. You pick your prisoner, kill the others, and beat feet."

Denver's method sounded good. It was apparent he'd

used it successfully in the past. But, I still had some apprehension about having to use gas masks.

I took a swallow of beer before voicing my skepticism. "The plan sounds great, if Murphy's Law doesn't get into the act. I don't like the idea of having to use gas masks. They're cumbersome, they limit visibility, and—"

Denver interrupted sharply. "Don't need 'em! What you do is wear gloves and a double set of fatigues. Tape the sleeves and collar tightly. Use double cravats over your face and neck and wear tanker goggles to protect your eyes. I'll make sure everybody has a pair of goggles. Just remember that you have to move in fast, do your thing, and move out quick. A short, protected exposure to the dust won't bother you. As soon as you get out of the area, halt the team, shuck off your outer set of fatigues and other protective gear, and ditch it. Trust me, Brett, you're gonna love it."

The look of confidence in Denver's eyes sold me. I lifted my beer in a gesture of acceptance. "Let's do it!"

Chapter 24

It was after chow before Denver and I began a target terrain study. Ski listened and took notes. After selecting the primary and alternate infil and exfil LZs, Denver made three suggestions for ambush sites. He assigned numerical priorities to each. His recommendations were good.

I listened and made check marks on my map to indicate approval. My interest was little more than courtesy. I couldn't tell him predetermined ambush sites were out of the question without tipping my hand about Baldy being my priority. For me to expect Baldy to waltz into a prepositioned ambush was as likely as snow in Saigon. I was going to have to comb the entire area looking for him. A search meant a lot of moving and monitoring different zones of enemy activity.

The best thing that could happen, and perhaps the most likely, would be to find Baldy traveling with a patrol. Once I'd sighted him, I'd stealthily advance the team ahead of the patrol, set a hasty ambush, and wait. When the patrol came into our sights and Baldy was in the capture zone, I'd detonate our claymores. When we rushed out of our concealed position and onto the trail,

I would only need a minute to ram my blade into Baldy's throat. The team, particularly Binkowski, would be stunned. I was counting on the intensity of the moment to remove the need for explanations. There would be none. We'd grab our prisoner, kill any survivors, and move out quick.

But, it was possible Baldy had been assigned stay-behind duty as a guard, or perhaps a radio operator in the new NVA headquarters area. If that turned out to be the case, I would have to go in after him solo. I couldn't risk the annihilation of my team, a team that had no idea what I was plotting.

By 2100 hours, Denver and I had finished a pot of coffee and the first phase of mission prep: target analysis. During the three-hour process, Ski filled up two large tablets with notes. I didn't have the heart to tell him all his data would have to be destroyed before we left. But Longstreath did.

Ski was still writing when Denver's condescending voice fell on him, an old pro talking to a rookie. "Binkowski, I hate to hit you with the news, but these notes are not going to be preserved in the Smithsonian. I gotta burn all that before you leave for never-never land."

Denver's sarcasm was quickly doused by Ski's cryptic reply. "No sweat, Sarge. I understand. It's the engrams that count. You don't mind if I take my engrams with me, do you?" He grinned as soon as he saw the question marks blinking in Longstreath's eyes.

Denver scowled, then muttered, "Engrams? What in the hell is—?"

Ski smiled. A hint of victory laced his voice. "An engram is a protoplasmic stimulation of the long-term memory cells. Taking notes accentuates long-term memory retention.''

I broke in. I didn't want a pissing contest started. ''I think we got the picture, Arnold.''

Denver quickly glanced at his watch, then gulped down his last swallow of coffee. ''Well, gents, after that engram information, I do believe it's time to piss on the fire and call the dogs in. See you in the morning.''

I shook his hand. ''Roger. Thanks for the help.''

He snuffed his cigarette out and strode to the door. Before leaving, he turned and looked at Ski. ''By the way, Binkowski, yes, it's all right to take your engrams. Just try and bring 'em all back in one piece, cherry!''

When the door closed behind Denver, I turned to Binkowski. ''You were probably right to whip that engram scene on Denver. But remember, he's on our side. Now let's hit the rack. We've got two days of work to cram into tomorrow, so it's going to be another sixteen-hour day.''

His response was positive. ''Roger, partner.''

I checked the yards. They were already bunked down, sawing logs. Ski sat on the edge of his bed taking his boots off.

''Brett, have you noticed how skinny Denver is? What do you think's wrong with him?''

I hesitated, shuffling through the letters on my bunk. I picked out the one from Tracy, then answered, ''Well, you're right, he's obviously lost a lot of weight. Maybe he's got a bad case of dysentery, or maybe he took a hit and he's recovering. Either way, if he wants us to know about it, he'll tell us.''

''Yeah. I guess you're right. Anyhow, skinny or not, the guy sure knows his shit about recon.'' Ski grinned widely as he glanced at the lavender envelope I held.

"That looks like another one of those sweet-smelling letters. Same girl?"

"Good night, Arnold."

After undressing, I turned out the light and lay down to read Tracy's lavender-scented letter by flashlight.

Dear Brett,

It's only been a few days since you walked out of my life and I'm already missing you. If that makes me a masochist, so be it. At night when I go to sleep, or try to, my mind fills with memories of our time together.

It may sound strange but I can still smell your scent. Silly me! It's probably just that strong Thai soap you showered with (ha, ha, just kidding).

I promised myself I wasn't going to get maudlin in this letter and already I'm breaking my promise. Sorry I had to give you the Claddagh ring via Ski; it was the only way I could think of. Please wear the ring. It doesn't mean you have to take me to the prom!

I'll be on assignment here for three weeks. If you can find a moment to write, you can send it to me, care of the Mai-lon Hotel, Room 203, Saigon.

I've managed to get an interview with Creighton Abrams and some members of his staff. It should go well, providing they don't ask me how I feel about this goddamn war. On the brighter side, my hat is partially off to Nixon. It appears he may be serious about his campaign promise to get us out of Vietnam. He's already withdrawn almost 100,000 American soldiers and he's only been in office nine months. Also, if you haven't heard, Ho Chi Minh died last week, Sept. 3. The Communists now have an official martyr and it's my guess they will dig their heels in for the duration.

So much for the news. I think I liked this letter better when it was maudlin. Thank you for the present. I love it. The wisdom in the book seems timeless. I particularly like the passage on love. It begins, "When love beckons you, follow him, though his ways are hard and steep. . . ." Gibran must have written that part especially for women who were destined to fall in love with soldiers!

I'll close this for now, honey, but keep in mind that if you have a chance to break away from "noble purpose" for a couple of days, I could be persuaded to fly up to Da Nang for a weekend. Take care, think of me (preferably not when you are looking through a gun sight), and wear the ring, please. Hope you like the picture. If the look on my face seems to say "Wish you were here," it's because it's true.

Love,
Tracer

P.S. As promised, I am enclosing the address of the Baptist agency in Dallas that handles Vietnam War orphan adoption. I checked on some of the regulations. Ming and Lon are eligible for the program, but Fousi, at sixteen, may be too old for the cutoff age. I want to assist you with this effort, so please send me some basic stats on them. Full names as well as dates and places of birth for starters.

Tracy's postscript tugged at my heart like pulled taffy. Damn it, was it possible I was beginning to love this woman? I lifted her square Polaroid snapshot from the envelope. She was sitting at a table by a swimming pool in a white one-piece swimsuit. One elbow rested on her typewriter. A breeze had caught a tress of her hair and lifted it. Her long tan legs stretched out, crossed in front. The top of her swimsuit revealed a modest hint of cleavage. She smiled but there was sadness in her eyes.

By 0900 hours the next morning, RT Texas, accompanied by Denver Longstreath, moved single file to the firing range at the base of Marble Mountain. Dark clouds blotched the windy sky, threatening rain. A strong ocean breeze lifted puffs of sand off our heels as we neared the base of the tall mountain.

Denver shouted through the cool wind, "Looks like a storm blowin' up."

I glanced skyward. "Yeah, but then, if the Air Force is right about the target-area weather, we'd better get used to it."

"Roger. Good training," Denver said sarcastically.

The prospect of rain seemed certain, but this was our last full training day before launch. I wasn't about to call it off.

We halted near the northern cliff edge of the mountain. I instructed Ski on the basics of arming and placing a claymore mine, then had him prepare one for detonation. Denver and the yards moved back to watch from a distance.

Beads of sweat formed on Ski's face as he attached the wire to the blasting cap and inserted it gently in the threaded arming well.

I coached at his side. I was glad he was a little nervous. I felt it was good for a man dealing with explosives to be just a controlled step on the near side of trembling. It kept him alert.

Ski completed arming the mine and placed it a hundred feet from the cliff wall facing the mountain while I set up several man-size cardboard targets against the cliff. He carefully fed the long wire back to our position behind a sand mound, then attached the hand generator.

I signaled for the others to get down. Lying prone, next to Ski, I said, "You ready, partner?"

He blinked several times, picked up the hand generator, and looked at me. "Yes, sir. I mean, roger." A drop of sweat dangled from the tip of his nose.

I took a quick look forward to make sure the blast area was clear. I spoke calmly. "All clear. Fire away."

Ski grimaced and jerked his grip tightly against the trigger arm. A second passed. Nothing. The generator had failed.

I couldn't have asked for a better chance to show him a critical "what-if" reaction to nondetonation.

Sand meshed into the side of Ski's blank face. "What happened?"

Staying prone, I took the generator from his hand. "What happened is, Murphy's Law just applied itself. If that occurs when we detonate our ambush . . . do this, immediately." I pressed my fingers between the lower edge of the trigger arm and the generator housing, then yanked upward, and opened my palm to display the re-armed trigger. "That quick movement repositions the trigger arm. See?"

Ski's face was grim. "Roger."

I stressed my next words. "The key word here is *quick*. You have to anticipate it may fail and be ready to re-arm the generator immediately. Then fire again. You can't fumble-fuck around with it, partner. We'll have four claymores in our snatch ambush. I'll be handling two of them and you'll have the other two. You'll detonate yours the instant you hear mine go off. So, if one of them fails, reaction time is critical. Otherwise we're startin' our show without a full band.''

I handed the generator back to Ski. ''Now, let's try it again. You can practice the re-arming procedure later.''

Ski brushed sand from his face and smiled nervously. ''I guess it's kinda good this happened, huh? I mean, I learned something here, right?''

Suddenly Denver's wry voice cut through the wind. ''What's going on up there? Did somebody forget their engrams?''

Binkowski flared. He jumped and ran toward the sergeant.

I leapt up and sprinted to catch him just a few feet before he reached Longstreath. I grabbed the back of Ski's collar and yanked him over my outstretched leg. He tripped backward, plummeting into the sand.

I glared down at him. ''Damn it, Binkowski, don't you fuckin' ever leave our position unless I tell you to. Get your ass back over there right now!'' I jabbed a finger toward the claymore site.

He rose and walked slowly away, brushing sand off his arms. I watched him for a second, then turned to face Longstreath. He was trying to light a cigarette.

''You're breaking a little hard on my partner, Sarge. So, understand this. If you're fuckin' with him, you're fuckin' with me.''

He didn't reply. I turned to walk away but couldn't resist adding some curt advice: ''By the way, if I were you, I'd be careful not to let my hippopotamus mouth overload my bumblebee ass. I might not be here to rescue you next time."

When I returned to the firing site, Ski was waiting. His eyes were anxious, as if expecting me to say something more. But there was no reason to dwell on the episode. Inwardly, I wanted to tell him he'd done exactly what I would have in the same situation. In that respect, Ski and I were alike—neither of us had much tolerance for bullshit.

I eased into a prone position near him. "You ready to give this another try, partner?"

Binkowski perked into a broad smile the second he heard me call him "partner." "Roger, Brett. Ready."

I gave a quick look to the rear, then forward. "All clear. Fire away."

His powerful grip seized the generator arm like it was Longstreath's neck. An earsplitting boom echoed off the cliff, hurling sand and debris high into the dark windy sky.

"It worked! Damn, that's a great sound." Ski's voice was excited, victorious.

Standing, I brushed the gritty residue off my neck and arms. "I'd say you're right, Ski. Great sound. Let's go check the targets."

Ski leapt up and hurried forward, ahead of me. The pungent scorched smell of burned plastic permeated the firing zone.

Binkowski stood inspecting one of the cardboard silhouettes as I approached. "In-fucking-credible," he murmured.

The once thick, stoutly fixed targets were now a shambles, drilled and shredded to pieces by a wave of steel balls from the claymore.

"Looks like you had it well aimed, Ski. Now, imagine an NVA patrol getting hit by four of these beehives at once. They go down quick." My words had a purpose.

He looked at me solemnly, not replying. A question flashed in his expression. He needed an answer to something, but he wasn't sure what it was. I knew exactly what it was. I had felt the same cold shiver wash over me when I first realized I had the sanctioned power to kill.

I caught a glimpse of Denver and the yards moving slowly toward us. I only had a moment to give Arnold Binkowski a justifiable motive to kill. He needed it, and he needed it now, while the stink of reality flushed through him. In less than two days he would be in Hotel-5 where he would come face-to-face with the gut-quaking decision to kill. Hesitation meant death.

My words cracked as I spoke them. "Ten months ago the NVA captured RT Nevada. With the One-Zero and One-One watching, they executed the Montagnards. Then, they beheaded the One-Zero, Glenn Neusome. They stripped him, strung him up by his arms, and stuffed a dog's head over the bloody stump of his neck. Bob Torres, Glenn's One-One, was forced to watch it all. When the bastards were finished, they took Torres, stripped him, tied his hands behind him, and strapped Neusome's head around his neck, just below his chin. Wc found Torres two days later, staggering around in circles in a clearing.

A month later Bob Torres committed suicide in a psycho ward at Walter Reed Hospital." I paused, wiped my eyes, and glared back at Ski. "Think of that when it comes time to kill."

Chapter 25

Flashes of lightning tore through the dark afternoon sky, unleashing the monsoon. I couldn't complain. Throughout most of the day we'd had only light rain. It had come and gone without interrupting training. Now the sky squalled in an unrelenting, pelting deluge.

We ran for cover. Huddling beneath an overhang at the base of Marble Mountain, we hastily yanked ponchos over our already soaked frames.

"Sar Brett, I think maybe time to call it day." Tuong's words were muffled by the plastic cloak he drew down over his head.

"You're right, Babysan. It's time to go to the house," I said while glancing at the team to make sure everybody had their ponchos on.

Lok was still trying to get his down over his field gear. He looked like a high-school girl attempting to straighten her skirt after a backseat rendezvous. I reached over and helped him. Then turning back to face the heavy downpour, I said, "Let's move out."

We ran single file toward the isolation compound. When we slushed inside, Denver, who had come in earlier to check on target intel updates, was waiting.

"Damn, looks like Buddha rained y'all out." Denver glanced nervously toward Binkowski, who was taking off his poncho. He waited a moment before walking over to Ski's side. He spoke softly. "Ski, sorry 'bout that bullshit out there this morning. I didn't mean anything by it. Anyhow, I was sure glad Brett stopped you before I had to whip your big ass."

Binkowski whirled toward the sergeant, but Denver was already backing away laughing. He held his open palm out to Ski. "Just joshin', Ski, just joshin'."

Ski laughed and accepted the hand in front of him. The Yards started without me this time, their laughter led by Tuong.

Reaching into a large sack on the table, Denver said, "How 'bout a cold beer? Just happen to have some here."

After handing a beer to Tuong, he replied with a grin, "Thank you, Sar. You a motley guy."

Rham and Phan busied themselves mopping up the puddles of water beneath our hanging ponchos. The rest of the team worked cleaning their rifles and field gear.

After changing into dry fatigues, Denver and I went into the isolation briefing room and began going over the intel updates for Hotel-5. There wasn't a lot of new information; however, one report did confirm the location of the NVA headquarters. The report included a six digit grid coordinate of the location, and an infrared aerial photo of the complex. The photo showed little more than thick jungle canopy with a trail leading out of the trees and through a clearing. I marked the location on my map. The report ended with a note saying the NVA headquarters area was scheduled for an arc-light bombing mission on September 19.

Ideally, we should have our mission wrapped up in two, maybe three days, and be out by the sixteenth, well before the arc-light. I didn't know how long it was going to take to find Baldy, but I knew we didn't want to be in the area when five-hundred-pound bombs started tearing up the landscape.

I underlined the scheduled bombing date and handed the report to Denver. "This arc-light could ruin my whole day if we're not out of there by the nineteenth."

Denver took the paper and placed it in a folder marked SECRET. He smirked. "Roger that. I hear those bombs can give a man a splitting headache."

He looked at my somber expression and dropped his grin. "Don't worry, Brett, I gotcha covered. I'll have my finger on the pulse all the way through this clusterfuck. If you're not outa there by the eighteenth, I'll have the arc-light postponed."

He lit a cigarette and leaned back in his chair. "By the way, I talked with Colonel Kahn today and asked him if I could work as your forward air controller when . . . I mean, if the shit hits the fan out there on y'all. He seemed to think it was okay. He told me to touch base with you on it first. You got any problem with that?"

Having a good FAC overhead was critical if a team was being chased by the enemy. He flew over the area in a small fixed-wing plane and controlled all necessary air support against Chuck. He had to be knowledgeable about the target area, enemy tactics, and Air Force reaction times. He also advised and guided the team on the ground, and was frequently the target of concentrated enemy ground fire. For Denver to volunteer as my FAC didn't necessarily mean he had suicidal tendencies. It only meant his elevator didn't go all the way to the top.

The decision was mine. The answer was no. I felt Denver could handle the job as well as anybody. He had the background, experience, and knowledge necessary to do it. But I didn't want him sticking his loyal neck out any more than he already had.

I looked at the proud emaciated man sitting beside me. "You know, Denver, after all the operations you've run, if you had nine lives to begin with, you've probably used up ten of them by now. Thanks for offering. I know you've got your shit in a tight condition. I just don't want you going out on a limb for us. Besides, I've always used Blister as my FAC. He'd probably feel left out if I didn't use him."

Denver leaned forward, placing his elbows on his knees. "I know Blister. He's good. In fact, he's helped me out of a crack or two. He's got balls of brass, and he's hard as woodpecker lips. But he ain't gonna be much good to you in Hawaii." Longstreath looked at me with a familiar smirk beaming off his face.

"Hawaii?"

"Roger that. Hawaii. He's leaving on R and R to meet his wife and kids day after tomorrow. Be gone seven days. Looks like you're either stuck with me or potluck, and I really don't think anybody knows that area like I do. At least nobody available to you as a FAC."

I shrugged. "All right, then it'll be you. But only if we're up to our asses in alligators. Understand?"

A wild, wide-eyed look slowly glossed Denver's face, like he was getting ready to tell a bald-faced lie. "Hell yes, only if you need me. Fuck me to tears, Brett, surely you don't think I like getting shot at without a purpose to it, do you?''

I leaned back and thought about his question. It was paradoxical, a man wanting to risk his life when he didn't have to.

I needed to find out what was winding Denver's clock. I placed the stack of intel reports aside and looked back at him. ''No, buddy, I don't think you like getting shot at. But I do think some people enjoy risk, even thrive on it. Back at school, we studied a theory that tried to determine why some people—like you and me, for example—prefer parachuting rather than tennis, snow skiing instead of golf, or even bear hunting over fishing. Our professor, Amelia Duncan, was convinced it all had to do with ego gratification. She said some people actually get high on risk.''

Denver's eyes were fixed, frowning at me, as if I were probing a sensitive nerve. He took a quick drag on his cigarette and changed his scowl into a smile. ''Yancy, that's bullshit. Pure college bullshit. With all respect to you and Amelia whatever her name is, she's pissed down your back and told you it was raining.''

He stood and mashed his cigarette into the ashtray, then spoke again. ''And by the way, just for the record, I happen to like both bear hunting and fishing. I've even played a little tennis. Go tell that to Amelia next time you see her. Damn it, I ain't some basket psycho case.''

Keeping my voice calm, I smiled up at him. ''Look, buddy, nobody is calling you weird. You're a damn good field soldier. I already know that. How long you been in 'Nam anyhow?''

''Thirty-three months. All C and C time.''

''You must have a reason for staying here that long.

Is it for Buddha, mamasan, and rice pie . . . medals maybe?''

He turned, shouting, while hurriedly unbuttoning his shirt. "Hell fuckin' no! You see these stitches?" He looked down at the dark jagged line of sutures across his chest. "The sons of bitches have tried to get me for almost three fuckin' years and they can't fuckin' do it. Oh, they've come close, the maggots, but they ain't got me yet, and I've cut down more of them bastards than you could bury in a football field. I got a job to do here, Yancy, and I do it well. As soon as these stitches are yanked outa me, I'll be back in the bush, working. Call it job satisfaction. Yeah, that's what keeps me here. Not fuckin' medals or anything else. It's fuckin' job satisfaction!''

It was obvious Denver Longstreath had a screw loose, maybe two. I didn't know how he managed to stay in 'Nam after taking the hits he had, although I'd known others who had done it. Perhaps they just didn't want to go home wounded. But the questions that hammered at me now were, Did I want a man who lived for killing flying above me as my FAC? And, with Blister gone, did I have much choice about it? I decided to wait and talk it over with Colonel Kahn.

Denver buttoned his shirt. I'd found out what I needed to know. I assembled words to cover my tracks. "Well, I'm sure as hell glad you're on our side. You're right. Job satisfaction's your motivation. How about we get some coffee.''

After returning to the team billet room, I asked Denver to give Ski a crash course on basic field-radio operation and procedure. Ordinarily the radio stayed with me; however, on this mission, I planned on having Ski carry it. If I had to suddenly leave the team to pursue

Baldy, I didn't want the team without a radio if I took a hit and didn't get back to them.

Although Denver was glad to be Ski's instructor, I could tell Ski wasn't exactly thrilled to be his student. Binkowski gave Denver his attention, but this time he didn't take notes.

The Yards played contact chess while I went to work on my brief-back presentation. My briefing was scheduled for 1100 hours the next morning, mission launch at 1300.

As I neared the end of my spiel, Denver came over and pulled a small white envelope from his pocket. He handed me the envelope along with an apology. "Sorry, Brett, I forgot to give this to you earlier. It's from that cute little Vietnamese girl who works down at the club. She gave it to me when I was by there gettin' beer for us this afternoon."

I looked up at him with a silent challenge.

He defended himself immediately. "Hey, don't ask me how she knew I was your AST. Shit, I get the feeling the VN know more about what's going on around here than we do." He shrugged, turned, and walked back toward Ski.

I opened the letter and removed two small pieces of paper.

Dear Brett,

I know you go field soon. For many day you no talk to me much. Maybe it best that way but we be friends like always before is OK. Ming and Lon and me saying thanking your very much for nice gifts. Ming and Lon draw bird for you I am send

you. They hoping you like and hoping war end soon.
Pleasing be careful.

You friend,
Fousi.

The picture was similar to the one they had etched in the sand that morning in Da Nang. This time they used their new crayons to draw a blue-and-green dove in flight. Below the picture was a heart drawn in red with their names on each side of it. My name was in the center of the heart.

By 2100 I had finished my briefing prep and written two letters, one to Fousi, the other to Tracy. I gave them both to Denver and asked him to mail the one to Tracy and give the other to Fousi tomorrow after we left.

In my letter to Fousi, I apologized for not visiting during the past week. I said we had been very busy training Ski. It was a weak excuse, but the only one I had. I also told her about my aspiration to try to get her and her sisters to the States via adoption, stressing the importance of Ming and Lon having an opportunity for a good education. I included Tracy's address and instructed Fousi to contact her if she didn't hear from me before long. Without sounding negative, I needed to provide Fousi with some contingency for initiating adoption proceedings if I didn't make it back from Hotel-5 in one piece.

In my letter to Tracy, I requested she help Fousi personally if I became "unavoidably detained and unable to do it myself." I place a short note and my Claddagh ring into a separate envelope addressed to Tracy.

Denver noticed my sealing the envelope. He walked over and sat on the bunk across from me. "More mail? Damn, you sure are writin' a bunch tonight."

I handed him the letter with instructions to mail it only if he had not heard from me in two weeks.

He pulled a pencil from his pocket and drew a question mark on the envelope while speaking. "I know all about these 'only-if' letters. I've written a few of them myself. But, you just wait and see. I'll be handing this one back to you before long." He stuffed the letter into his pocket, yawning. "Think it's about time for me to hit the rack. By the way, Binkowski checked out okay on the radio." He scratched his head. "But he didn't take notes on anything I said. See you in the morning."

Moments after Denver left, I poured the last of the coffee into my cup and unplugged the pot. Just as I lifted the cup to my lips, a shout echoed through the room. It was Binkowski.

"A-ten-shun!" Ski's near scream almost knocked the cup out of my hand. Turning, I saw Colonel Kahn closing the door behind him.

"At ease, gents. Go on with what you're doing." He spoke while crossing the smoky room.

Shifting the coffee cup into my left hand, I saluted. "Evening, sir."

The colonel returned my salute while glancing at the chessboard. He pointed at one of the chess pieces and winked at Tuong, who was playing Rham. Tuong looked back at him, returned a wink, and said, "Thank you, sir. You looking very motley tonight."

I cringed, trying to sip my coffee. Somehow I was going to have to disarm Tuong of that word.

Colonel Kahn smiled while looking down at his muddy boots, then glanced back at Tuong, who was clad only in underwear and a T-shirt. "Thank you, Tuong. You look kinda motley yourself."

I interjected quickly while looking at the colonel's dry beret, "Looks like the rain's let up."

He turned back to me. "Yeah, and none too soon. The mortar pits all look like backyard swimming pools. I just dropped in to see how you're coming. You about ready?"

"Roger, sir. And I think Binkowski's ready to piss on tall trees with the rest of the big dogs." When Ski looked up at us with a grin, I added, "I'm scheduled to brief you and the staff tomorrow morning at 1100 hours."

"Don't worry too much about that briefing, Brett. If it was being done my way, you could tell me your plan over a cup of coffee. Sure as blazes if I did it, one of the staff would bitch about it."

I turned and looked at the empty coffeepot. "I'd offer you some coffee, sir, but we're out."

"Thanks. I've had more than I need today, anyhow. Let's go next door for a minute." He motioned toward the briefing room.

Entering the cool room, I decided now was as good a time as any to get Colonel Kahn's idea about how many cards were left in Denver's deck. But I knew he'd directed us into the room for another reason. He had something to say. I withheld my question and sat down. What I expected from him was the usual pulse check he always performed on a One-Zero before he left on a mission, and his lighthearted but serious words, designed to instill confidence.

I was wrong. I knew it the second he removed his beret, like he was lifting a burden from his head.

He remained standing. "Brett, I had a few drinks

with Swede Jensen last night. I do that every now and then so Jensen can update my education on what's happening out there.'' He nodded toward the wall map. ''He's the best team leader I've got. Don't get me wrong, all my One-Zeros are at the top of the page or they don't stay team leaders.''

I remained silent while he lit a cigarette. I felt the small of my back tighten, remembering the conversation I'd had with Jensen the night after Will's death. The memory of those words swarmed through me and stopped on the sentence ''I won't leave this fucking war until it's done.'' That had been my response to Jensen when he asked if I'd killed the sniper who'd hit Will. I sensed what Colonel Kahn was moving toward. I didn't know if Jensen had accidentally let it slip that I planned to pursue Will's assassin, or if the colonel was simply trolling me.

Chapter 26

Colonel Ivan Kahn sat on the edge of the briefing table, smoking a cigarette. He was silent. Seconds passed like the slow pounding of a hammer striking an anvil.

Finally, he glanced at me with a pensive eye and broke the silence. "Your AAR said Washington was hit first by assault fire, but it was a sniper who killed him. You mentioned you returned fire. Did you hit the sniper?"

"No, sir. I don't think so."

"So, the sniper escaped, or do you know?"

He was watching for any twitch in my face, any involuntary movement that might betray the truth. The tension of the moment told me if I didn't have the answers he was looking for, RT Texas was going to be pulled off the mission. Colonel Kahn wasn't about to turn me loose on a personal vendetta. If I was too casual in my answer, he would know I was cloaking the truth. He was like a clever attorney who doesn't ask a question in court that he doesn't already know the answer to.

Frowning, I replied, "Yes, sir, the sniper got away."

"Why didn't you pursue him, kill him?"

The memory of those agonizing seconds boiled up inside me. "Damn it, sir, I wanted to. But Will was torn up bad. I had to get to him, try to save him."

My eyes blurred. My mission depended on this interrogation. Suddenly, everything was at stake. If I blew it, if I wasn't convincing enough, he would scrub it all, and I'd have to live with the cancer of Baldy murdering Will and getting away with it.

The colonel's words brought me back into focus. "You'll be back in that area tomorrow afternoon. You planning on getting him? The sniper?"

The question floated down over me like a net. I searched through my memory, back to the conversation with Jensen. Had I told Swede the sniper was bald? If not, the colonel had no way of knowing I could distinguish Baldy; so, pursuit would be next to impossible. I drew a blank. I couldn't remember what I had said, except that I would get the assassin before I left Vietnam.

I looked directly up into Colonel Kahn's eyes. "I'd love to get the bastard, sir. But that's impossible. He was a typical, average-height, khaki-clad NVA. I only got a glimpse of him from a distance. Shit, I couldn't identify him on a police lineup."

He stood, exhaled his smoke, and smiled. "That's right. It would be a damn needle in a haystack, wouldn't it? But don't go in looking for a body count either. Remember, this is a snatch mission, not a search-and-destroy. All we need is one warm NVA body, that's all. The sooner you get in and out, the better."

Breathing a restrained sigh of relief, I replied, "Roger, sir. The quicker, the better." I changed the subject immediately.

"By the way, Denver Longstreath wants to work on-call FAC for me, says Blister's going to be on R and R. What do you think about it?'' I stood and walked over to the wall map.

The colonel shifted his position toward me, stayed seated. ''He's a good field soldier. In fact, according to Colonel Sims at C and C Central, Denver's one of the best in the business. But right now, he's a loose cannon. Longstreath lost his entire team a few weeks ago, got cut up pretty bad himself. They wanted to send him back to the States, but he convinced somebody somewhere that he'd heal just as fast here in 'Nam. So, they assigned him to us as an AST. You probably already know he's asked me about being your FAC.'' He stood and walked over to my side, glancing at me warily. ''You might just need a loose cannon out there.'' He looked at the map, then back at me, and winked.

I couldn't help grinning. The colonel had just endorsed Denver, with a disclaimer attached.

''Roger, sir. Let's let him do his thing. But, like I told him, only if the defecation is already in the cooling apparatus.''

He laughed. ''Since I posted that new dialogue notice, the whole damn camp's been picking up on it, you included. We're starting to sound like a gang of religious perverts around here. I sent a copy of that notice to the good Senator Shortel, but he hasn't said thank you yet. Fornicate the anus if he can't take a joke!''

The colonel's disposition had returned to normal. My performance had been successful. It was the first time I'd ever lied to him and I didn't like the feeling. But this was a matter of priorities. Baldy was at the top of my list.

Ivan Kahn took a final draw on his cigarette and

snuffed it into a butt can. He put his beret on, looking at me. "Brett, I'll see you in the morning at the briefing. You got anything else you need to run by me now?"

He immediately understood my change in expression, answering before I spoke. "I'm still pushing on Will's decoration. Nothing yet."

Smiling, he extended his hand. His strong calloused grip conveyed confidence. Releasing my hand, he grinned and added, "You know, if you just happen to run across some typical, average-height, khaki-clad bastard out there, it really wouldn't put any holes in my parachute if you fired a few rounds into him for Will. Call it an eye for an eye."

The colonel's grin and voice dropped back to dead serious. "Brett, I'm fighting the bureaucrats in Saigon, trying to get Will's award approved. So far, they're not budging. But, if you bring me a prisoner, a bone to throw at their feet, it just might do the trick . . . for Will." He winked without smiling. "Good night."

I watched him walk down the hall, then closed the door and sat down. The stale haze of his cigarette smoke lingered, surrounding me with his presence. I had just lied to a man who had never let me down, a man I respected and depended on.

Colonel Ivan Kahn was doing everything he could to get Will's Medal of Honor approved. He needed this prisoner, this "bone."

Now it became clear to me that slaying Baldy, and the acquisition of a prisoner, were of equal importance for Will.

Chapter 27

The whine of our chopper's engine pierced the cool afternoon wind, raising a sandy cloud over CCN. All the preparation, training, briefings, and bullshit were over—it was time to go to work.

Arnold Binkowshi's faded green scarf danced in the rotor downdraft as we rose from the sandy mouth of the launchpad into a cloud-patched sky. We watched Trung-uy run, following the shadow of our chopper. He barked helplessly, trying to leap the chain-link gate as we passed over the camp entrance. Finally, he sat and watched us rise westward and away.

Ski leaned forward, looking around Tuong, seated between us, and gave me a confident, brow-furrowed smile, and a thumbs-up. Painted streaks of green-and-black camouflage contoured his face. I returned the thumbs-up, and sent the same silent signal to Hector Gomez, seated beside his M-60. Hector patted the brightly linked snake of machine-gun rounds draped over his torso. A second later, he raised both fists and flipped two thumbs-up.

There was something different about Hector today. I studied him more closely.

As our chopper lofted full-speed over Da Nang, I yelled above the noisy rotor draft, "Hector! What the hell happened to your mustache?" I pointed to my upper lip.

He grinned and shouted back, "I shaved it, man! I'm headed home in a few days. I don't want to put any runs in my girlfriend's panty hose."

My laughter was muted by the rotor blast, but Hector saw me and returned his wide ivory smile. He had remembered my joke.

I nudged Ski's shoulder and shouted while pointing toward Hector, "That's Hector Gomez! He's one of the best door gunners in the business! Hector, this is Arnold Binkowski."

Ski smiled and shouted emphatically, "Call me Ski."

Hector grinned and quietly acknowledged Ski with a circled forefinger-and-thumb okay sign.

We had climbed to our cruising altitude now, three thousand feet. I looked forward and saw the drab silhouette of our escort Cobra gunships dotting the distant sky. This time, if all went well on insert, we wouldn't need them. My plan was to get into the target as quietly as possible. I had instructed the Cobras to stay well away from us when we went in, in order to keep fanfare to a minimum. The pilots assured me they would stay several minutes off-target, close enough to give us quick reaction time if we were hit and suddenly needed them.

I studied the distant northwest horizon. It was clear. My hope was that the Air Force weather report was right this time. The sooner we had rain cloaking us, the better. Denver had not only gotten us tanker goggles as he'd promised, he also managed to scrounge us a rain jacket a piece. The jackets wouldn't keep our asses dry, but they would make movement through the bush much easier than ponchos. Moving through the jungle wearing a poncho was like trying to get through a crowded elevator with an open umbrella.

A voice shouted, "Hey, Yancy. You like jalapeños?" Hector leaned toward me with an outstretched hand holding a small jar of jalapeño peppers.

I took the jar as he spoke again. "These are for you, man. I thought of you when I started cleaning out my wall locker. I figured they might go good with long-range patrol rations. Be careful, those are three-alarm peppers, man."

I tucked the jar into a side pocket of my rucksack. It had been months since I'd eaten a jalapeño. "Thanks, Hector. I'll have a couple tonight with my gourmet rice and fish heads."

"Enjoy, Yancy."

Tuong watched us. He was already familiar with the hot peppers. He like them about as much as I liked sea snake. It was Ski who asked the question this time. "Brett, what was that he gave you?"

"Texas hot peppers. They're great."

"What did he mean by three-alarm?"

"Three-alarm means they're very mild. I'll let you try one tonight." I grinned.

Ski cast a skeptical smile. "How did Hector know you like peppers?"

"He's from El Paso. Jalapeños are damn near the national fruit of Texas. Kinda like baked beans are to Boston."

I leaned back out of the lapping draft, against a large green pile of coiled ropes stationed in the center of the troop cabin. Hector had everything pre-rigged for Stabo, if we suddenly had to use it to get out. I glanced at him, leaning against his machine gun. His dark, vigilant eyes studied the terrain below as we approached the Laotian border. I looked around at the team. Nobody was sleeping this trip. Everyone was alert.

"Five minutes out, Yancy!"

"Roger!" I shouted back to Hector, pulling my thirty-round magazine out. I held it above my head and yelled, "Lock and load!" I thrust the metal case into the magazine well of my rifle, hit the bolt release, and flipped my selector switch to full-automatic. Five metallic snaps resonated through the noisy cabin. The team was loaded.

Our slick began a rapid descent. Warm earthbound air flooded over us. I yanked binoculars from inside my shirt and scanned our approach. I quickly found the pale green speck of our LZ.

Handing the field glasses to Ski, I pointed toward the infil area and shouted, "Check the LZ! It's just left of that ridge line." Binkowski pulled the glasses to his eyes and peered forward. I said, "If we get hit on the LZ, we'll move due east toward high ground."

Ski returned the binoculars, nodding seriously.

Two miles out, our slick began a serpentine treetop contour flight to the target. The low-level route would help keep us cloaked from enemy ground observation until the last minute. Leaves and branches rippled just beneath our dangling feet as if we were speeding over a vast green sea.

Hector jerked his M-60 bolt to the rear and swung the muzzle of his weapon forward. "One minute!" he shouted.

I looked up at the sparse puffs of clouds. Where was the fucking rain we were promised?

Our chopper surged forward over the thick edge of dark trees, then suddenly pitched upward, braking to a slow stop. We gently descended into the windblown mouth of the LZ. A swirling haze of leaves, dust, and grass clouded my vision. I strained to scan the tree line for khaki, rifle muzzles, any movement. Nothing.

The silence of Hector's M-60 told me he hadn't spotted anything either. I glanced at him, gripped my CAR-15 against my chest, and thrust my free arm forward. The chopper hovered inches above the ground. I leapt outward through the downdraft and sprinted toward the near edge of the line of trees. The team followed.

Upon reaching the trees, I knelt and peered with darting eyes into the dark tangle of jungle. The windy thudding noise of our slick quickly ascended, leaving us surrounded in silence.

Ski huddled near me while Rham and Lok moved cautiously, deeper into the cavelike shadows beyond us. Tuong and Phan covered them.

I pulled the radio handset from Ski's shoulder strap and whispered into the mike, "Raven, this is Texas. Over."

"Roger, Texas. This is Raven."

"All clear on infil. We're moving in. Over."

"Roger, Texas. We're going to stay in commo range in case you guys get in a bind. If we don't hear from you in fifteen minutes, we'll head home. Over."

"Roger. Copy, Raven. Thanks. Texas out."

I returned the handset to Ski, then lifted my arm and took a wrist-compass reading.

Tuong relayed a silent okay signal from Rham, indicating it was clear for us to move deeper into the bush.

"Brett, I gotta shit." Ski's whisper was emphatic, almost pleading.

I glared at him. "Damn it, Arnold, this isn't a roadside rest area. Shit later. Move out."

I glanced quickly back at the clouding sky, then motioned for Rham to lead us north. One by one, at close intervals, we slipped into the dark tangled labyrinth of Hotel-5.

We had lucked out. We got in without making contact. But Chuck knew we were here. The chopper had alerted him to that. He just didn't know where we were or in what direction we were headed.

A hundred yards later, Rham halted the team. I crept forward to his side and peered beyond the thick vegetation. We had intersected a small path winding through the thicket in a northwesterly direction. I sent Rham to check it for tracks.

Moments later he returned, pointing toward the trail. "*Beaucoup* bata-boo tracks," he said softly.

Chuck had been here, and recently. Rham estimated the tracks were less than a day old. I decided to wait and watch the trail for a while before crossing it. I was tempted to use the path because it headed in the exact direction we needed to go, which was toward the NVA headquarters area. But it was too soon to get bold.

I dispersed the team along the trail, making sure everyone was well concealed, then crawled back to Binkowski. "Okay, Ski. Move back into the thicket and shit, but make it quick."

He gulped before speaking. "I can't. . . . I mean, I already did."

I looked at his somber eyes, then involuntarily glanced at his crotch. "Where? Where did you shit?"

His voice quivered. "I . . . I shit my pants."

"Fuck! Well . . . well, move back there and clean up, but make sure you bury it good." I turned to crawl away, then looked back at him. "And don't shit your pants again, damn it!"

I crept back to a concealed position near Rham, pulled the target map from my pocket, and located our position. I drew an abstract northerly line on the map along the eastern edge of the LZ to indicate the new trail location. Studying the map, I noticed that the general direction of the uncharted trail could possibly intersect a trail leading to the NVA battalion area. I decided our best bet right now was to stay off the path we'd discovered and parallel it northward. Movement would be slow and arduous in the thicket, but as long as we stayed concealed and quiet, we could see any NVA using the trail.

I tucked the map away and looked back toward Ski. He had returned to his position.

Easing to Rham's side, I whispered instructions for him to lead us along a route near the path, making sure he stayed three to four meters away from the winding course at all times.

Rham's dark eyes widened. He grinned like a child who had just been told a secret. He raised into a crouched stance and moved stealthily into point position. The little people always seemed less tense in danger situations. Perhaps it was because they had grown up in the jungle and were more at home there. I sometimes felt like this fucking war was a game to them. At times, I envied their childlike attitude under stress.

An hour later, Rham halted the team. We hadn't covered much ground, maybe three hundred meters. The tangled vines, limbs, and blades of grass made every step a struggle.

As I crept forward to Rham, I could feel sweat saturating my collar. He pointed at the trail and drew my attention to his wrist compass. The trail had turned due east, away from the direction we needed to go. Crawling, I edged nearer to the path for a closer look. I dug my fingers down through the leafy surface and gathered a handful of dirt. The dark soil was damp but loose. It appeared no rain had fallen in the area for some time.

I gazed down the dark tree-shrouded tunnel. I needed to know how far the trail continued east. Did it hook north again toward the NVA headquarters? The thick overgrowth cloaked the distance in darkness. I signaled for Rham to move forward and cover me while I reconnoitered the path.

Staying crouched, I stepped slowly onto the trail and moved eastward down the dim tube. The only sound breaking the silence of my easy steps was the occasional rustle of birds high in the trees.

I'd never seen a trail this straight for so long a distance. It would be a perfect ambush location, I thought.

Fifty meters into the path, I peered forward and saw what looked like a trail junction. A few careful steps closer revealed a *T* junction leading north and south from my pathway.

I began stepping carefully backward along the cavernous path, keeping my tracks oriented forward. I'd learned what I needed to know. The trail was a well-traveled artery leading to the headquarters complex.

Upon reaching Rham's position, I eased back into the thicket and made a *T* sign with my hands, then motioned for him to lead out, paralleling the trail again.

As we turned to creep back to the team, a tossed pebble struck my chest. My eyes found Tuong waving me toward him. He quickly held a cupped hand to his ear, then pointed south. I turned to listen for a moment, but heard nothing.

I edged quietly to his side and whispered, "What you hear, Babysan?"

Tuong's usually confident face was frowning. He gazed intently southward. A second before he answered, I heard it: the hideous, distant yelping of dogs. They had our scent. I reasoned it was Binkowski's shit they'd picked up on, and now they were firmly locked in on us. The ominous barking grew closer.

I turned to the hunkered wide-eyed figure of Rham beside me. Time was critical. We had to use the trail to put some distance between us and the trackers fast. "Rham, go trail. Turn north one hundred meters." I slapped his shoulder. "Go fast!"

Rham turned and motioned the team onto the trail. Having just walked a portion of the trail, I felt we didn't have to be too concerned about booby traps in the area. I yanked my rucksack off, dug my hand beneath the canvas flap, and pulled a canteen from inside. I stood while drawing my arms back into the pack straps.

Binkowski's heavy breath neared me. "Brett, what the hell is going—"

"Not now, Arnold. You head east with the team. When you reach that trail junction go north a hundred meters, then pull off into the left side of the thicket and wait. I'll be along in a minute."

"What . . . what are you—"

"Move out!"

Ski turned and ran, following the team down the dark throat of the path.

I unscrewed the canteen lid and quickly bent, scattering the pale yellow CS dust along the trail while edging backward. Denver had suggested I bring the extra powder just in case we needed it. Now I hoped it worked.

I pulled my cravat over my nose and mouth as a whiff of the acrid stench seared into my nostrils. My eyes teared and burned. I snorted, trying to blow out the stinging residue. I ignored the pain and continued hastily scattering the powder over a large section of the trail. The jaundice dust rose like a fog around my feet. Coughing, I fumbled to screw the lid tightly back on the canteen and thrust it into my pocket. I turned and ran. My labored breathes drew the CS sting farther into my throat. Finally, I stumbled off the path and leaned against a tree, gagging. I yanked my hat down over my face and belched globs of puke into it. I couldn't leave my vomit tracing our withdrawal.

I spit the sour scraps of puke into my hat, gripped the brim around it, then stumbled toward my team. I could hear the rasping barks of hounds nearing. Soon their prowling hungry noses would dip into the acrid dust.

I halted near the trail junction, waiting, listening.

Suddenly, the jungle trembled with the agonized howls and awful piercing yelps of dogs gone insane. The hideous yelping frenzy mixed with violent growls. Wild human screams tore into the morbid chorus as though the mad animals were attacking their masters.

Gunshots ripped through the air, followed by the dying yelps and fading whines of hounds.

I smiled and leaned into the thicket to pour the puke from my hat. Wiping the residue from inside the hat, I heard the distant violent shouts of men. They seemed to be yelling at me for some reason. My smile broadened. "Fuck 'em if they can't take a joke."

Chapter 28

After rejoining the team, we moved swiftly along the dark corridor. We soon found a suitable well-concealed bivouac position thirty meters in from the path and began setting up our night claymore defense. I posted Lok near the trail to observe and report any signs of NVA movement. As nightfall approached, we hadn't heard from Chuck.

The distant roar of thunder, followed by strong winds stirring the thick tree cover above us, were welcome sounds. The rains were near at last.

I tore the plastic top off a bag of dehydrated rice-and-fish-heads ration and poured water into it. Ski watched me slice pieces of jalapeño into the bag then stir it with my pocketknife.

After opening his ration, he edged near me and whispered, "Brett, can I have one of those peppers? I'm starved."

Withholding an urge to grin, I pulled one from the jar and handed it to him by the stem. The Yards watched warily while Ski sliced part of the pepper into his rice bag, then popped the remainder of the jalapeño into his mouth, pulling the stem from between his teeth like it was a cherry.

Seconds later his eyes flashed. His cheeks began to puff like something was expanding inside his head. He swallowed, then clutched his canteen and poured gulps of water into his mouth. Finally, he withdrew the canteen, gasping heavy breaths.

I cupped a discreet hand over my mouth to hold my laughter in. I could tell Ski wanted to yell out at me, but wouldn't. Instead, he jerked the canteen back to his mouth and began gulping again. The Cowboys were jolting with silent laughter. They knew the water wasn't going to douse the blaze in his mouth. Grinning, I handed him a large cracker from my meal packet and signaled for him to eat it. He accepted the cracker with skeptical eyes, implying he wasn't sure he'd ever trust me again.

The cracker would help extinguish the burning in his mouth; however, it would be a while before the fire was out. Ski quickly began picking the pieces of pepper from his ration while he chewed the cracker. He tossed the bits aside with a jerk of his hand, like he was pulling cactus needles from a wound.

Violent winds swarmed into the jungle. Within moments, heavy drops of rain penetrated the overgrowth. We hurriedly donned our rain jackets and drew ponchos hoodlike over our heads.

By 1930 hours, RT Texas was cloaked in the chill of monsoon darkness, cracking thunder, and a cold pelting downpour. I directed the team to move into our standard wagon-wheel sleep formation, then left to bring Lok in from his vigil on the trail.

I had trouble finding Lok in the deluge-tangled blackness. Blue flashes of lighting finally illuminated his huddled silhouette. He crouched beneath his poncho, peering faithfully toward the trail. I crept near him and whispered through the howling wind and rain, "Lok box."

The huddled figure turned slowly. I gripped the trigger of my rifle, aiming the muzzle directly at the covered, turning figure. *Lok box* was a personal challenge to him in order to be certain the obscured figure wasn't an enemy decoy. Each team member had a different challenge and reply.

"Lok box open," he whispered back to me.

I relaxed my rifle grip and crawled to his side. "You see Chuck?"

He brought his face to mine and grinned. "No see Chuckie," he whispered, "No doggie."

"Number one. We go now."

Standing, he took a lengthy piss while I waited. I was glad he hadn't seen any NVA. Evidently the absence of their dogs, combined with the heavy rains, had dulled Chuck's enthusiasm for night hunting.

Returning to the team, I again initiated a challenge and reply. A moment later, Lok and I moved carefully into our position in the human-wheel sleep formation. I took the first one-hour watch and radioed our position to Moonbeam. The lightning made communication difficult, but after repeated blind transmissions, I finally got an acknowledgment from them.

The heavy rains poured through the darkness all night. I was already soaking wet from my excursion to find Lok. Memories of Tracy Gibbs warded off the urge to shiver as I faded into sleep.

Dim first light slithered through the twisted dripping shadows around us. It wasn't the unfurling light that awoke me, it was the silence.

I raised quietly from beneath my poncho and glanced at my watch: 0515. The rain and wind had stopped. We were surrounded, engulfed in the damp cloudy breath of waist-high ground fog. Ten feet across from me, I saw the silhouette of Phan. He was squatting, smiling at me. I ignored his face and turned to listen. Nothing stirred. Only the soft occasional splatter of water dripping from the trees above us broke the eerie silence.

After awakening the remainder of the team, we held a fifteen-minute stand-to vigil, then rose from the fog and moved quietly toward the trail.

We skirted the path north again, staying several meters off the corridor.

An hour later the fog had dissipated. I was about to call a rest break when suddenly two sharp jabs struck my shoulder. Tuong had sent up the signal that something was approaching from the rear.

I quickly relayed the signal to Lok, then dropped into a prone position with my eyes focused toward the trail. The chill of wet earth soaked into me. I tried to edge forward to get a better view of the path, but my rucksack caught a low vine, locking me into place. I struggled to break away from the vine but soon decided the noise I was making wasn't worth getting a closer view. If it was NVA coming up the trail, I knew they'd have their ears well tuned for sound. I lay still. The strong adrenal beat of my heart seemed to penetrate the dead silence.

A moment later, I saw the dull ominous profile of a pith-helmeted figure easing through the shadows toward me. Now his khaki torso came into view. His finger was poised over the rifle trigger. The man's cautious steps were accented by the searching concentrated movement of his head, first studying the trail for tracks, then glancing left and right into the bush, looking, smelling, listening, for any looming hint of our presence. As the point man moved into my sights, I studied the outline of hair below his helmet. This one wasn't Baldy.

He stopped abruptly, whiffing the air, then slowly gazed into the thicket toward me.

Damn it! I had concentrated on him too long. He sensed me. Experience had taught me better than to look at the enemy too long. Something in a person's psychic perception alerted them to it.

Now he was on to me. I tensed my trigger finger while his probing eyes peered into my camouflaged face. If his rifle barrel moved even an inch toward me, I'd have to cut him down. I could feel beads of sweat gathering, straining to drip from my forehead. In the eternity of a second, I wondered if my blue eyes would give me away. I narrowed my vision to a slitted squint.

Finally, his glaring face turned away to look back down the path at another soldier approaching him. *"Tat-ca-sach,"* he said to the approaching man.

I relaxed my grip and breathed softly while he stepped away from me and onward down the path. Within moments, the catlike steps of disciplined jungle fighters were moving along the trail. I counted eleven hard-faced NVA. The absence of backpacks told me they were a local patrol. I scanned each man passing by me. All had close-cropped, thick black hair skirting beneath their helmets. Baldy wasn't with them.

I remained still for several minutes after the last man was out of sight, then edged backward through the wet musty leaves, trying to free myself from the grasping vine. After pulling away from it, I glanced up at the snakelike branch and pondered for a moment. Was it the benevolent hand of fate or just geographical coincidence that had kept me from moving closer? If I had been only inches nearer the path, the NVA bastard would have spotted me. I stood and shrugged. It was simple coincidence combined with the mistake of keeping my eyes fixed on him for too long.

Crouching, I motioned for the team to follow me back deeper into the thicket and away from the trail. A light drizzle veiled the jungle ahead of us.

"There, Sar Brett. You lookie close. You see." Tuong's soft words traveled down his pointing arm as he handed the binoculars to me.

I wiped the lenses with my cravat and raised the field glasses to my eyes. After a moment of straining to see through the drizzle, I made out what he was talking about. Several figures were emerging from a round thatch hut. I hurriedly brushed beaded drops of rain off the plastic covering of my map and noted the location. This was the right place all right. But a damn hut did not make a battalion headquarters, I thought.

The structure was located seventy meters in front of us at the end of a long easterly-oriented path. From our position, the path lead up from the south then hooked due east, directly into the hut. I reasoned the hooch was perhaps a checkpoint entrance for the complex, possibly even a shelter entrance for a tunnel. At this point I didn't know, but I intended to find out.

I tucked the binoculars into my shirt and looked at Tuong. "You go team," I whispered. "Bring here."

I had stationed the team along a section of trail to observe, while Tuong and I tried to locate the NVA headquarters.

Tuong stepped quietly back into the darkness and

away. It would be at least an hour before he returned with the team. I reached for the field glasses to study the hut again. This time the hut was obscured behind the huddled movement of four enemy figures walking single file straight toward me.

I blinked and looked again. Their rifles were at sling arms. Two of the men were carrying a basket suspended between them on a bamboo pole. I eased backward while continuing to keep my binoculars focused on the men. They were clad in what appeared to be American ponchos, but there was no mistaking the pith helmets or the AK-47s. Then I saw what looked like a trace of hairless scalp beneath the last man's helmet.

I quickly wiped the watery residue off the lenses and jerked them back to my eyes. The man walked with a limp. I studied his cold expressionless eyes, then looked at the bare temples around his ears as he moved closer. It was fuckin' Mr. Baldy in person, just fifty meters in front of me.

My wet hands gripped the binoculars harder. I peered toward him, whispering, "Make your peace with Buddha, you heathen glob of spit."

Chapter 29

I tucked the binoculars away, slowly removed my ruck-sack, and stretched into a prone position. Peering through the wet foliage, I watched and listened to the approaching figures. They seemed to be arguing. Every few steps one of them would point to the trail, jabber-ing.

"Ngung-day!" Baldy's voice was curt, authoritative.

The group stopped abruptly and set the basket, along with their rifles, to the side of the trail. They were only fifteen meters in front of me.

Baldy's cold dark eyes looked up the trail in my di-rection, then turned to examine the rear approach. *"De-day!"* he directed.

I raised my head higher, trying to get a better view. Two of the soldiers withdrew small shovels from the basket while another pulled a thick circular object from the same container.

"What the hell are you little bastards doing?" I thought to myself as they began to dig into the center of the trail. Then it hit me: They're planting welcoming mines for us. They know we're in the area. Evidently, this trail is a primary approach to their headquarters complex.

I glanced at their weapons. The AK-47s were well out of their reach. Baldy lit a cigarette and stood watching the men dig a small hole in the center of the trail.

The fact that Baldy had been limping up the trail told me he'd probably sustained a leg injury when he fell through the tree after I'd fired at him. He had hobbled during his escape. The limp also told me it wasn't likely he was working with patrols. NVA patrols moved fast at times, always covering a lot of ground. No, Baldy was working stay-behind duty and this might be the only fucking chance I was going to have at him.

I glanced at my watch: 0933 hours. It would be at least another half hour before Tuong returned with the team. There was no time to wait for them.

I looked back at the work crew. Baldy had laid his rifle aside and was taking a piss. The others carefully placed the mine into the hole and began covering it.

Reaching into my rucksack, I withdrew my long knife from its sheath and gently slid it underneath the backside of my fatigue pants. A chill ran through me when the cold steel nestled against my buttocks.

Slowly, I raised into a crouched stance. My searching eyes moved over the huddled kneeling figures, then back to Baldy. He hadn't picked up his rifle. Instead, he stood chiding over the others, as if directing them to camouflage the mined area.

I tensed, gripped my CAR-15, and peered through the mist with caution, first beyond the four men to make sure no one else was approaching, then to my right to ensure the trail was clear.

My plan was to kill two of the workers and take the third prisoner. I'd have to knock him out and recover him after I jammed the steel into Baldy's throat. I knew the shots from my rifle would alert the whole NVA nation to my presence, so there wouldn't be any time to fuck around.

I readied my rifle. Adrenaline began to pump as I stepped cautiously out of the bush. Suddenly, just as I stepped onto the trail, a vine dropped across my face. No! It was a deadly temple viper! I quickly bent to dip beneath the thick green serpent, knowing I was now fully exposed to the enemy. The viper's head instantly drew into strike position. In the flicker of a second I saw its glaring elliptical pupils aimed right at my neck. I jerked my muzzle upward, triggering a burst of fire into the snake. Warm blood spurted against my face as I spun toward the three workers now scrambling to their weapons. I fired directly into two of them, sparing the third for my prisoner.

My fire pelted across their backs like jolts of electricity biting into them. Screams exploded from their twisting death spasms. The third man grasped his rifle and swung the black barrel toward me, spewing full-automatic lead. I triggered a burst into him. My fire ripped across his chest, heaving him back atop the others.

I hurried forward through the cloud of muzzle smoke, looking at the bloody heap of bodies, then searching madly to find Baldy. Fuck! The bastard had run. But he'd stayed off the trail. He knew he'd be a perfect target if he ran back toward the hut. My ears caught the near sounds of branches cracking, leaves shuffling, beyond me.

I moved quickly, nearer the sound. Through the mist, I saw the silhouette of Baldy's poncho-draped figure struggling to pull free from a tangled snarl of vines and limbs. His now helmetless shiny head glowed like a beacon in the misty shadows.

My eyes glanced to see his AK-47 where he'd left it. In his panic, he'd thought of only escape and survival. I lowered my rifle to rest on the sling and reached behind my back to grasp the contoured bone handle of my knife. I walked forward, staring, smiling at the bastard rat, caught in the snare of his own jungle habitat.

Suddenly, he jerked one arm free from the tangled web and swung his head toward me. His dark eyes flashed panic. He struggled frantically to pull his other arm free while groping at his pistol holster.

I sprinted forward and seized his free arm, twisting it with all my strength up behind his back. My knife arched around his neck, prodding the point of my blade beneath his quivering chin.

The foul stench of his hot breath rolled over my face, crying, "No kill. No kill! *Chieu-hoi, chieu-hoi!*"

"No fuckin' *chieu-hoi*, you scum-suckin' bastard. You fuckin' die. You fuckin' die for Will Washington!"

My raging flow of adrenaline blurred my vision. I blinked, fighting to clear my eyes while still grasping my struggling prey.

Then, suddenly, the words of Ivan Kahn came through. "I'm fighting the bulldog bureaucrats in Saigon to try and get this award approved. Bring me a bone to throw at their feet, for Will."

I felt Baldy's left arm grasping my knife hand, fighting to pull it away from his jugular. I clinched my grip on his other arm with all my strength and yanked it farther up his backside.

His grappling hand dropped away from my wrist as I felt his right arm crack.

"Aheeeee!" His agonized scream quickly faded into quivering whimpers and moans.

Turning the blade away from his neck, I rammed the bone-crushing hilt of my knife hard into his yelping face, then dropped him to the matted ground at my feet. Straddling his wreathing, gasping body, I quickly tucked the knife into my belt, then reached and flung his pistol aside.

I glared down into his terrified eyes, shouting through my heavy breaths, "Okay, you glob of spit, you're going with me. I'm trading your stinking ass for a Medal of Honor."

Clutching at his broken arm, he squirmed into a fetal position. *"Chieu-hoi, chieu-hoi,"* he jabbered.

"Fuck a bunch of *chieu-hoi*," I shouted while yanking a Syrette of morphine from my first-aid pouch. I broke the plastic cover off with my teeth, then thrust the needle into his neck, and squeezed the Syrette.

He yelped as I withdrew the needle. I slapped him hard across the face. "Shut the fuck up."

I quickly rigged a cravat sling over his broken arm and tied a loop of rope tightly around his neck to lead him with. Using the rope, I jerked him to his feet and began dragging him toward the trail.

I approached the trail cautiously, scanning the area for signs of enemy. None. Pulling Baldy onto the path, he almost stumbled over the sprawled pile of bodies and damn near stepped on the planted mine. The morphine was numbing his senses.

Returning to my rucksack, I grabbed a strap and heaved it up on one shoulder, scarcely stopping. I trudged onward in the direction where I'd left the team tugging my starry-eyed prisoner along behind me.

Fifteen minutes into the thicket, he collapsed.

"Shit!" I said, dropping to my knees beside him. I yanked a canteen from my web gear, poured a good dose of water over his head, then drank, catching my breath between gulps.

My ears alerted for sounds of pursuit. None. I looked back at Baldy, then emptied the rest of my canteen over his head.

He winced and began muttering with his eyes closed, as if praying. *"Chieu-hoi, chieu-hoi."*

I spit at him. "Fuck you and *chieu-hoi*. You didn't surrender, you heathen puke. I fuckin' took you, and if I didn't need you, I'd kill your sorry ass. Now shut the fuck up."

I pulled my knife and began cutting the poncho away from his body. His dazed eyes flashed at me while I tore away the shredded pieces and tossed them aside.

"There," I said, tearing away the last piece, "now it'll be a little easier dragging your ass through the bush. Get up!"

Standing, I yanked on the leash around his neck and pulled him up to his feet. I wasn't sure how much English he understood, but I was about to make damn sure he understood me in any language. I wasn't going to kill him unless he tried to escape, he was too valuable. But I didn't want him knowing that.

I pulled his grimacing face up to mine, and prodded the tip of my long knife under his chin. "You're going with me, puke, and if you even scratch your balls wrong, I'll jam this steel so far into your gut, my bloody fist'll come out the other side. *Biet?"*

"Biet . . . biet," he muttered while keeping his eyes focused nervously down on my knife hand.

A half hour later, it started to rain heavily again. I still hadn't located the team, even though I knew I was in the area where I'd left them. I skirted the trail. The dense jungle was now cloaked in wet shadows, making visibility poor.

I was about to move back into the bush when a muffled voice called out a challenge to me: "Brett foget."

I smiled. The omission of an *r* in the second word told me it was the voice of my favorite Yankee. I spoke back quietly. "Brett forget nothing."

A hurried rustling noise near my feet brought my eyes down toward the black ground. Arnold Binkowski rose up from beneath the dark foliage, like a giant tearing out of a grave. In the murk, I'd almost stepped on him.

Rain beaded over his smiling camouflaged face. His excited voice shivered. "Man, am I glad to see you. There's . . . there's been all kinds of shit running up and down this fucking trail. We heard gunshots back—" Suddenly, his eyes caught the hunched figure of Baldy standing behind me. Ski jumped back, mumbling, "What the hell . . . who's . . . ?"

I ignored his stupefied gaze. "Where's the team?"

His eyes stayed fixed on Baldy as he pointed blindly into the shadows. "Back there, hidden along the trail."

Turning, I looked at my prisoner. His head was bowed as though he were trying to sleep standing up. I jerked on the leash, snapping him from his stupor. His head moved upward. Gaping, he stared wide-eyed at Ski.

Ski turned to me with a silent questioning expression.

I focused a hard frown into Binkowski's eyes. Leaning closer to his face, I whispered, "This is the bastard that killed William Washington. I'm taking him back with us."

Ski's eyes squinted in disbelief. "But how did you—"

"No questions. Listen. If anything happens from here on in, anything, and it looks like this son of a bitch is going to escape, kill him! Don't hesitate. Kill him. I need this bastard, but if I lose him, I lose everything. I'll be handling him most of the time, so you shouldn't have to worry about it. Just remember what I'm telling you. Understand?"

"Roger, Brett. Understand."

"Also, it's vital that the Cowboys don't know this is Will's assassin. If they find out, they'll cut him to pieces no matter what we say or do. Do you understand that?"

"Roger, Brett. One question?"

"Shoot."

Ski's eyes glanced toward Baldy, then back to me. "Does this mean we're not going to get to blow our claymore ambush?"

I couldn't believe my ears. I tilted my face up into the cold rain. The wet chill cooled my anguish and reminded me of what I'd told him during his training: "The only stupid question is an unasked one."

I looked back at Ski. "Arnold, this is our prisoner"—I held up the rope leash leading to Baldy's neck—"so we don't need to ambush anybody now. Our next miracle is to try and get the fuck outa here alive. Where's the radio?"

"Right here." He reached into the shadows and pulled his ruck up and onto his shoulder.

"Follow me," I said, yanking on the leash while moving farther back into the thicket.

An hour later, after repeated frustrating efforts, I finally contacted Sunburst. I told them our situation and requested immediate exfiltration at our alternate LZ.

Even though the storm was beginning to subside,

Sunburst couldn't confirm my exfil request until they checked with Da Nang Air Base. I moved the team into a tight well-concealed defense position and waited.

I monitored the radio while the team ate rice and rainwater. After checking our position on the map, I estimated we were roughly three hundred meters from the LZ, about an hour of movement time. I knew it would take Hector and company better than an hour to get there, so I decided to wait until we got confirmation on exfil before we headed in that direction. There was no reason to go to the ballpark if the game was going to be rained out.

So far, Baldy had been quiet and cooperative. But I could tell the morphine was wearing off by the new alertness in his eyes. He studied us, carefully observing our moves. I noticed his eyes occasionally glance upward to the trees and move slowly from side to side as though analyzing the sounds. Strangely, and even though the morphine was wearing off, he registered no pain in his expression. I knew his arm had to be hurting. I figured it was his hardened Oriental discipline, or perhaps his displaced pride, that wouldn't let him demonstrate his pain. Whatever it was, I didn't like his new alertness. It was time to put him back on the dark side of the moon.

I pulled out a fresh Syrette of morphine and handed it to Ski, seated on the left side of the prisoner. Pulling Baldy's khaki collar back abruptly, I said, "Hit him here, Ski." I nodded toward the neck.

Baldy's eyes got big while he watched Ski remove the needle cover. I'd already given Ski some training in administering morphine, but up until now, his only victim had been a sandbag.

Baldy gulped, resolving himself to the forthcoming sting.

Ski grimaced, thrust the needle deep into Baldy's neck, and squeezed the Syrette slowly. He yanked it away, glancing at me as if looking for my approval of his first live fire application.

I nodded to Ski, smiled, then looked at Baldy. "Have a nice trip, ugly."

A cracking voice sounding in the handset drew my attention to the radio. "Texas, this is Sunburst. Over." The voice was urgent.

"This is Texas. Over."

"Roger, Texas. We've got a few holes in this cloud cover, so we're going to give this exfil a shot. Confirm exfil at lima zulu Bumfuk at 1430 hours. I say again: lima zulu Bumfuk at 1430 hours. Do you copy? Over."

"Roger, Sunburst. Bumfuk at 1430 hours. Tell Raven to bring his guns on this one. It's gonna be hot. Over."

I'd let Ski assign code names to our LZs. Suddenly, I was wishing I'd done it. There was something about the name, Bumfuk, that just didn't appeal to me.

The voice replied, "Roger guns, Texas. It wouldn't be no fun any other way, buddy. Give me a call if you guys have a flat on the way to the station. Over."

"Roger Sunburst. Negative further. Texas out."

I motioned for the team to get ready to move out while giving Rham the new compass azimuth. I told him to keep the pace slow and quiet. It bothered me that we hadn't heard from Chuck.

I knew they had to be at a maximum alert for us. Ski's info about high-volume movement of the trail had verified that. I didn't know if they'd discovered Baldy missing, but if they had, they were now well aware this was a snatch mission. If they started putting two and two together and coming up with anything resembling four, they would have our escape LZ covered. We were going to have to approach it and check it thoroughly before I could bring a chopper in.

After thirty-five minutes of slow movement through the bush, the rain stopped, and with its absence our noise cloak lifted. I became aware of the sound of our steps pressing into the foliage, the rustling noise of my wet legs against the leaves, and the swishing of branches springing back into place. Even the droplets of water falling from the canopy seemed to reverberate as they splattered against the shoulders of my rain parka.

Then I heard it. A single, muffled rifle shot cracked in the distance. I froze in place. Baldy bumped noisily into my back.

Turning, I quickly pulled him down into a kneeling position beside me and looked forward to Lok. Lok's pointing hand confirmed my reading. The shot had come from our left side, approximately forty meters off.

I listened. Soon, two more shots echoed from behind us. The sounds were closer. The bastards were on to us now. They were trying to channelize us, move us to the right, away from the rifle fire. If we moved to the right, we'd be going exactly where they wanted us to.

The NVA pursuit tactic of channelizing a team was clever. I'd been duped once before. By using prepositioned personnel to fire shots, they reasoned we would move in the opposite direction, allowing them to eventually herd us into an ambush zone.

They now knew our general position and had baited their hook. What they didn't know was, Texas wasn't going to bite.

I pulled a new cravat from my pocket and tied a gag

tightly around Baldy's mouth. There was no sense in taking any chances on him crying out, now that he knew his little-prick cronies were in the area.

I sent up the signal for Rham to take us obliquely left. I put Baldy in front of me and nudged him along with the muzzle of my rifle.

Fifteen minutes passed before we heard another shot. This time it came from the right, but more distant. I halted the team near a huge fallen teak tree and motioned for everyone to take cover against it. I estimated we were only ten minutes from the LZ Bumfuk. To move any closer could give away our destination. I wanted to keep Chuck scratching his head as long as possible.

I decided to send Ski and Phan forward to recon the LZ while the rest of us moved right to keep the enemy from second-guessing our intended direction.

Before moving out, Ski crept back to my side. His whisper was emphatic. "Brett, I gotta ask—"

"Ask, Arnold. What?"

"Well, who's in charge of this LZ recon, me or Phan? I mean contact. What if—?"

I exhaled an exasperated breath, trying to keep my voice soft. "Damn it, Arnold, don't start what-iffing me. You're in charge. If you make contact blow the bastards away and hold your ground till we get there. You've got the radio, but don't bring the chopper in till we're there." I grinned, tapping his shoulder. "Just don't shit your pants, partner. You'll do fine. Now go."

Ski turned to crawl away, then looked back. "Roger."

I leaned back against the tree, pulled a canteen out, and began drinking.

A muffled sound came from the slumped figure beside me. I looked down into the pleading eyes staring at my canteen. I pulled his gag down below his chin and poured water into his gulping mouth.

As I tucked my canteen away, a stone struck my hand. I looked up and saw Lok pointing into the shadows beyond the tree. I pushed Baldy down against the bottom edge of the timber and raised slowly upward.

Termites scurried along the top edge of the bark as if evacuating the area. I peered over the hurried procession and into the shadows. Forty meters ahead, I saw sunlight stabbing through a break in the canopy like a floodlight glaring into a clearing. My eyes caught a glimpse of movement.

I pulled my binoculars out and focused toward the light. It was Chuck and gang. My pulse quickened when I spied the ominous horizontal silhouette of a B-40 rocket being carried by a crouched figure like a long log tucked under his arm. I counted eight men. I was certain I hadn't seen them all.

I turned to the team hunkered along the length of the tree and signaled for them to get ready to move out.

Standing, I started to pull Baldy up to his feet, then heard hurried movement coming toward us. I knelt, centering my rifle in the direction of the noise. It was Binkowski crawling to me.

"Brett, we couldn't get far." His voice flushed through heavy breaths. "We got about ten meters and saw *beaucoup* fuckin' NVA. They're just ahead over there. I think we're surrounded, partner!"

I yanked my ruck off and pulled the flap open. "We're not surrounded, Ski," I whispered while pulling a claymore from the ruck. "If they hit us it'll be from there." I jerked my head backward to indicate the direction while hurriedly unraveling the detonation wire. I unfolded the anchor legs of the mine, then stood, leaning over the girth of the tree, and jammed the mine into the soft earth.

I glanced back at Ski while quickly feeding the det wire back to my generator. "Move to the far end of the tree and do the same thing now. Move!"

Suddenly, my eyes caught flickers of muzzle flashes sparkling through the darkness, just a split second before I heard the riveting chorus of enemy fire.

I slammed downward, frantically pulling a grenade from my web gear. Yanking the pin free, I hurled the grenade back over my head and grabbed my rifle.

The explosion from my grenade boomed like a clash of thunder through the jungle, signaling us to raise and return fire into the face of the assault. Together our rifle barrels swung over the top edge of the tree, spewing heavy fire back into the enemy.

"Reload!" I shouted, dropping swiftly downward. My hurried fingers ejected my magazine then clutched another and jammed it into the empty well.

I pivoted upward again and poured rapid-fire bursts into the enemy's dark mouth. Stinging bark fragments bit into my face as the unrelenting NVA lead riddled wildly over the teak tree in front of me. My eyes caught the launch flash of a B-40 rocket. A thunderous, savage explosion ripped into the teak, hurling me powerfully backward. I struggled, clawing blindly into mud, trying to reach the generator arm of my claymore. The charred, raping stink of agony jabbed into my senses, flooding, numbing me . . . into darkness.

Chapter 30

The stench of burning wood and rifle smoke swirled above me like a macabre carousel revolving with the growl of automatic weapons fire. The rain had stopped. Blood cloaked my head.

I moved a hand over my face and torso, feeling through the blood for holes. None.

"Blow your claymores now!" I shouted. I groped blindly through the mud, trying to find my claymore generator.

Grasping it, I seized the arm. The earth trembled from the jarring explosion. The sounds of other claymores exploded through the crimson darkness.

Our mines silenced the NVA fire, but I knew it wouldn't be for long. I tried to get up but seemed nailed to the ground. Pain scraped my torso like a mass of animal claws raking over me.

"Break contact! Break contact!" I yelled.

I heard a tremulous voice at my side. "You're hit, partner! Oh, shit! You're hit!"

"Baldy. Where's—?"

"I got him. Don't worry, Brett. I got him. He tried to escape but I got—"

"Good . . . good," I muttered. "Get us to Bumfuk, Will. Get us to Bumfuk fast."

Orders shouted. "Lok, Tuong *la dai*. Take prisoner! Rham, Phan, Move out to LZ. Go! Go!"

Will's voice lowered. "I'm going to have to carry you, Brett. There's no time to treat your—"

"No sweat, Will. Get the fuckin' show on the road."

Strong arms lifted me. Heavy breaths whispered, "Okay, buddy, if you start hurting tell me."

"Let's move."

Distant weapons fire and grenade explosions reso- nated through the jungle as I bounced in darkness draped over my partner's shoulders. I felt the handle of my knife prod my right side. No feeling in my left side—eyes seeing only vague shadows. I drifted in and out of consciousness, feeling branches and vines drag across my back. A chill numbed me—lured me into sleep.

I felt myself being laid on wet leaves. Hard slaps stung my face. "Godammit, Brett, don't go to sleep!"

"That's . . . that's what I told . . . told you. Don't go to sleep. Remember, buddy? Don't let shock get you, Will. Where are we, partner? Are we home?"

Will's words hurried. "We're at Bumfuk. I just got commo with Denver. He's working FAC for us, bring- ing in tac-air. Hang on, Brett. I'm gonna hit you with some morphine."

"Sar Brett. Sar Brett. We got *beaucoup* Chuckie come. I think maybe nee cla-mo!"

Tuong's urgent voice stirred me. He didn't ask for anything unless it was critical. I reached up, moving my fingers over the blurry outline of a face. "Where's Will, Tuong? Where's Will?"

"Will no here, Sar Brett. Skee here."

"Ski here?" I muttered.

I dug through my cloudy mind and tried to remember how many claymores we had left. One—the CS.

In the same seconds I heard Arnold Binkowski. "Brett, we only got one claymore. The one Denver took apart and taped the CS powder to."

"That'll do it, Ski. Get out there and plant that claymore facing the movement. . . ." I felt a strong breeze lapping at my collar. "And, Ski, make sure you place it facing downwind. We don't need that shit blowing back in our faces. Tuong, you and the team cover Ski. Go!"

"Rogee, sar Brett."

"Didi mau."

I felt the sting of a needle bite into my shoulder. "Brett, it'll have to wait. I gotta get some bandages on you. Your bleeding like hell—"

I grabbed at his shirt and jerked him down to my face. "Goddammit, I'll tell you when I need help. Now, you do what the fuck I say, Yankee! Move out!"

A strong hand gently pulled my clinched fist away from the shirt. His voice cracked. "All right, all right. We'll do it your way. Just don't fuckin' die while I'm gone or . . . or, I'm gonna be pissed off. You remember that, Yancy!"

A rustle of noise through the grass, then I heard the drone of mosquitoes swarming over me. I felt the morphine creeping through me—dulling me.

"Fuck mosquitoes," I mumbled. "Suck it up, you thirsty whores."

Slowly, I drifted to thoughts of Tracy lying at my side. Soft, fragrant hair nestled against my shoulder. A warm hand caressed my chest with gentle motions, massaging me. I could hear calliope music in the distance as her voice comforted me. "I love you, Brett. I'll love you forever, and ever, and . . ."

Will's voice joined in soft chorus with Tracy's. "We don't likely have no real choices about how we die. If we're lucky, we may just have a little choice about the cause we die for. If the cause is noble, and your life is right with God, then he's got a slot waitin' for you in his army."

I struggled to raise up, but could barely move. My eyes searched through blurred shadows. "Oh, Will! I thought you were gone, buddy. I've missed you, partner. Tuong said you weren't here. I guess he didn't see you. But I knew you were here."

Water patted my face and eyes. It wasn't rain. The wetness was laced with words that seemed to rise from the bottom of a well. I felt something press against my chest as the voice spoke. "I gotta move you, Brett. Hold this cravat on your chest. Hang on, buddy, you're gonna make it."

I felt myself lifted, carried, bounced, then lowered to the ground again. My fingers touched the abrasive texture of wet elephant grass.

"Baldy . . . we still got Baldy?"

"Roger. He's right here, Brett. I got the claymore in position, but—"

Suddenly, the hideous scream of full-auto AK-47 fire erupted near us. An explosion bellowed in the distance. CAR-15s returned riveting heavy fire. Expended brass rained over me.

Struggling, I pushed my right arm against the ground and strained to sit up. I blinked madly, trying to clear my eyes. Amid the dim ghastly smoke I saw the silhouettes of hunkered figures. Muzzle flashes sparkled

in the darkness. Then I saw a shadowy figure lurch
forward, attacking a man near him.

"Ahhhh!" The scream cried wildly above the weapons fire. Again it screamed. "Ahhhh!"

Through squinted eyes I saw the hairless outline of a
head—Baldy!

Adrenaline exploded through me with the fury of a
cannon blast. I yanked the knife from beneath my belt
and lunged toward the heathen bastard. With raging
strength I rammed the steel into his gut. I twisted the
long blade, driving it deeper into his belly until I felt
the warm greasy flow of blood melt over my fingers.

As he fell away, I released my wet hand from the
knife and raised on my knees, screaming, *"Anh chet!
Anh* fuckin' *chet*! You die, you scum-suckin' chancre
scab. *Anh chet! Anh chet!"*

A thunderous flash of light exploded in a wall of
flames, ripping through the jungle as Will's God swept
his wrathful hand across the jagged horizon. The sweet
gasoline stink of napalm caressed my nostrils. Then, I
saw the dim profile of a plane rise out of the billowing
smoke like an airborne sword withdrawing from its victim's wound.

Suddenly, the violent boom of a claymore detonation
rocked me backward. Falling, I saw Ski's huge figure
run forward into the jaundice cloud of CS smoke. His
rifle spewed full-auto fire as he disappeared into the
haze.

"What the fuck are you doing, Arnold? What the
fuck . . . ?"

Slowly, darkness engulfed me. As the last embers of
my strength faded I wilted forward over Baldy's blood-
soaked corpse. *"Anh chet . . . anh chet,"* I murmured.

Chapter 31

"Sergeant Yancy . . . Sergeant Yancy, can you hear me?" The voice sounded feminine, soft, concerned.

I tried opening my eyes but darkness stayed, as if I were in a cave. My nostrils caught a heavy odor of antiseptic mingled with perfume. A cool breeze floated over me. I could hear the fading sound of a chopper somewhere in the distance.

The soft voice spoke again, this time with a warm hand touching my neck. "I know you're probably drowsy, Sergeant Yancy, but please don't go to sleep. You've just come out of surgery. It's important you stay awake. Also, you have an IV in your right arm, so try not to move it abruptly."

I raised my arm slowly and felt the gauze texture of bandages cloaking my eyes, my head, my entire face. My fingers touched the dry skin of my lips, then my tongue.

"Please don't try to move much right now." The voice was more distinct this time.

"Just take it easy for now, okay? I'm going to slip a thermometer under your tongue now and take—"

264

I pushed the hand away. "Wait . . . wait. Where am I? What the hell's wrong with my eyes?"

She withheld the thermometer, offering words instead. Words spoken like a preacher during an invocation. "You're in the 95th's medevac hospital, Da Nang. You've had some eye injuries, Brett. May I call you Brett?"

I didn't like being stroked. "Look, whoever you are, just tell me what's wrong with my eyes. I don't need any sugar coating, just tell me, damn it!"

The voice remained polite but more stern in tone now. "You mustn't get upset. You're very lucky to be alive. The doctors will be along shortly and answer your questions. As far as who I am, my name is Goodwin, Lieutenant Goodwin. I'm a nurse. Now let me take your temperature please."

Relenting to the thermometer, I retorted, "Yes, sir."

A moment later she removed the small tube from my mouth. "Aren't you going to take my pulse? Isn't that kind of standard procedure?"

"I did take your pulse. You just didn't feel me holding your left wrist. You sustained some spinal injuries, which caused a partial paralysis on your left side. The paralysis should subside within a couple of days."

"That's good," I said, touching my eye bandages. "Now, how about my eyes? I'm a little worried about my tennis game."

The voice smiled. "Yeah, I can see . . . I mean, understand . . . that it could slow you down a little." She then gave me the standard put-off again, saying the doctors would answer my questions.

Suddenly, I flashed back to the firefight. "Where's my team?" I demanded, jerking forward in the bed. A sharp pain stabbed into my back.

Authority snapped, "Don't try to move, Yancy! If you insist on moving, I'll have you strapped. Understand? It's for your own good." The soothing hand touched my neck again.

I lowered my voice. "I need to know the disposition of my team. Do you understand?"

"Your team is okay. One of the pygmies sustained a shrapnel wound and a fracture in his arm. He's in the indigenous ward.

"How long you been in 'Nam?" I said dryly.

"Two weeks, but I was at—"

I butted in. "Then it's time you updated your vocabulary, Lieutenant. They're not pygmies. They're Montagnard tribesmen. Don't call them pygmies."

Her reply was sincere. "Thank you. The Montagnard tribesman is being treated. I'll go and inquire as to how he's progressing. But don't go to sleep while I'm gone. I'll be right back."

"Thank you, and try to find out his name."

I lay still, staring into the darkness, determined not to get into any panicked second-guessing about blindness. I reminded myself the important thing here and now was the team.

I focused back on the moment when I'd jammed my blade into Baldy. It had felt righteous, but what ached inside me now was a feeling of defeat. I knew that without a prisoner my chances of getting Will's Medal of Honor slid further away. A sense of helplessness gripped me.

I began to wonder how Ski had gotten us out of that hornets' nest. I remembered Baldy attacking him. After I'd killed the scum I saw Binkowski run into a cloud of CS. But everything else was a blank. Evidently my favorite Yankee did good. The question nagging at me now was: Why would Arnold run into a CS fog!

Hearing footsteps, I turned my head toward the sound. I sensed two figures.

"Sergeant Yancy, I'm Lieutenant Colonel Ostrum. I'm the resident neurosurgeon. With me is Major Madden. He's an ophthalmologist. How you feeling?"

"Like my face and chest caught fire and somebody put it out with a track shoe."

"That's pretty close to the truth, Brett. You took a hard lick, several as a matter of fact. But we didn't use a track shoe on you. Right now you're experiencing some temporary paralysis on your left side. It should abate before long."

"That's obviously the good news, sir. Now, how about my eyes? Am I still a candidate for the Army rifle team, or are you about to tell me how easy it is to learn Braille?"

The colonel ignored my wit and shifted directly into an esoteric medical dialogue, telling me that I'd sustained multiple lacerations and bruises over most of my face and upper body. He said that the impact trauma from the rocket explosion had caused partial blindness but that my vision should recover. He also told me that I had some nasal fractures, which would now make my voice a lot less than baritone. They weren't sure about retina damage yet but they were "optimistic." Other than that, everything was just wonderful.

I took in a deep breath, exhaled, and put my wit on the shelf. "Okay, sir, how about taking this mask off and let's find out if my headlights are functioning. Any problem with that?"

The colonel repeated my request softly to the major. "Any problem with that?"

Clearing his throat, the major replied, "No . . . no, we might as well see where we stand." His voice turned in another direction. "Lieutenant Goodwin, would you pull the curtain shut please?"

"Yes, sir. Sir, would you tell Sergeant Yancy his Montagnard tribesman's name is Lok and he's doing fine."

I smiled. "I heard you. That's great. Thanks."

As they began cutting the bandages away from my eye, the major provided some layman's instruction about ocular resiliency, as though he were already counting on my eyes being functional. His optimism eased my tension.

"It is incredible how much trauma the human eye can sustain and still function. Although, in your case, some good old-fashioned luck played a significant role. We removed some forty wood slivers from your face and neck region alone. If one of those had been only a half centimeter closer to either eye it would have caused irreparable damage."

As he removed the gauze a dim light peeked into my eyes around the protective shells positioned over them.

The major's voice was tense. "I'm going to lift the eye shields now. You may experience some pain from the eyebrow sutures."

The moment went silent. I smelled perfume again as more light flooded over me. I blinked, feeling only a minor sting and tightening along my eyebrow. Then I saw the dull outline of white-cloaked figures come into blurry view.

I blinked again, turning my head toward the fragrance near me. Within seconds I focused on the nurse's smiling face.

My first words choked. "You know . . . you're every bit as good-looking as you smell."

Raising my right hand, I wiped a tear away and saw the glowing path of another on her cheek.

"They're blue," she murmured, sniffing. "Your eyes are blue." Reaching past the major, she gently grasped my hand.

I winked at her, feeling a slight sting from the sutures. I squinted up into her glistening eyes. "I'd say yours are brown."

She sniffed again, then exhaled a sweet breath over me. "Not bad, Sergeant Yancy. I'd say you're doing fine. Great!"

The major interrupted, raising a penlight over one eye, then the other. "Splendid! Your pupils respond well." He replaced his light in his pocket. "Tomorrow morning, I'll need to conduct a thorough retina exam on you. For now, just take it easy and—"

"With all respect, sir, I'm hungry. Any Mexican food on the menu here?"

The colonel answered with a half smile, "If there is, I haven't found it yet. We'll see what we can dig up, Sergeant Yancy. But it's going to be a few hours yet before you can eat."

When they left, the room fell silent. I drifted off to sleep.

The soft grip of a hand, interlacing fingers into mine, stirred me from sleep. For a moment, I ignored the sensation. Then a familiar fragrance nudged my senses to wake. My eyes moved over the small dim room, then squinted, not really believing the vision seated beside me. Was I dreaming? It looked like Tracy.

I spoke hoarsely, slowly, as my gaze shifted over her

face. "Damn, you smell good. You look like a girl I remember dancing with not long ago."

She sniffed, trying to smile while brushing her eyes with a quick hand. She leaned closer, kissed my fingers, and lifted her tearstained face upward. "I seem . . . I seem to recall the same memory. Was it in Chiang Mai, handsome?" Her voice trembled.

"Could have been. I spent a whole year there one day."

She tried to laugh, but squeezed my hand and withdrew, crying, "Brett, I'm so happy you're alive. I don't want you fighting this god-awful war anymore!"

"Hey, darlin'," I said, gripping her hand, "I don't think we have to worry too much about that. I only have about six weeks left here."

She frowned. "Six weeks! Brett, don't you understand, you're wounded. You'll be going home, honey. Home!"

I smiled silently back at her. Now was not the time to tell her that if I had any choice about it, I was staying in 'Nam. I knew I needed to let Ski get at least one or two more missions under his belt before I could feel confident about turning the team over to him. Binkowski had performed well on his first combat mission, but there was still a lot I needed to teach him.

No, I didn't have suicidal tendencies. I owed it to Ski and I owed it to my Montagnards. They'd given their all to Will and me. They never once let us down, and I wasn't about to.

I decided it was time to change the subject. I raised my hand to slip my fingers through her soft hair. "How long have you been here? How did you find out I was here?"

Denver Longstreath had called her at the Mai-lon

Hotel in Saigon. He'd gotten her address off the envelope I'd given him, called and told her I'd been hit, and where I was. Somehow she wrangled a flight out of Saigon. She'd been at my bedside since early morning.

As she talked, the morning light began to filter through the window, illuminating her green eyes. Tracy's spirits soared when she told me her publisher was going to help with the adoption process for Fousi, Lon, and Ming.

I watched her caring face, comforted by her presence.

Moments later, Lieutenant Goodwin strode into the room. "Good morning, Brett," she said cheerfully. "They told me you had a special visitor with you. From the gleam in your eye, I'd say she's improved your morale considerably."

Smiling, she offered her hand to Tracy. "I'm Lieutenant Goodwin. Glad to meet you."

Tracy responded politely. Standing, she leaned and kissed me gently, then excused herself, saying she needed to leave to change clothes and make some phone calls. "I'll be back in an hour. I love you."

"You're a lucky man, Yancy," Lieutenant Goodwin said, pulling a thermometer from her pocket. "They told me she's been here most of the night. Now, I'll trade you a big breakfast for a temperature and pulse."

By 1100 hours I'd been given a fifty-thousand-mile checkup and pronounced alive and on the road to recovery. The best news was, no retina damage to my eyes. I was starting to get feeling in my left arm again.

The hospital chaplain insisted on wheeling me back to my room. He talked, moving the chair through long, crowded corridors. His condolences sounded like a form letter.

"Actually, Sergeant Yancy, it was not luck that saved you. You see, God works in strange and wonderful ways. He has smiled on you, my son."

I only half listened, giving my interest instead to the hall traffic. The tone of passing conversations were serious. Smiles were few.

Ahead of us, a man hobbled along on crutches. He was obviously just learning how to use them. An empty pajama leg was pinned up to his waistband. He wore an olive-green Marine Corps sweater. Below the gold eagle emblem were the words *Semper Fidelis*.

Ironically, my eye caught the message of a small sign hanging near the nurses' station as we passed the tall, hobbling Marine. It read, I ONCE CRIED BECAUSE I HAD NO SHOES, TILL I SAW A MAN WHO HAD NO FEET.

Thirty meters from my room, a familiar voice spoke from behind us. It was Tracer. "May I take over the navigation of this wheelchair?" She leaned and kissed the top of my head.

The chaplain touched my shoulder, yielding to Tracy's request. "God bless you, Brett. I'll be by to see how you're doing later."

"Thank you," I said, turning my attention to Tracy. "You look good, lady. Let's take the long way home."

"Not now, Yancy. You've got visitors waiting for you," she said, pushing me onward.

Entering the small room, I saw Fousi, Lon, and Ming dressed in the bright-colored dresses I'd brought them from Thailand.

I smiled. "Wow, this is a welcome surprise."

Seeing my smile, they dropped their sad faces. Lon and Ming hurried to my wheelchair. Talking at the same time, they pointed to a picture they had drawn, which now hung above my bed. "Look, Sar Brett. You see? You like?"

I beamed at their latest artwork. Once again they had given me a picture of their favorite subject, a dove. But this time they'd drawn an outline of the United States around the dove, with an American flag colored in above it.

"I do believe you two are getting better." I glanced up at Tracy and whispered, "Do they know about the adoption?"

"Yes," she whispered back.

I widened my smile. "I think you're both going to be great artists. Who knows, architects maybe." Their expressions told me immediately that I'd used a word they didn't understand.

Fousi stepped between them, touching their hair as she spoke. She smiled, glancing first at Tracy, then back to me. "We happy you are okay, Yon-cee, and we happy to be going America soon. And we thinking this lady Tra-cee is number-one. I also thinking she love you *beaucoup*. She making good wife for you if you smart."

I felt Tracy's fingers touching my shoulders. I tried to change the subject without sounding too obvious. "I probably ought to get into bed before Lieutenant Goodwin comes—"

Fousi interrupted me with a polite emphasis. "Bed can wait! You needing to asking her now for marry you. You know, many man liking to have pretty lady liking her." She dramatized a wide-eyed look into the hallway full of passing soldiers to make her point. "You asking her now, please."

I was beginning to feel pinned down, surrounded. I pleaded back, "Fousi, maybe Tracy doesn't want a Green Beret for a husband."

"No chance, Yancy. She knows I love you."

Ming nudged my hand and spoke softly. "You asking her, Sar Brett."

Tracy stepped quietly near the huddled trio and looked down into my eyes. Her gentle expression let me off the hook, if I wanted out.

Looking up at her, I said, "Tracy, don't you think it's a better idea to live together first? Hell, you don't know, maybe I squeeze the toothpaste tube wrong, or put the toilet paper on backward, or—"

"Idiosyncrasies don't bother me, Brett. But don't feel like you have to—"

"Damn it, will you marry me?"

"Yes, damn it!"

"Yes, damn it!" Ming sung out happily, clapping her hands.

Suddenly an amused voice echoed from the doorway, like she'd been listening to us unnoticed. "What's all this profanity in here? You need to be in bed," Lieutenant Goodwin announced, lifting my IV bottle off the wheelchair rack.

I glared up at her, wondering why she couldn't have arrived a little earlier. Then I started to feel like lying down wasn't a bad idea after all. Without intending to, I fell asleep.

I awakened to the smell of fried chicken and a strong voice. "Sergeant Yancy, can you handle some chow?" the slender black orderly questioned.

"Roger," I answered groggily. "What time is it?" I asked, noticing a note tucked into my hospital ID tag.

"Chow time, 1600." He positioned a bed tray across me. "Take your time. I'll be back later."

I ignored my food for a moment and read the note:

Brett,

You dozed off and we didn't want to wake you.
I've gone with Fousi and the girls into the city. I
need to pick up their birth certificates and make
some copies, so I'll be gone for a while.

Thank you for your proposal. Yes, I would marry
you anytime, anywhere. But understand, your foot
isn't nailed to the floor. Men say strange things
under the influence of medication (it would never
hold up in a court of law. Ha, ha, just kidding).

I love you,
Tracer

Smiling, I lay the note aside and picked up my fork.
There was a presence in the room. Turning my head
farther to the left, I saw Lok beaming up at me from
his wheelchair. "Damn, Babysan. How long you been
here? How you feel?"

Lok ran his hand along his cast, tapping his fingers
over it while answering, "Feel okay, Sar Brett. Heavy."
He raised his casted arm slightly.

"Number-one. You hungry?" I asked, motioning to
my tray.

"No hungry. You eat."

We talked while I ate. He didn't ask about my wounds
and I understood why. With the little people wounds
were a way of life. No matter what one's condition, if
he was alive, that was good enough.

I wasn't able to find out much about how we'd gotten
out of the target area, but Lok's admiration for Ski was
evident as he related some of the action. "Ski number
fuckin' one," he repeated several times.

The orderly's voice intruded emphatically. "Man, I

ain't sure, but I think you got visitors comin'. There's four of the baddest-lookin' dudes I ever seen comin' down the hall.'' Quickly retrieving my tray, he added, ''All wearing green berets. I'll see you later, Sergeant Yancy.''

Colonel Kahn was the first through the door, followed by Arnold Binkowski, Swede Jensen, and Denver Longstreath.

I spoke first, smiling, while I reached to shake Colonel Kahn's hand. ''It's about time ya'll got here. I'm hoping somebody can fill in some blanks for me. Sir?''

Colonel Kahn grinned, still gripping my hand, as everyone gathered around the bed.

Smirking, Denver handed me the envelope I'd given him with the Claddagh ring inside it. ''I told you I'd be giving this back to you.''

Before I could answer, Colonel Kahn spoke. ''Brett, as far as filling in the blanks, let me just say these two guys here did one hell of a good job out there.''

''Yeah, you went to sleep during the best part of the show,'' Denver said. ''Ski here was a regular one-man crowd down there.''

''Don't try and make me sound like a hero,'' Ski countered. ''I was scared shitless, and if it hadn't been for you directing napalm to the right places we would of been up shit creek!''

Swede pulled a small cigar from his mouth. ''What they're sayin' is, Brett, the defecation definitely hit the cooling apparatus, but together y'all kicked Chuck's ass so far up between his shoulders he'll have to open his mouth to shit for a while.''

Ski laughed, then suddenly exclaimed, ''Oops! I forgot about the Yards. They're outside waiting. Do you mind if I bring—''

"Go get 'em, partner!"

After Ski hurried out of the room, Denver and Colonel Kahn began filling me in on the details of the exfiltration.

Now, at last, I learned why Binkowski had run into the CS fog. He'd grabbed us another prisoner. Ski had seen me kill Baldy. He knew how critical it was for me to bring back a prisoner.

I was proud of my new One-One. No one could take Will's place, but Ski had gone a long way in that direction.

It was Denver who pulled them out of the tiger's teeth. As FAC, his knowledge of NVA tactics, combined with a sharp eye for enemy movement, allowed him to direct the tactical air support into key locations, beating the enemy back long enough for the chopper to get to the team.

Listening to Denver's enthusiastic portrayal of Ski's courage under fire, it appeared he'd developed a new respect for Binkowski during the extraction from Hotel-5.

Suddenly, Ski and the Yards stormed through the doorway, crowding into the room.

Tuong moved forward, ahead of the others. He glanced up at the dove picture above me. His childlike eyes glistened as he looked back at me and touched my arm. He gripped it to emphasize his words. "We missing you, Sar Brett. Skee say you maybe go home soon. We missing you more if you go."

I winked at him, then looked directly at Colonel Kahn. "Sir, you know, these superficial wounds heal fast . . ." I glanced at Denver. "And I'm really not in any big hurry to get home—"

Ivan Kahn stopped me short. "Stop beating around

the bush, Brett. Are you saying you want to hang in here until your tour is up?''

"That's exactly what I'm saying, sir.''

"Okay, I'll see what I can do. No promises. But I'll see what I can do.''

Denver butted in, grinning. "Don't worry, Brett. I just happen to have a couple of captured AKs. You'd be surprised what they can do as trading material to swing a doctor's mind in the right direction, get him to approve you stayin' here. Shit, it worked for me.'' A smirk lit his face. "Works on nurses too.''

I looked into the anxious eyes of Lok, Phan, Rham, and Tuong. "Okay, gang, you heard the man. Don't go packing my gear yet!''

"Now, I seem to remember talking with Will one day not long ago, and you know what we decided you guys need?''

"What?'' Tuong questioned.

"What?'' Lok mimicked.

"Boots!'' I answered.

"Boots? We already have,'' Tuong replied, looking down as if to make sure he had his on.

"No. Cowboy boots. You know, like in the movies. How would that be if I send ya'll some boots? You know, when I do go home in a couple of months?''

Rham moved forward quickly. "Number-one, Sar Brett. I like same—same Clin Eez-woo.''

"Okay, you got it,'' I said, pointing back to him. The words "Me too'' resounded in chorus from the others.

Moving closer, Colonel Kahn rested a hand across Tuong's shoulder. "Brett, I was on the horn with General Anson this afternoon. He's the deputy director of combat operations in Saigon. Anyhow, he said the prisoner you brought back couldn't stop talking. It looks like they're getting all the information they wanted, and then some. While speaking with the general, I just happened to mention we were running into some foot-dragging about Will's Medal of Honor approval. He assured me that he'd escort the award through personally. They're going to need an NCO to make the presentation to Will's family. The ceremony will probably be sometime around Thanksgiving and you'll be home by then. I recommended you.''

I felt my jaw tighten; tears welled up in my eyes. I looked out the window toward a semicircle of fading sun. ''Every now and then, if we're lucky, and smart enough to realize it, a truly noble person comes along and touches, changes, our lives. For me, William Washington was such a person.

''To present his award to his family will be a privilege and an honor.''